YA. Goobi. 2004. F.

Flux

Flux

BETH GOOBIE

ORCA BOOK PUBLISHERS

National Library of Canada Cataloguing in Publication Data:

Goobie, Beth, 1959–
Flux / Beth Goobie.

ISBN 1-55143-314-1

I. Title.

PS8563.O8326F58 2004   jC813'.54   C2004-901023-9

Library of Congress Control Number: 2004101754

Summary: Deep in another reality, while using her ability to travel to parallel worlds, Nellie uncovers a conspiracy to abduct children for an experimental laboratory.

Orca Book Publishers gratefully acknowledges the support of its publishing program provided by the following agencies: the Department of Canadian Heritage, the Canada Council for the Arts, and the British Columbia Arts Council.

The author very gratefully acknowledges the Canada Council for the Arts grant that funded the writing of this book.

Design by Lynn O'Rourke
Cover Images: www.eyewire.com
Printed and bound in Canada

Orca Book Publishers
1030 North Park Street
Victoria, BC Canada
V8T 1C6

Orca Book Publishers
PO Box 468
Custer, WA USA
98240-0468

08 07 06 05 04 • 6 5 4 3 2 1

Quote from *LUH, Man's Cosmic Game*, published by Edizioni Noesis, © Giuliana Conforto. www.giulianaconforto.it
Used with permission. All rights reserved.

for Melanie

Memory is a goddess because
it is our sense of identity:
if we couldn't remember our past
we wouldn't say 'I'.

—Giuliana Conforto
LUH: Man's Cosmic Game

Part 1

Chapter 1

IT WAS DUSK, the stars beginning to show, a low song along the horizon. The first moon had appeared and among the doogden trees the breeze was growing sleepy, a wickawoo bird giving out its last cry of the day. Shadows dreamed themselves across the landscape, taking it deep into sepia and pewter gray. In the still heavy air only the doogden leaves seemed awake, like those parts of the mind that wait on the edge of things, whispering as the body slides toward sleep. Suddenly a snapping of twigs erupted along the treeline, followed by a loud grunt as a twelve-year-old girl came careening down the steep slope of a nearby hill and landed in a withered dengleberry bush, her body clenched, absorbing the shock of impact.

Slowly Nellie uncurled, each movement a stifled groan. Thin electric lines pierced her lungs, she'd been running for over an hour since she was spotted coming out of a corner store on Borovan Avenue. Nothing had distracted her pursuers, not even a pack of cigarettes dropped early in the chase—the Skulls had merely scooped them up and come after her, their bodies streamlined for tracking as they ducked through the late afternoon crowd. Now she was in the warehouse district, a haphazard collection of concrete buildings that had sprung up on the northern edge of the city. In the two years since she'd fled the Interior with her mother, Nellie had learned that everything about the Outbacks was haphazard, a scornfully discarded handful of chaos for which the Interior had no use. At least, not officially. During the time she'd lived in the city of Dorniver, she'd seen the slick gray vehicles that identified the Interior Police less than ten times. The first had directly preceded her mother's disappearance, the rest had clustered in the following weeks, tapering off within two months.

A hoot from the hill alerted her. Starting to her feet Nellie watched a boy peak the crest, followed by three more. Huddled briefly, their dark outlines conferred, then took a simultaneous slide down the steep slope, braced for the five-foot drop at the bottom. Whirling, Nellie took off along the outside of the nearest warehouse. Beyond it lay a network of dirt-packed roads and warehouses that had closed down for the night, but perhaps she could find a place to hide, or a door someone had been stupid enough to leave unlocked. Heading home wasn't an option, not until the Skulls left off tracking her. No way was she leading them to the only place that held the quiet beating of her heart, her one true sanctuary.

Grunts punctured the air as the Skulls hit ground. Increasing her pace, Nellie veered around the end of the warehouse and collided with a chain-link fence that enclosed a large loading area. Beyond this she could see the next warehouse, completely fenced in, and beyond that a dirt road and an open field. Wherever she looked, the evening sky poured down a long brown-gray emptiness. With nowhere to hide, the Skulls would tackle her before she was halfway across the field. There was nothing to do but climb or turn back. Quickly she swung herself up the fence, the moonlit mesh clattering against the metal posts, a heart gone wild, tearing at itself. Perched on the top rail, she was about to start down the other side when a low snarl rushed across the yard and a sleek black dog launched itself toward her, its legs swimming air. At the same moment the Skulls skidded to a halt outside the fence, their mouths hanging loose as they stared upward.

Twisting itself into a frenzy, the dog shifted its attention to the Skulls. Momentarily forgotten, Nellie studied the animal's growling contortions and a slow grin eased her scowl. With those teeth tearing at the mesh the boys wouldn't be able to climb the fence, they couldn't even touch it. Swaying high above the ground each time the dog launched itself, she pondered her options. For one succinct raw-breathing moment, she was safe. Beside her the warehouse wall rose ten feet above her head, but the opposite side of the building appeared to be lower. If she crawled along the top of the fence, she might be able to access the warehouse roof from the other end and wait the dog out there until it was penned at daylight.

Straddling the fence she dug her feet into the mesh and began inching forward, the dog keeping pace underneath. "Get something," yelled a voice. "A long board." It was Deller, leader of the Skulls, and the rest of the gang faded obediently into the sepia dusk. Quieter now, the dog paced and panted, watching the boy who stood silently staring upward. Ahead of Nellie the fence stretched so taut it was like crawling her own panic, but she thought she could make it through anything the Skulls might throw in their attempts to knock her down. What else could they do? No one could get at her directly with the dog so intent on keeping them at bay. If she got out of tonight's mess in one piece, she was going to return sometime soon with a raw steak and fling it over the fence as thanks.

The boys reappeared, dragging a large tree branch, and levered it up against the mesh.

"Not there," hissed Deller. *"Ahead* of her. Where she's *going."*

Clinging to her perch, Nellie absorbed the shock as the heavy branch hit the fence a second time and Deller shimmied its full height, well out of the dog's reach. Crouched and grinning, he faced her. Fourteen, wiry and strong, he was tuned to every pulse of his body. Violence sang in his blood, sky met earth, and he was a lone dark figure dancing at their center point. At the base of the fence the dog went manic, vaulting itself upward, spiraling into a high-pitched whine. Leaning down, Deller teased it with a dangling hand.

"Gotcha, Bunny," he sneered.

They'd never trapped her like this before—alone, way out nowhere. In back alleys, Dorniver's crowded streets, there had always been some adult—not her own mother perhaps, but *someone* who'd come sharp-eyed and yelling to her rescue, providing the few seconds she'd needed, the frantic escape-line of heartbeats that had mapped her way home.

"Just come on down," Deller said softly, "and we'll go easy on you."

Praying her worn runners wouldn't slip, Nellie brought her right foot to the top rail and sprang, angling her shoulder so it would knock Deller into the enclosed area and deflect her own body outward. But as she leapt so did the dog, and the force of its body against the fence sent both girl and boy tumbling over the opposite side. Grabbing Deller's shoulder, Nellie hung on as his fingers clutched and slid the length of the mesh. They landed, Nellie on top, Deller taking the full force of their fall, the fence belling out as the dog threw itself at them in another savage rush. As she clambered to her feet, Nellie saw Deller's hand still clinging to the fence, the dog's muzzle rushing to meet it. Turning, she exploded through the shocked Skulls as an eerie scream rose behind her, slippery and lonely as moonlight.

At the bottom of the hill she glanced back to see the Skulls crowded around Deller's writhing body. Just beyond them the dog continued to throw itself at the fence like a heartbeat, sending the wire mesh into long clattering waves around the yard. Then she was in among the doogden trees where the air breathed differently, a breeze slipped like forgetfulness down the back of her sweating neck, and she could fade between the quiet coppery trunks, their sighing cobweb of leaves so delicate one might have thought their sadness nothing at all.

IN THE ONE-ROOM SHACK, Nellie lit a black candle and prepared to remember the dead. Carefully she covered the only window with a gauzy material she'd chosen for remembering purposes because she liked the soft wings it formed on a breeze. The material floated, a haze of purples and greens, its lower edge brushing an upended crate that held a margarine container and the black burning candle. Night came early to the shack's interior. Although it had originally been built in an open area, small trees and foliage had grown up around it, so dense the crumbling structure could no longer be seen, even from a few feet. No path led to it and Nellie made sure she never defined a trail, working her way through the surrounding bush by alternate routes. Often she crawled tree to tree, feeling her way along the strongest branches. She'd even created a hidden passage to the shack's front door by forcing a crawl space several feet in length that began midway through the dense foliage. Soon after moving in, she'd nailed some rusty screening over the window and covered the dirt floor with blankets in a vain attempt to keep back the bugs. Her single other home renovation was a piece of rope which she used to tie shut the ill-fitting door, closing herself into a small private space that tilted in the gusting candlelight, taking greedy leaps into the unknown.

Pushing aside several tea towels that were piled in a corner, Nellie lifted a folded gold-brocaded cloth that had been stored underneath. It was a slow, awed gesture, her eyes solemn and tranced, as she let the cloth fall into a loose swinging dress. In the small shadowy room the brocade flickered, veined with light and whispering with angel voices. The dress had instantly been hers the moment she'd first seen it floating on a laundry line, shining white and gold, pure as mother love, and she wore it only on those extra special, holy occasions when she sent herself out in search of the minds of the dead.

Peeling out of her grimy T-shirt and shorts, Nellie kicked off her runners and stood naked, the dress clasped to her small breasts as she watched the candle flame weave in and out of itself. Sometimes the light seemed weary, as if an unseen weight pressed upon it. At other times a wicked energy rose through the candle stub and she danced naked in the tilting light, grunting as flux entered the shack and everything that was known undid itself. Before moving into the shack she'd never experienced flux, hadn't been aware it existed. Since she knew of no one to ask about these experiences, she'd decided they were a gift sent by the Goddess Ivana, moments in which Her divine mind touched directly upon the material world, causing a quirk in the molecular field. Then Nellie's surroundings would shapeshift, the air suddenly filling with smoke, quick-twisting forms and the call of drums. At other times there would be only her body taking strange wild forms, and she would dance until exhaustion dropped her panting to the ground, her face wet with tears she didn't understand.

If only, she thought, stroking the gold-brocaded dress, she could shapeshift at will and didn't have to wait for the Goddess to send some flux. Sometime soon she was going to have to learn the proper incantation to grab Ivana's attention good and hard, and *make* Her listen. Slowly Nellie pulled the dress over her head, the sensation of the heavy cloth shivering deep into her skin, then knelt and spread the skirt into a glowing circle. Folding her hands in her lap, she focused on the question of candlelight that lit the small shack and whispered the beginning words.

"Blessed Ivana, come to me." One afternoon about a year ago, she'd slipped into a small church on a Dorniver street corner and seen a clutch of old women rocking in the pews, mumbling similar words. Now as she chanted the memory came back to her, heavy and weighted like sleep. "Blessed Ivana, come to me," she repeated, the words taking the shape of something lonely—dark doves flying from the mouths of old women stinking of garlic and missing teeth. "Blessed Ivana," Nellie whispered, twisting her lips into old women's lips. Her own mother's name had been Lydia but no matter, the Goddess Ivana was everyone's mother and all missing mothers returned to touch their children through Her. "Blessed

Ivana, blessed Ivana," Nellie chanted, her eyes squeezed tight, and suddenly her brain pivoted on its axis, the shadowy shack took a crazy tilt to the left, and it happened—a hand appeared, reaching through a long darkness toward the candlelight. Gently the palm pressed itself against her hot forehead. Pale fingers stroked her cheeks and touched her wailing mouth.

"My child," a voice whispered and it was her mother's voice, Nellie's own mother named Lydia, the mother who'd disappeared sixteen aching months ago, her voice deep with the echoes of what could not be understood. Then the hand withdrew, retreating into the long darkness. Lunging after it, Nellie knocked over the crate. The candle toppled, hissing out, and the gate to the mother-world disappeared, leaving a twelve-year-old girl collapsed in a gold-brocaded remembering dress beneath the sighs of a floating gauze curtain.

Chapter 2

NELLIE WOKE LATE, to a dull pain that throbbed at the base of her brain. Shifting and muttering in her nest of dirty blankets, she hovered between sleeping and waking, letting her eyelids drift repeatedly open, then closed. Sometimes the morning sludge in her head was a gutter thick with mud, and there was no one to help pull her out of her dreams—no nagging mother knocking at a bedroom door, no bus driver waiting at a corner stop, no schoolteacher summoning up a nine a.m. smile as her students walked into the room. The grimmest and most basic fact of Nellie's life was the first to attack her every morning—if she decided to lie without moving until breath left her and her body rotted into the shack's crumbling floor, no one would notice. Each day she came awake daydreaming about the pleasures of dying, of slipping gradually backward into the comforting world of the dead where she wouldn't have to try anymore, could simply accept the way things had gone and let everything rest as it was. No more endlessly trying to make things come together again, trying to make sense of what could not be understood. And no more endlessly hungry belly, with the deeper emptiness that threatened beyond it.

Outside the shack, a flock of squawking wickawoos descended into the foliage and prepared to do battle over a patch of dengleberries. Grunting irritably, Nellie rolled over and focused on the window. The sagging rectangle of light was a dim haze of purples and greens that swelled gently on the incoming breeze. With a start she realized she'd forgotten to take down the gauze curtain after last night's remembering session and came fully awake, riding the thundering of her heart. This was blasphemy, a major trespass against the Goddess who treasured any ritual object used to invoke Her presence. Ivana's tokens were sacred, set aside for divine purposes, and couldn't be left lying about. What if She'd noticed the holy veil floating carelessly in the morning light while Her twelve-year-old devotee slept? What if She took offence and decided to never again bless the shack with Her presence?

Quickly Nellie sat up, intending to return the gauze curtain to its customary hiding place under the stack of tea towels with the gold-brocaded dress. But as she pushed herself upright, the shack spun into a dizzy ooze, forcing her to drop back onto her pad of blankets. For a long moment her mind rippled and whirled, and then it opened onto a great humming darkness full of stars that shifted in and out of mysterious complex alignments. The stars glowed in a wealth of unfamiliar colors, and they seemed to be calling to one another in shrill piercing voices. The sound was unearthly, surrounding and resonating through Nellie's body until she felt as if the physical world was about to dissolve into one vast singing wave.

Gradually the vision faded from her head and she opened her eyes with a cautious whimper. This wasn't the first time she'd woken, still carrying intense dreams of stars in flux, nor was it the first time she'd felt those dreams shuffle her physical reality like a deck of cards. Sometimes the stars seemed to transport her to unfamiliar places, and she would open her eyes to find herself in a room with arcing white walls, a tropical garden, or a mechanical cubicle with sleepy blinking lights. At such times she would hold on desperately with her mind, trying to imprint what she saw into memory, but the images remained only for a heartbeat, then faded. Still, Nellie couldn't convince herself they were mere fantasy. The places seemed more real, more *solid* than the dilapidated shack she called home— as if they held more of her, were keeping the most important part of herself just beyond reach. *Was that what a soul was?* she wondered. *A part of you that lived somewhere else?* Lifting a hand to the dim window light, she was relieved to see it was human. Her dreams cast her in such weird forms—batlike, reptilian, or furred like a bear—and sometimes she seemed to be made of light, changing shape as easily as thought.

Muttering fervent apologies to the Goddess, Nellie took down the gauze curtain and slid it under the stack of filthy tea towels. Then she stood waiting, one hand braced against the windowsill, but the shack's walls remained firmly in place and no further craziness swung through her head. As with most of her morning swoons this one was short-lived, but she knew what it foretold. Nights of odd dreaming were inevitably followed by days of flux. When the stars danced in her dreams, the morning air vibrated strangely, people's brain waves changed, and it was a time of subtleties with new words suddenly appearing in the language, unfamiliar viruses surfacing and a universal slipperiness to the eye.

When she'd lived in the Interior, there had been no singing stars and no days of flux. There, nothing had been erratic and every aspect of a child's life had been organized to the minutest detail. Family, school, religion and hobbies—it had all been as orderly as the night sky. In fact the slow overhead shift of the stars had dictated everything from the seasons, with their predictable weather patterns, festivals, and holidays, to each individual's school, playmates, career, and breeding partners. Nellie clearly remembered charting the major constellations in class and studying the nine signs of the zodiac and their caste rules. Her star sign had been the Cat constellation, which represented one of the lowest castes, but it hadn't meant much to her. Back then the stars had seemed irrelevant, nothing more than meaningless pinpoints of cold brilliant light, just as the blue constellation tattooed to the inside of her left wrist had held no significance, being simply the identity tattoo she'd extended like everyone else to be scanned at the security entrances to her school and apartment building, nearby stores, rec center, and library branch. All across the Interior, electronic billboards constantly flashed the message: YOUR GOVERNMENT CARES ABOUT EVERY CITIZEN. YOUR GOVERNMENT NEEDS TO KNOW WHERE YOU ARE AT ALL TIMES.

The Interior had held no days of flux, but Nellie remembered the constant feeling of secrets, as if another layer of meaning lay hidden behind everything she saw. As if, she thought, shivering in the shack's early morning coolness, those secrets had somehow crept inside her and were growing there, like an innermost eighth skin. *Creepy, creepy. Ooly-goolies.* Muttering further incantations to the Goddess, she pulled off the man's dress shirt she used for sleeping and dipped a grimy tea towel into the bucket of rainwater she stored in a corner. Then she gave herself a perfunctory sponge bath. A thorough morning wash had been something her mother had always insisted upon. While Nellie's efforts could hardly be called thorough, she continued to obediently trickle handfuls of water over various parts of her body and rub herself dry every morning. Sometimes she used soap, but usually reserved it for her infrequent dips in a nearby brook. This morning she splashed water liberally here and there, then stopped to press her hands firmly against the small curve of her breasts. Eyes narrowed to slits, she considered. Had they grown since yesterday? She pressed harder, ignoring the pain. Maybe, maybe not, but one thing was certain—she was going to have to come up with a new solution for keeping them flat. Sleeping on her stomach wasn't working, and neither was the thought-management program she'd invented after reading a newspaper article. The article had been about stress, and the small jiggling blobs on Nellie's chest were certainly stressful, but the managing thoughts she'd directed at them hadn't had any noticeable effect to date.

Nor had the bra she'd filched from a department store. The damn thing had stuck out of her chest like the front ends of two canoes. Well, one canoe—the bra had been so large, one of the cups had dangled ineffectually at her waist. Nellie hadn't known anything about sizes, she'd just grabbed the closest package off the shelf. How was she supposed to know if she was a 48D or a 32A?

Muttering under her breath, she released her breasts and began to explore the hair at her crotch with curious fingers. When it had first appeared she'd tried to pull it out, thinking flux was finally taking over her body and she was about to be permanently transformed into a bear or a large hairy dog. Then she'd come across a discarded magazine full of naked women, and discovered every one of them sported a bearskin between her legs. The magazine gave no reason for the bearskin, nor did it explain why Nellie also had fur in her armpits and the magazine women didn't, but she'd relaxed a little, realizing she wasn't about to grow claws and fangs and start foraging for bugs in rotten logs.

She'd found other magazines since, in garbage pails and back alleys, and kept them as a reference for the changes her body was experiencing. Though she'd never seen her mother naked, Nellie could remember the electric razor she'd used to shave her legs. There were no electrical outlets in the shack, and the fine blond hairs on her own legs continued to grow. The mother she remembered had belonged to a small girl with smooth hairless skin. Day by day Nellie felt herself losing her mother more completely, through each small change in her growing body.

The one thing she continued to share with the mother she remembered was a small scar on the inside of her left wrist. Tearing open a package of oolaga candy, Nellie munched steadily as she studied the shiny pink mark on her skin. In the Interior her mother had never commented on their identity tattoos except to say "Stick out your wrist for the scanner, honey," but the first thing she'd attended to upon their arrival in the Outbacks had been the removal of the Cat constellation tattoos. Both Nellie and her mother had been born under the sign of the Cat, and their tattoos had depicted a small crouched cat outlined in tiny blue stars. Nellie had been fond of hers, nicknaming it Starpurr, but no indigenous Outbacker sported a tattoo, and they were regarded with suspicion. Nellie's memory of the operation that had removed her tattoo was vague, consisting of little more than a dimly lit kitchen at the back of a sparsely furnished house. She remembered perching on a creaky chair and sipping a sweet drink as a whispered conversation passed between her mother and an unfamiliar man. Money had rustled, changing hands, and then a sleepy darkness had enveloped her. Several hours later she'd woken to find her bandaged wrist throbbing painfully and her mother, wearing a similar bandage, smiling tearfully from across the room.

"We're free, Nellie," she'd whispered. "Now no one can tell who we are, and out here no one cares."

When she'd removed the bandage several days later, the tattoo had been gone along with the small bump that had always sat beneath the skin on her wrist, slightly distorting the cat's head. Though Nellie had pestered her mother, she'd never received an explanation for the removal of their tattoos or their escape from the Interior, but she knew they were somehow connected to flux and the dreams that drove Outbackers wild, tussling with their minds like a storm wind among trees. Signs of it lived in their faces, their startling tempers and wary manner, clues that revealed the way other realities kept tugging at the boundaries of this one, taunting and pulling tricks. True Outbackers walked as if the ground beneath their feet was always about to be transformed into the raging Funnerbye Sea, and they trusted nothing—not the things they were told, not the rumors they overheard, and certainly not the confidences they passed on to others. All in all, Nellie figured, she'd choose an Outbacker for a friend over someone from the Interior any day. The people you wanted to steer clear of were the ones who *expected* you to trust them and toss your own brain into the nearest garbage heap.

Having tallied up the new bug bites she'd gotten overnight, she tugged on a pair of jeans and a T-shirt, and spread the tea towel to dry. Then she tidied her nest of blankets, skewered her blond hair into a short ponytail and slid a small blue knapsack onto her back. Slipping out of the shack, she swung up the nearest doogden tree and crawled a well-known network of branches to the edge of the trees, where she dropped into ground-level foliage. Depending on the route she took through the tangled copse, she could emerge near a deserted quarry, a highway that traveled south toward the Interior, or the scrub that stretched toward Dorniver's outskirts. Much of the area was used for bootlegging, dirt biking and romance, but in the year she'd spent living in the shack no one had ventured into the wooded area that enclosed it. Still, she remained cautious when coming into the open, remembering the way her mother had hesitated in door-ways those last few days, so tense her nostrils had flared.

Today Nellie crouched as always, scanning the surrounding scrub and sniffing. The smell of exhaust coiled thick in the air— some kind of vehicle must have recently passed—but the only sound was the rustling sunburnt grass and a scattering of siccna crickets. Crawling through the long grass, she tracked the scent of the exhaust to a set of tire marks that led to a burgundy van parked near the old quarry. Through the weaving grass, she could see several men smoking cigarettes as they set up delicate complex instruments that resembled mechanical birds, their long necks straining toward the sky. The men worked meticulously, checking and rechecking everything they did against instructions displayed on a small computer.

With a soft grunt, Nellie pressed closer to the ground. The bur-gundy van was sleek, a newer model that would be inconspicuous in the Interior but spoke volumes in the Outbacks. The Interior frequently dispensed officials beyond its borders to scrutinize the surrounding area, take notes and report back. When sleek uniden-tified vehicles were spotted cruising Dorniver, everyone laid low. Usually these officials were after someone specific, but they had the authority to apprehend anyone on a whim, and no one who disappeared into the Interior's bureaucracy was ever heard from again.

The men's voices were a vague murmur in the mid-morning heat, too distant to be made out clearly. Still crawling, Nellie had begun to back away when the approach of a second vehicle sent her flat to the ground. The dry earth throbbed as another van passed and pulled up beside the first. As she watched, a man got out and called to the others. Then he opened the back of the second van and crawled inside. Nellie's stomach growled, but all thoughts of heading off in search of lunch disappeared as she saw a small child lifted from the back of the van into the arms of a waiting man. The boy was around five years old and obviously sedated. Blinking, he stood where he was placed, displaying no interest in his surroundings. Next a young girl appeared, followed by two others, until four children stood in a quiet line—three girls and one boy, all under the age of eight.

Nellie's heart thundered and she was suddenly wired with fear. Bright rooms ... she was remembering bright rooms in the Interior, soft straps that trapped her arms and doctors and machines that brought many kinds of pain. Pain was a story. In those bright rooms of long ago, she'd learned to take pain and set a girl inside it, then give her something to do—crawl into an underground cave, mount a backyard swing and pump herself above the trees, or turn her into a free-winged bird—anything that would take that girl of pain and send her so far away, she would vanish into nothingness.

The bright rooms of the Interior, and what had taken place inside them, had faded years ago to a fuzzy blur in Nellie's head. No matter how she struggled to remember the details she couldn't, but now as she watched the children and the birdlike machines, she recognized the doctors of her memories—different men perhaps but the same kind of pain-makers, the same evil intent. Taking the hand of the five-year-old boy, one of the men led him to the centerpoint between the three birdlike machines and placed a wire-mesh helmet on his head. Then the man stepped back, leaving the boy alone, his eyes fixed in a dull stare, his hands relaxed and dangling as if there was no danger, as if the fear stiffening the hair on the back of Nellie's neck had nothing to do with him, his life, its possibility.

One of the men held up a small device that emitted a series of electronic beeps, and the boy's eyes closed. Slouched and nonchalant, the men smoked silently. Beside them the line of girls stared listlessly at the ground. Only the tall blond grass moved, swaying in the wind, whispering sweet-scented incantations to the Goddess. Without warning Nellie felt her mind buckle and give way, dropping her into a roaring darkness full of strange wild stars that pivoted around a central point. As she watched, radiant lines of energy connected and a central star blazed. At the same moment an electric current shot between the birdlike machines and the five-year-old boy stiffened, his eyes flying open, staring at something Nellie couldn't see. A wave of iridescence passed through him and he vanished, his wire-mesh helmet thudding to the ground. One of the men started toward it, but another called out sharply, pointing to the laptop. The first man paused, waiting until the man with the laptop nodded, then moved in and picked up the helmet.

Crouched like a spitting cat, Nellie watched as one of the girls was led among the machines. Like the boy, she stood dully as the helmet was placed on her head and the man stepped back. Again the blond grass rustled, whispering between worlds; again Nellie's mind buckled and she watched strange wild stars align as the birdlike machines hissed and another child vanished. The next girl was led into position, and the process repeated. None of the children protested—they seemed barely alive, drugged too heavily to whimper on their own behalf.

When all four children had disappeared, the men dismantled the machines and placed them in the back of the first van. Then they climbed into both vans and drove off, passing so close Nellie was certain she would be seen; but the vehicles continued on, leaving only the wavering scent of exhaust and a flattened area of grass struggling to lift itself, inch by broken inch, toward a thin blue sky.

Chapter 3

NELLIE LAY A LONG TIME beneath a bleached canopy of rustling grass, watching it ripple in the slurred rhythms of her brain. Ants crawled up the inside of her pant legs; a tiny red spider ran across her stomach. Gradually she began to stir, then sit up, feeling the oddness of her body as if she was a stranger to it, as if she'd been absent a long time and had just returned in order to relearn its meaning. Slowly the shifting pieces of her mind floated together and she was once again Nellie Kinnan, twelve years old and without a mother, and the men from the bright rooms had been here, right in front of her, wracking their evil on the bodies of innocent dull-eyed children. She remembered being that dull-eyed, she remembered the machines that had towered above her, their gleaming invasions of pain.

Getting to her feet, she followed the van tracks to the flattened area of grass where the birdlike machines had stood. With precise venom, she spat on each tire mark. Then she knelt, placing her palms on the blurred footprints the children had left at the center point between the machines. A coldness sang through her and she wanted to pull back, but forced herself to remain crouched in position, sending herself as far as she dared into the vibratory trail emitted by the children. Like a long ago thought, she could feel their passage to some distant place, their crossing abrupt and full of pain, tearing at the veils of vibrations that separated the different levels of reality. They were still alive, she could tell that much, but the vibrations they'd left in their wake throbbed with fear, and their destination was obscured. Grumbling and muttering, Nellie tossed handfuls of dirt over the place the children had stood, trying to cleanse the small vague footprints. No words could give meaning to this terror, no words could take it away.

DORNIVER WAS AN HOUR'S WALK. Moving quickly, Nellie steered clear of the main road that led to the city center, ducking into the undergrowth whenever she approached one of the shacks that dotted the area. Though she knew most of the local residents by sight, she'd never spoken to any of them. No one who'd seen her in the past sixteen months knew her name, though the Skulls had nicknamed her 'Bunny.' She'd read enough discarded magazines to know what that meant. "Nellie Joan Kinnan," Nellie sang low in her throat as she approached the city's outskirts. "Nellie Kinnan, Nellie Your-Mother-Loves-You Kinnan."

Dorniver was a rambling sprawl that had grown out of itself like a tumor or a plague. Each building pressed against its neighbor in a vaguely menacing fashion, roads veered like quickly told stories, and the electrical system was so frequently on the blink that many residents relied on kerosene lamps and wood-burning stoves. It hadn't taken Nellie and her mother long to learn Dorniver's basic rule of survival: depend on nothing and no one but yourself. Each municipal department operated within a larger system of bribery and fraud that extended throughout the Outbacks, the city's tiny police force accepting payment from the same variety of sources as the City Hall clerks. Most of these sources could be tracked to a competing network of gangs, but some led directly to the Interior. Nellie's first lesson in the relationship between the Outbacks and the Interior had come several days after she and her mother had arrived in Culldeen, one of the neighboring Outback cities. They'd been standing in a slow-moving checkout line at a corner store, and when they'd finally reached the till Nellie's mother had asked, "Could you give me directions to the city housing registry, please?"

"Now what d'you want that for?" the dumpy middle-aged clerk had asked, shooting her a narrow glance. Cigarette smoke wreathed her head. Though it was mid-afternoon, she was wearing pink sponge curlers and a brilliantly flowered, short-sleeved housecoat. Fascinated, Nellie had watched the huge blankets of flesh fold and refold above her elbows.

"We're new here," Nellie's mother had responded quietly. "We're looking for an apartment to rent."

The clerk had nodded, her eyes flicking across their bandaged wrists. "Take my advice, dearie," she'd advised bluntly, ringing in their purchases. "Go to City Hall and you'll be selling your soul to the devil. You'll never get their noses out of your ass and they'll be sniffing from a long ways off, if you take my meaning."

Nellie's mother had taken her meaning, paling noticeably.

"Best just to walk around and look for signs in the windows," the woman had said, handing over their bag of groceries.

"But I haven't seen any For Rent signs," Nellie's mother had said wearily. "We've looked everywhere."

The woman had given a slight grin, then glanced around the store to see if anyone was within earshot. "What you're looking for," she'd said quietly, "is a susurra. A small blue flower. If a house has rooms for rent, you'll see a potted susurra in the front window."

They'd located rooms within half an hour. Several months later, when they'd moved to Dorniver, they'd found much the same system in place, the local inhabitants presenting an impassive, almost stupid, face to city bureaucrats and outsiders, all the while entertaining a complex level of insider communication through coded phrases, gestures, and objects placed casually in a window. No one who knew anything volunteered contact with city officials. More business was done through barter than the common currency, and only the naive used credit cards. Technology was viewed as a means of surveillance and avoided wherever possible. This applied even to the hospital, whose connections to the Interior were well known, and most utilized the services of neighborhood witches and healers. School attendance was erratic at the best of times—colleges and universities existed only in the Interior—and the majority of students dropped out in favor of part-time jobs long before they'd reached the legal age. Mail was delivered only to those who purchased post-office boxes, as street signs were constantly disappearing, and many of Dorniver's residents refused to display numbers on their houses. Census takers faced an impossible task. Inhabitants pressed for information were likely to grow hostile, send a child for the carving knife, and stand silently stroking the blade until the census taker backed off in the interests of his or her own throat.

It was an atmosphere that suited Nellie—wary, silent, and sharp-edged. Arriving at the city's outskirts she headed into the Waktuk district, Dorniver's oldest suburb. Experience had taught her that flux was strongest here. Even on the days no stars sang in her dreams, she could spot turbulence bubbling to the surface through sudden gusts of light from windows or doorways that had nothing to do with the city's unreliable electrical system, or in the face of a passerby that momentarily blurred and took an entirely different form before regaining its usual features. Fearful Outbackers called this a 'doubling' and wore the root of a nevva bush on a chain around the throat to ward off those moments of flux that allowed curious entities from other levels of reality to temporarily merge consciousness with someone in this one. Others raved about the visions the experience brought them, claiming they found them-selves flying with angels or fused with the energy of stars.

Slipping carefully through the mid-morning throng, Nellie watched for signs of flux—a display of oranges rolling off a table, a cat bolting from a doorway, a curtain in an open window to her right that rose on a gust of wind while its partner hung flat. Gleefully she noted the window's location at the side of a house, set back from the street and partially obscured by a doogden tree. Ducking behind the tree she waited and soon felt the ripple of flux leave the curtain and enter her body. With a delighted giggle she rode a rush of changing sensations as her body began to shift rapidly through an astonishing array of forms—demon, gargoyle, two-footed reptilian, strange-singing bird, star, and angel—culminating in a figure of light that seemed to be made entirely of small crystals.

Finally the surge of energy left her and Nellie found herself once again in the body of a twelve-year-old girl, standing beneath a limp set of window curtains. To her left, the street scene progressed as usual. No one seemed to have noticed her rapid-fire shapeshifting experience, but most Outbackers preferred to put on blinkers when flux entered their lives, grabbing at the hunk of nevva root around their throats and muttering incantations to the Goddess. This was both sad and stupid, Nellie had decided. Sometimes, as she passed from one shape to another, she could have sworn she felt Ivana's delighted laughter rippling through her body. The Goddess didn't mind Her children exploring flux, Nellie was certain of it, though the idea of being doubled left her less keen. *Imagine something from another level sticking its snout through yours so it can take a casual look around,* she thought, shuddering, and reminded herself to dig up a hunk of nevva root as soon as possible.

About to head back onto the street, she glanced to her right and froze. Just on the other side of a small hedge stood a corner store, and there on its sunlit wall a shadow was shifting in and out of itself, unattached to anything solid. Peering through the hedge, Nellie gasped softly as the shadow stepped free of the wall and solidified into a casually dressed man who carried signs of the Interior in the heavy-lidded watching of his eyes and the trained nonchalance of his shoulders. Everything about him said *Interior Police, violence waiting for release.* Nellie had never seen an agent of the Interior step out of a moment of flux, hadn't realized they knew anything about manipulating the molecular field or traveling the levels. Spinning on her heel she darted into the crowded street, giving the fluttering hand signal as she went: *Interior Police. Beware, Interior Police.*

Everywhere hands took up the signal, a silent nervous system rippling outward: *Interior Police in the area. Red alert, red alert.* Halfway down the block, Nellie ducked behind a parked car and peeked over the hood. From her position she could see the Interior agent stroll casually past the store's front steps and out into the street, oblivious to the hands that fluttered and gesticulated on all sides. From this point onward, wherever he went Outbackers would be tuned to his presence, watching him from the back of their heads. Everywhere the rippling hand signals would precede him, without a word he would be identified: *Interior Police, beware, beware.*

When she was certain the agent had passed on in search of other prey, Nellie returned to the corner store from which he'd emerged. It was obviously a building in flux, which made it worthy of a second glance. On top of this, it was a building that could supply her with everything she needed for several days. Entering the store she picked up a basket and moved along the aisles, selecting packages of candy, nuts, cold cuts, some bread rolls and fruit. Two women had followed her in and she waited them out, dawdling and scratching at fresh bug bites until they'd completed their purchases. As the clutch of bells tied over the door signaled their departure, she grabbed a large bottle of nevva juice and approached the till.

Everything seemed quiet and she could see no sign of the flux the building had displayed when the Interior agent had emerged from its east wall. Briefly Nellie considered hanging around in the hopes of another shapeshifting rush, but she had more than one goal to accomplish today and needed to act quickly. Besides, she and the clerk were alone in the store, and that simplified her next task greatly. Nellie had never seen anyone else do what she was about to do. No one had taught her this skill. It had come to her, startlingly, after her mother's disappearance, born out of necessity, out of flux. Setting her basket of purchases on the checkout counter, she smiled at the clerk.

"Hi there." The girl behind the counter looked young, perhaps fourteen, her left wrist unblemished and free of scars. Heavy green makeup accented her eyelids, tapering into long wings that scooped across each temple, and silver rings swung from her nose and lips as she punched the first price carelessly into the till. She hadn't given Nellie more than a cursory glance.

Here we go, thought Nellie, letting her own eyelids sink heavily over her eyes. *Slow it all down, turn it inside-out.*

"Inside-out" was her term for it, knowing no other way to describe the sensation of flipping backward into the darkness of her head, where she dissolved into a deep throbbing hum. At the same time she remained conscious of her position in front of the till, staring at the oblivious clerk through the narrow slits of her eyes. It was a little like being in two places at once. Anchored inside her physical body, Nellie also floated within the deep hum of her mind, sending herself beyond her own skin like an electrical field that permeated everything in its path and converted it into a vast pattern of shimmering bits of energy. As she did, solid objects lost their outlines and the molecules within each box and can of food, the counter before her, even the clerk's body, came into focus, humming and throbbing like a massive swarm of bees.

Or souls, thought Nellie, vibrating at the center of the vast pattern that surrounded her. *Rocks and water and walls and tin cans all have souls. Most people just can't see them.*

Tuning into the molecular plane of existence was a little like being shifted into high gear, and her thoughts raced as she scanned the throbbing pattern. As far as she'd been able to figure out, the molecular field served as a buffer—a kind of intermediate stage you had to tune into in order to be able to see the exit points leading to the next level of reality. If you didn't know how to locate these gates you were stuck in your home level, the one into which you'd been born. Probing the shimmering bits of energy that lay before her, Nellie quickly found what she was seeking—three, no four tiny seams that ran spiderlike through the quivering mass that surrounded them. Four gates. This corner store had obviously been used for inter-level traveling before.

Slowing her thoughts, Nellie tuned partway back into her normal view of reality. As she did, the shelves of tin cans and baked goods swam into focus, overlapped with her view of the molecular field so each object hummed and shifted within its outline. Across the counter the clerk now radiated such a mass of energy that it drifted, free-form, from her arms and back. Nellie grinned, thinking of angels she'd seen pictured in children's books. Superimposing realities made them much more interesting. It also meant she could now figure out how the four gates aligned with solid reality. A quick scan of the overlapped realities located one seam snaking horizontally along the wall beside the store entrance, another laid across the floor, and two that hovered vertically midair—the closest at body height and a mere two steps to her right.

Perfect, Nellie thought with a burst of satisfaction. The Goddess was definitely looking out for her today. Traveling between the levels was much easier if a ready-made gate stood waiting in a convenient position. All she had to do now was stop time in this level, open the gate and step through. But first she had to position herself so she was standing directly against the gate. A foot too far to the right or left and she would miss her chance.

Taking two steps to the right, Nellie positioned herself so the vertical midair seam ran directly through her body. Then she fixed on the hum at the base of her brain and moved deep into its vibrations. *Slow,* she thought. *Slow it all down, take it toward sleep. Sleep, sleep, everything sleep.* Obedient to her thoughts, the hum deepened. As it did, the room's molecular field began to lose its intensity, a swarm of bees settling for a long winter nap. *Dream,* Nellie whispered into the quieting pattern. *Dream a snake sunning itself, dream a drowsy stone.*

On the other side of the counter, the clerk sagged against the till and yawned. Through the molecular field that connected them, Nellie could feel the other girl's heartbeat thicken and her mouth take on the taste of sleep. *Falling, falling,* she whispered into the clerk's mind. *The air is growing heavy and you are falling down a long dark tunnel toward sleep.*

Drowsily, the clerk glanced at the clock above her head, watching the arrow-tipped hands that dragged between seconds. "Geeeeeeez, I'm sleeeeeepeeee," she slurred, her index finger drifting over the till.

Let her add everything up first, Nellie told herself. *Wait until she's opened the till.*

The hum at the base of her brain deepened yet again, slowing the room's molecular field further. A fly buzzed sluggishly past the clerk's nose, but the girl barely lifted her eyes. About her head dust motes were slowing, and the second hand on the clock was barely moving. Her heavy-lidded eyes skimmed lethargically over Nellie's pile of purchases, checking one last time, and her index finger settled onto the 'Total' key.

"Okaaaaaaaay," she yawned. The till gave a long drawn-out click, the money drawer inched outward, and Nellie sent one last message into the room's molecular field. *Stoooooooop,* she whispered, and the clerk's mouth froze, mid-yawn. Dust motes stopped moving about her head, the fly droned to a halt above her nose, and the clock on the wall came to a standstill—every molecule in the room caught and fixed in a pattern, the pattern of one specific moment.

Carefully Nellie focused on the seam that ran midway through her body. What she had to do now was tricky because she couldn't afford to confuse the gate's molecules with her own. Fortunately the pulse rate of a gate was so unusual, it could immediately be distinguished from any surrounding molecular field, even one that had been locked in time. A gate felt like dead space, a scar of solid nothingness. Sending her mind into the thin line of nothingness that dissected her body, Nellie began to push outward.

The seam divided cleanly, creating a human-sized doorway that stretched several inches beyond her arms. Immediately Nellie sent her mind into the blur that could be seen through the gap, assessing its vibratory rate and bringing her body into sync with it. The process took less than a second. When it was competed, the blur had disappeared and she was stepping into a reality that existed one level beyond the one she'd just left, a virtual copy: same grocery store, same clerk with the same green-winged eyeshadow, and, two steps to Nellie's left, a duplicate of herself, standing with her eyes riveted to the till's money drawer. The only noticeable difference between the two levels was the slightly quicker rate at which this one vibrated, but that was normal. As far as Nellie could tell, the different vibratory rates were what kept the levels separate.

Deeply involved in a heated argument over the price of the bottle of nevva juice, neither the clerk nor Nellie's double appeared to have noticed her. Moving swiftly toward a pyramid of tinned fruit that had been stacked at the front of the baked goods aisle, Nellie yanked a corner can out of position. Instantly cans began toppling onto the shelves of baked goods and cascading to the floor. Without a backward glance she took off for the aisle's other end, then turned and ran up the next one, just in time to see the clerk dart from behind the till, intent on saving the doughnuts. Unguarded, the till loomed wide-open. *Perfect*, Nellie exulted as she slipped behind the counter. There was enough money here to keep her fed for weeks. Ditching her excitement, she reached for the nearest wad of bills.

But another hand beat her to it. Oblivious to Nellie, her double was sprawled across the counter, fumbling and snatching at anything within reach. With a hiss, Nellie raked her fingernails across the back of her double's hand. As it withdrew, she began ramming bills and coins into her pockets. The fact that her double had seen her was of little concern. This often happened when she traveled the levels, but her doubles were usually so stunned by the experience that they did little more than gawk. This double was more active than most, but the person Nellie figured she had to keep an eye on was the clerk, who was moaning loudly and plucking cans out of the dengleberry tarts. If *she* turned around, the molecular field would really start jumping. Lifting the cash drawer, Nellie scrabbled for coins that might have slipped underneath.

"Hand it over, all of it," hissed a voice, and suddenly a knife appeared beneath Nellie's nose. Startled, she glanced up to see her double leaned toward her, reaching for the money she hadn't yet shoved into a pocket. As usual they were mirror images, dressed in the same T-shirt and jeans, their blond hair pulled back into the same short ponytail and glaring at each other with the same unusually slanted gray eyes. But the knife dancing beneath Nellie's nose was definitely out of sync with the mirror image. Just as she'd thought, this store was in flux. That was the intriguing thing about flux—you could never predict the way it would reveal itself.

And then before Nellie's eyes, her double began to shapeshift. Openmouthed, Nellie stood fixed in her human form, watching her double rotate rapid-fire through a variety of threatening forms— ghoul, vampire, gargoyle, demon. But how was that possible? Nellie could feel no flux in the air, no quirk in the molecular field. Her double seemed to be manipulating her own physical reality entirely at will.

Returning to human form, the double glowered at Nellie. "I don't know who you are or where you come from," she said grimly, "but this is *my* store. *Everything* in it's mine."

There was no need to panic—shapeshifting and a knife were mere technicalities against a gate to another level. Jabbing a finger in the direction of the clerk, Nellie shouted, "Look out!" Then, as her double whirled to see what was behind her, Nellie darted around the counter toward the gate. Stepping into the gap, she drew the two halves of the gate together and sealed them, then synchronized her vibratory rate with her home level's. Gradually she brought the surrounding molecular field back into time. Dust motes began to drift and the fly buzzed away from the clerk's nose.

On the wall the clock dragged itself through one second, then another. Slowly the clerk took a deep shuddering breath.

"I need a coffee break," she muttered, one hand pressed to her heart as if to make sure it was still beating. "That'll be fifteen dollars and ninety-four cents."

Pulling a crumpled bill from her pocket, Nellie handed it over. Without hesitation the clerk gave her the change and packed her purchases into a bag.

"Thanks." Untroubled by guilt, Nellie headed for the exit. Perception created reality and as far as her home level was concerned, she'd left everyone well-paid and satisfied. If this clerk remembered anything out of the ordinary, she would dismiss it as a wild dream, and if a fourteen-year-old girl in the next level was fired due to money that had gone missing on her shift, it was none of Nellie's concern. Flux upended everyone's life, whether or not you clued into its existence. This time it had left her with the task of figuring out how her double had been able to shapeshift when there was no sign of flux in the vicinity. Once she'd solved that question, Nellie would also be able to shapeshift whenever she wanted.

Whistling, she leapt off the store's front porch and swaggered down the street, munching contentedly on a bread roll.

Chapter 4

S HE HAD ONE MORE GOAL for the day—to buy a metal canister for food storage. Digging out a candy bar, Nellie swung the grocery bag over her shoulder and slipped into the busy street. Already the corner store theft was fading from her thoughts. One last memory of her shapeshifting, knife-carrying double crossed her mind—now that had been a real rush, a double that made her think for a change—and then she ditched the incident completely and focused on the surrounding crowd.

On all sides street pedlars bartered with women who were keeping sharp eyes on the children that darted shrieking about their knees. Eagerly Nellie's gaze flicked over the scene, taking in everything she saw and filing it as information that could be used to shore up her shrinking store of memories about her own mother. These related mostly to the time they'd spent in the Outbacks before her mother disappeared, for Nellie could recall very little of their life in the Interior, and the urge to fill those missing years with some kind of story had her continually searching her environment for details from the lives of other children. Had her mother, for instance, ever grabbed Nellie's arm and yanked her out of a spit fight like the mother scolding her seven-year-old son across

the street? Probably. Had she braided her daughter's hair with red
ribbons and bells like the small girl seated next to the vendor selling
animal-head balloons? Probably not, and it seemed like a surefire
way to drive a kid crazy, but still Nellie followed every twist and
turn of the little girl's head, listening as the bells sent out their faint
tinkle. This would make a lovely bedtime story to tell herself about
her own mother, she decided wistfully—the two of them walking
through a bustling market, Nellie's hair tinkling down her back,
her small hand engulfed in her mother's large palm.

A new thought struck her. Why not buy a few ribbons and braid
them through her hair? Thoughtfully Nellie tugged at the ragged
tendrils hanging over her ears. Generally she attacked the stuff on
her head with a pair of rusty scissors when it got too long, but today
she had enough money, more than enough—and there was a barbershop nearby. She could get it done *professionally*. Grandly Nellie
played with the word on her tongue, tasting its importance. Already
she could see herself sitting in the barber's fancy chair, pretending
it was actually her mother cutting her hair, or better yet, that her
mother had sent her there to get her hair done *professionally*. Yes,
that was what she would do. Excitement mounting, Nellie headed
toward the barbershop, sketching out the scene in her head. She'd
just come home from school. *My dearest darling*, her mother had
said lovingly, stroking Nellie's lovely waist-long locks. *I think it's
time you had a haircut. You're the star in the school play tomorrow
night, and you'll need to look your best. Here's some money. Go get it
cut and come home quickly, so I can see how beautiful you look.*

Yes, that was it—her mother was at home right now, waiting for
Nellie to return with her *professionally* cut hair. Cheeks flushed,
breathing anticipation, Nellie pressed against the barbershop
window. As far as she could see there were no customers in the shop,
the barber standing alone in front of the mirror, rearranging bottles
of shampoo. Why not go all out and get her hair washed too? Her
mother would like that. She would pull Nellie close, bury her nose
in the fresh shampoo scent of her hair and say, *Nellie darling*—

"Where ya going, Bunny?" a voice sneered behind her.

Nellie whirled but the Skulls had already surrounded her, breathing heavily as if they'd been running for blocks. Hornets of fear swarmed her brain but she managed a frantic head count that took in everyone but Deller.

"Barbershop, eh? Think you're going to get pretty?" jeered Pullo, a large heavyset boy who seemed to be Deller's second-in-command. Slit-eyed and intent the boys pressed closer, staring at the blobs on Nellie's chest. With a grunt she shoved the nearest one. He shoved back and she coughed, winded.

"Look, she bought us dindin," yelled the boy next to him, a kid with a mean yellow squint called Snakebite. Snatching Nellie's grocery bag, he opened it.

"We'll eat later." Ducking down, Pullo grabbed Nellie around the knees and upended her over his shoulder. Immediately she exploded into a frenzy of kicks and punches. Someone shoved her face into Pullo's back, muffling her cries. Enraged, she bit deeply into his T-shirt, worrying the flesh underneath until a punch to her head dissolved her into a whimpering mass. The ground arced dizzily beneath her, taking a pendulum swing as Pullo rounded a corner. Coins rained from her pockets, the boys pushing and shoving to get at them.

"She's got money?" grunted Pullo. "Check her pockets."

She was ransacked, the boys whooping as they brandished fifty-dollar bills.

"All right," said Pullo. "Let's keep going."

She tried clawing her way up Pullo's ponytail, but her head was punched a second time and she sank into a jarring upside-down swoon. Blood collected thickly along her eyelids and pounded in her upper lip. She thought she could feel Pullo starting to tire, a stagger creeping into his walk. Maybe he would set her down soon and she could make a run for it. Tendrils of an upside-down plan began to form in her dizzy brain, but all thoughts of escape vanished as Pullo passed through a doorway, banging her knee carelessly against the

doorjamb. Dumping her onto the floor he sank, gasping, beside her.
A door slammed shut behind them.

"You got her."

Still swaying inside the darkness of her head, Nellie recognized
Deller's voice. Someone kicked at her back. She didn't move.

"What, you kill her already?" Deller demanded.

"Playing dead," panted Pullo.

"I'll give her dead," said Deller. "Dead meat."

This time she rolled to avoid his foot and the room danced a half
circle, skittering as she tried to sit up.

"She was going to get herself pretty at the barbershop," jeered
Snakebite.

Nellie squinted, fighting the swing in her head. So this was the
Skulls' headquarters, a dim shabby room lit by a single candle that
burned on a nearby table. Several broken-down chairs leaned at
various angles against the opposite wall, and the single window was
covered with cardboard. Turning her head slowly, Nellie scanned
for exits. Immediately behind her was the doorway through which
she'd been carried, and to her right was another that led further into
the building. The only other exit was the black cave that loomed
inside her head, threatening to engulf her completely. Should she
try tuning into the molecular field to locate a gate to another level?
No, too dizzy. Wait a bit.

Sinking carefully into a three-legged armchair, Deller watched
her survey the room. A tiny thrill of satisfaction shot through
Nellie as she saw the heavily bandaged hand in his lap, and she
let go a tiny grin. "Shake and make up?" she asked softly, and a
collective gasp rose from the boys behind her. Deller's eyes widened, but he raised his good hand as someone grabbed Nellie's
shoulder.

"She needs kicking," Pullo protested.

"She'll get kicking," Deller promised, "but first she gets a
haircut." Pulling some money from his pocket, he held it out.
"Snakey, fetch some shaving cream and a razor."

Nellie's eyes narrowed, darting between Deller and the rest of the gang. "They got money," she spat contemptuously. "They stole a hundred and forty off me."

Deller's gaze shot dangerously toward the other boys.

"We were going to show you," whined Snakebite, giving Nellie a swift kick in the leg.

"*Show* me?" Deller hissed.

"Give it to you." Reluctantly the boys handed over the money and Deller made an awkward one-handed count.

"You got your own private bank account, Bunny?" Deller asked, granting her a curious glance.

"Found it," she said tersely.

"You got real lucky. Then we got lucky." Grinning, Deller handed Snakebite a bill. "And bring back the receipt," he ordered, giving the fidgety boy a long stare.

They came at her without warning, and once they'd grabbed her there was no longer any chance of tuning into the molecular field. She needed calm for that kind of focus, a moment separate and breathing at its own pace, not screaming wild in her face like this one. Once their hands were on her she became a cyclone of fear, biting, scratching and kicking, and they had to work to get her into one of the chairs, then tie her sloppily to it with a few odd ends of rope. Finally they backed off, muttering and nursing their bruises. Immediately Nellie fixed on Deller, riding the thin electric vibe she could feel humming between them. Tilted in his three-legged chair, he'd watched impassively as the other boys tied her up. Now he sauntered over to inspect her fastenings. Though his eyes never quite met hers, she felt him watching her like she watched him. If that vibe faded between them, if he lost interest, she was a goner. Not even the Goddess would be able to save her then.

The outer door slammed open and Snakebite rushed in, flourishing a receipt. Handing a paper bag to Deller, he demanded, "Who's going to do it?"

"I am," Deller said calmly.

"But your hand's wrecked," Pullo protested.

"I got my best one left." Pulling out the can of shaving cream, Deller leaned into Nellie's face and grinned. "Just don't make any sudden moves, and there won't be no accidental brain surgery, right Bunny?"

The gang dissolved into raucous laughter as he squirted a mound of foam into her face, then covered the rest of her head. Blinking hard, Nellie fought to keep her eyes open, but the sweet-smelling foam was liquid fire and she was forced to sit in searing darkness as the razor tugged at her hairline. Her heart lurched at every sound and she tried to track the circling boys by their voices, but the shaving foam crept into her ears, its bubbles popping madly. Pain slivered her scalp as the razor snagged. Someone's arm brushed her ear, wiping away some of the foam, and sounds came back into focus, Deller swearing as the razor snagged again.

"Should've cut it with scissors first," muttered Pullo.

"Now you tell me," Deller snapped. "Anyone got scissors?" When no one responded he changed his shaving technique, asking Pullo to hold up Nellie's hair while he sawed it off in small bunches, then went at what remained with short harsh scrapes. Gradually the last of her hair began to give, the cool air nuzzling her scalp.

"C'mon Deller, give her a slash," someone jeered. "Something to remember us by."

"She'll remember, all right." Tiny nicks of pain dug into Nellie's scalp as Deller worked his way across her head. Every now and then he would pause, as if contemplating his handiwork. The last pause had been the longest, and then he'd started scraping at the left side of her head. Pausing again, he let out a long whistle.

"Sweet sweet Goddess," someone whispered.

"Where'd she get that?" asked Snakebite.

"Lobotomy, man," muttered Pullo.

They spoke in awed whispers then fell silent, intent as a cat licking its hind end. Fear sang through Nellie's skin. Something weird was being uncovered on her scalp, something she didn't know about and yet she did too—a long ago secret that had something to do with the bright rooms of the Interior. Even though she couldn't remember the details, the fear of it was like a sickness gnawing at her gut. Whimpering, she tugged against her bindings.

"Hold her," snapped Deller and someone grabbed Nellie's head, holding it fast. Scraping carefully, Deller worked his way across the secrets on her scalp. Tears slipped through Nellie's tightly squeezed eyes, moans twisted her mouth. Finally the razor clattered to the floor and a T-shirt was rubbed roughly across her face and head, clearing the foam. Opening her eyes, she focused on the raw blur of Deller's face hovering inches from her own.

"What happened to you, Bunny?" She could hear the airy hook of fear in his voice. "There's scars all over your head," he said softly. "Like you've been ... cut open. Like they siphoned out your brains."

No one snorted.

"Let me see," she choked, avoiding his gaze.

"Get the bathroom mirror," said Deller. Feet pounded out of the room and Snakebite's voice came hollering down a hallway.

"It won't come off the wall."

"Smash it," Deller yelled impatiently.

A crash followed and then Snakebite called, "There's a hundred pieces. Someone come help."

Two more boys ran from the room. Returning with various-sized fragments, the three gathered around Nellie, holding the glass to her shorn scalp. The air pulsed with their damp breathing. She thought she was about to pass out among the scattered images that danced around her head.

"Hold still!" she grunted, and her scalp's scattered reflections slowed their giddy weave, merging into a discernible shape. What she saw then was unrecognizable, her head a bare bulb decorated with tufts of hair and streaks of blood, but it was the scars that sucked her breath away—four thick worms that angled across the top, down the back and along one side.

"All right," she whispered finally. "I've got it."

The boys stepped back, the air growing immediately cooler.

"So," said Deller, leaning in again. "What happened to you, Bunny? Who did it?"

Wordless she stared, and his green eyes glinted. "You don't know, do you?" he said. "Someone's been digging in your brain and you don't know why."

"Yeah, I do." Thoughts ricocheted through Nellie's head. "I'm just not telling."

A corner grin tugged at Deller's mouth. "Well, I'm telling you something, Bunny. This is payback for my missing finger. Pain for pain, a bit of your body for a bit of mine. Not a bad deal, really. At least this time you'll know who did it to you, and why." Pulling a jackknife from his pocket, he waved the blade in her face. "I'm giving you a new scar for your head—the letter D, for Deller. I'm putting my mark on you. You'll be branded." Straightening, he raised the knife.

Fear exploded across Nellie's brain and the words burst unchecked from her mouth. "Okay, I'll tell you what they did," she blurted. "It happened when I was little and lived in the Interior. They put a bomb inside my head. That's the kind of experiments they do to kids who live there."

In a single motion the Skulls drew back, their mouths sucked in, their bodies taut. Everyone in the Outbacks knew someone who'd disappeared into the Interior. Every Outbacker had heard of the experiments.

"You're joshing," Deller challenged cautiously.

Nellie fought to keep hope from surfacing onto her face. A way was opening before her, the tiniest chance at escape. This time her eyes didn't skitter, she nailed Deller with a raw red stare. "A secret code will set it off," she said, fixing on the lie, growing more certain. "I just have to close my eyes and *think* it, and the bomb'll explode. It's nuclear." As slowly as possible, she lowered her eyelids.

With a hiss, Pullo began shuffling toward the door. "I'm outta here."

"No one leaves until I'm untied," Nellie snapped, jerking against the ropes. "You can't get away by running. The blast from my brains'll take out the whole city."

"Let her go, Deller," whined Snakebite. "I don't want to get blowed."

Deller stood, his green eyes in slits, the jackknife still open in his hand. "You're fibbing," he sneered.

"Walk out that door and see," she invited.

His eyes flicked to the exit, and she watched every rumor he'd ever heard about the Interior flash across his face. He didn't believe her, she knew this, but he wasn't willing to gamble on common sense, not with those scars sitting thick and ugly on her head.

With a loud snort Deller cut her free, then backed with the others against the far wall. Hunched and slit-eyed, they waited in silence as Nellie straightened and stared at them. She was free and it was so unbelievable she wanted to laugh, throw back her head and crow. Instead she got to her feet and stared significantly at each Skull in turn. "From now on, you just watch your step around me," she said menacingly. "Now you know my secret, I won't have no mercy."

"Give her back the money, Deller," whined Snakebite, peering over Pullo's shoulder. "Don't let her leave mad."

"C'mon, Deller, give it to her," Pullo urged hoarsely.

"She's lucky to walk out of here alive," snarled Deller, his good hand creeping protectively toward his pocket.

Nellie took a step toward him. "*Kaboom*, Deller," she whispered. "*Kaboom*."

Deller's face leapt with panic. "Okay, okay." Digging into his pocket, he handed her a wad of money. She thought about counting it, but decided not to push her incredible luck.

"Keep the change," she said grandly, stuffing the money into her pocket. "And remember." She traced her fingers slowly across the scars on her shorn scalp. "I'll be thinking my own special thoughts about each one of you."

Drawing out the thrill of a last meaningful glance, she turned and walked out the door.

Chapter 5

CROUCHED BY THE BROOK that ran close to her shack, Nellie traced her fingers slowly over the top of her head. Tiny hairs bristled and a scattering of scrape marks smarted, still raw, under her touch. Deller had shaved her scalp with deliberate carelessness, leaving erratic tufts so her hair would grow back ugly and uneven. *Not such a major penalty to suffer*, thought Nellie, scowling at her watery reflection. *If you considered his missing finger*. Obviously he blamed her for that, and maybe it was partly her fault. With a shiver of unease, she recalled the snarling dog and Deller's eerie moonlit scream. Tit for tat ruled Dorniver's streets, and no one who'd been violated like Deller could have rested until he'd claimed his revenge. The shaving of her head had been a matter of honor, she understood this. But if the Skulls hadn't found the scars on her head, and if she hadn't come up with the lie about the bomb, what would have happened after Deller had carved the D into her scalp? Would they have set her free? Would they?

She was going to get herself pretty at the barbershop. Covering her ravaged scalp with her hands Nellie clucked softly, talking to herself in the wordless sounds she used when alone. Any vague memories she'd had of her mother brushing and braiding her hair had been blown to smithereens by her ordeal with the Skulls. They were gone now; she would never get them back, and her scalp felt like an orphan, like loneliness, an ugly open-mouthed wail. She had to find some way to cover it, hide all that sadness so it wasn't living in full view for everyone to see. That would mean sweating out the summer months under a stupid hat, and where was she going to find one that would cover her entire scalp? She couldn't let any part of it be seen, she couldn't let anyone see the *worms*.

Worms was how she thought of them—four thick worms that writhed silently across her head. Why couldn't she remember how she'd gotten them? *Why?* Hands trembling, Nellie ran her fingers over her scalp yet again. Tracing the scars was like reaching into a coffin to touch the dead, some lost part of herself she couldn't remember. The scar tissue felt different from the rest of her scalp— dense and smooth, an alien presence. Once upon a time in the Interior long ago, doctors in white rooms had cut her open, dense thick worms had crawled out of her brain onto her scalp and died there.

Nausea twisted Nellie's stomach, bile rose in her throat and she gagged. Leaning forward she ducked her face into the brook and drank deeply, letting the water wash the tears from her face. She'd come to this quiet place, knowing she had to get out of the shack to think her way through this or her terror would settle into every crack and cranny of her home, coming out at night and making it difficult to sleep. Outside was the best place to work through these kinds of thoughts, where they could be mulled over, then released into the far blue sky.

And so she had chosen this half-circle of kwikwilla trees, whose twisted trunks leaned over a slow-moving pool the brook had carved into the bank. The place was her favorite bathing spot, the quiet pool curtained off by the kwikwillas' thick green fall of wispy branches. This morning she'd been here for over an hour, crouched on the bank, riding the frightened thud of her heart. Grimly she retraced the long lines of deadness in her scalp. The scars felt like the gates in the molecular field that she used to pass between the levels. Did that make the scars on her scalp some kind of a gate too?

They contained secrets to her past, that was certain. But did she want to open those secrets and explore them more deeply? The short blurred memories she retained of the white rooms were already enough to leave her whimpering with fear. Whatever the pain doctors had done to the inside of her head was over and done with. Was it important to remember the exact details?

Most of her memories of the Interior revealed scenes from a very normal life—an average-looking, squirmy, loud-mouthed kid goofing off on the school playground or eating supper with her mother. But the scenes changed so often—Nellie could remember what felt like an endless stream of apartments and schools. Looking back, it seemed as if she and her mother had been on the run throughout the last few years they'd lived in the Interior, but had pretended nothing unusual was going on, even between themselves. *Why?* thought Nellie, hugging herself and rocking. Why had her mother never explained their frequent moves, or the long moody silences that had filled their last few apartments? Every time she looked at these memories, Nellie filled with an overwhelming sense of deadness, as if the memories themselves were playacting at being alive, as if they'd never been the real thing even when they were happening.

Sometimes, in odd quiet moments when she was least expecting it, she would feel a shift inside her head and a different kind of memory would surface—something that felt real, that almost explained things. Like the time she was four years old and visiting a neighbor's newborn with her mother. The new mother had been sitting on her living room couch, smiling and cradling a tightly wrapped blanket. "Come here, Nellie," she'd called, and Nellie had run toward the woman, a sweet scent of milk and baby powder rising to meet her as she'd peeked into the blanket. A tiny wrinkled face had blinked unfocused eyes at her and waved a delicate red fist. Immediately Nellie's gaze had slid to the inside of the infant's wrist, and a sudden vivid knowing had sung through her brain. Pointing to the infant's fresh tattoo, she'd declared, "That's so they know where she can go to."

Silence had dropped on the room then, so thick and intense it had seemed to swallow the very air. Confused, Nellie had turned from the neighbor woman to her mother, but both women's eyes had flitted away as if they'd no longer wanted to see her, no longer wanted even to remain in the same room. When they'd gotten back to their own apartment, her mother had started packing. At bedtime Nellie had been given a pill and when she'd woken, they were somewhere else. In the weeks that followed, she remembered waking each morning in a different place, her mother's body curled around her own like a warm hand. Nothing had been explained, but she'd felt the fear her words had caused. Lying beside her silent mother she'd thought back to that moment, trying to remember why she'd spoken those exact words, but their meaning had come and gone like the blink of an eye, a turn of the head. Like flux.

That's so they know where she can go to. Crouched beside the brook, Nellie rested her chin on her knees and stared into the rippling water. The newborn's tattoo had been a Cat, like her own. They'd been of the same caste, which meant the infant would eventually attend the same schools, use the same public swimming pools, and choose from the same narrow range of career options. Everyone knew this, so why had her words caused so much dread?

Unless I was talking about the levels. The thought exploded across Nellie's mind, thundering her heart. *But how could I?* she thought wildly. *I didn't know about levels back then. The Interior doesn't have levels, just like it doesn't have flux.*

Or did it? Was it possible her inability to remember much about her life in the Interior was connected to the levels that existed there, and the way flux was used to travel them? After all, she'd seen an agent step out of a pocket of flux in a corner store wall, so someone from the Interior obviously knew about it. And the experiment she'd seen by the quarry, with the children and the birdlike machines—that had been about traveling too. Nellie's heart plummeted. What if the mysterious scars worming across her scalp were also connected to experiments with flux and the levels? Getting quickly to her feet, she stripped and waded into the quiet pool. It wasn't good to do too much thinking in one day, especially if she wasn't sure what she was thinking about. And it couldn't be healthy for a brain to work too hard, especially one that had been cut open like hers. She'd better give it a rest and think about something easy, like getting hold of a stupid hat.

Eyes closed she floated on the murmuring water, trying to forget the worms on her scalp and the white rooms that hid behind them. Turning onto her side, she whispered softly to the flecks of light that speckled the water's surface: *Have you seen my mother? She disappeared sixteen months ago. She never said goodbye, but sometimes she still comes to me and tells me she loves me ...*

A WICKAWOO CRIED LOW in its throat and Nellie stiffened, hugging the shadow of a backyard shed. Up and down the alley a ripple passed through the air as Outbackers turned in their beds, following the bird's warning cry through their dreams. Pressed against the shed Nellie counted heartbeats and waited, but nothing moved in the stillness. The night had turned deep into the hour past midnight, and the wickawoo had caught her creeping through one of Dorniver's southern districts, a neighborhood known locally as 'Snake Eye' due to its many witches and healers. All things considered, it was a perfect place to be on the first night of Lulunar, the month of the twins, the only time of year the two moons came together to ride the night sky in a parallel arc, and the air breathed flux.

During the year's eight other months the moons could be seen at various positions in the night sky, separated by vast distances. *By loneliness*, thought Nellie, staring up at them. After all, the moons were human, the souls of the Goddess's twin sons. Separated at birth, they'd spent their entire lives searching for each other without success. Upon their deaths the gods had granted them immortality for their perseverance, and now their pure shining souls rode the heavens every night as a reminder of the gods' wisdom and love. What would it be like, Nellie pondered from her position in the shed's shadow, to be immortal and ride the skies like that? The Goddess's priests were always talking about how the faithful would become stars when they died. She scowled. And pagans would fall into utter darkness and vanish into nothingness. Serve them right for not believing in the Goddess and living in filth and wickedness.

What was weird, she thought, *giving the moons one last glance, was the way people thought of Lulunar as the month of insanity, when everything became its opposite and chaos reigned.* Already Outbackers were posting small statues of the Goddess over doorways and in windows as protection against the doubling that was said to attack even the clearest of minds at this time. Why Lulunar was considered the month of insanity, when it was the only time the twins' souls were united, was something Nellie hadn't been able to figure out. Certainly her schoolteacher hadn't explained this aspect of the myth when they'd studied it in the Interior. She shrugged. Back then she hadn't paid much attention to the Goddess and Her sons. Sure she'd gone to church on major holidays and paid obeisance to the gods and the stars, but she'd had a mother then, and she'd thought she always would. She hadn't *needed* the Goddess, not really. Fiercely Nellie blinked back the tears stinging her eyes. Fortunately, Ivana was the Mother of all mothers, and willing to overlook mistakes of the past. Otherwise there would be no one to love her now.

Easing out of the shed's shadow, she waited, but the troubled wickawoo seemed to have subsided into sleep. Still, she knew enough to be cautious—the twin moons might be in their crescent phase, but they were currently riding the center of the sky, casting everything into sharp relief, and the city was a restless sleeper at the best of times. With a last glance up and down the alley she started off, lifting the kerchief wrapped around her head and scratching irritably. A week had elapsed since the Skulls' attack and her scalp itched constantly as new hairs pushed through the skin. Sometimes the urge to scratch drove her frantic and she would claw at her scalp, wanting to dig the itch out by its roots. Sniffing her fingertips for blood, she licked them clean, then tied the kerchief securely into place.

A doogden tree loomed to her right and she slipped behind it, then peered out at a domed structure that sat at the alley's far end. A wealth of arches and gables, the Sanctuary of the Blessed Goddess was one of many small parishes dedicated to Ivana that were scattered throughout Dorniver's poorer suburbs. Rising from the center of its domed roof was a spire tipped by a pair of brass hands—the Goddess's hands, cupped and lifted high above the city. Again tears stung Nellie's eyes. The Goddess never rested; all over Dorniver Her hands lifted from church spires, continually beseeching the heavens to gaze upon Her followers with mercy.

Leaving the doogden tree, she trotted down the alley toward the church. A quick run across a small parking lot, then along a short wall brought her into a narrow courtyard that nestled against the back of the building. Sharp-edged shadows slanted down the parish walls. In the radiant moonlight each cobblestone was clearly etched and the silvered air hung motionless, waiting within itself. As far as she could see, everything was on schedule, which meant she was early.

Darting across the courtyard, she ducked behind a large rain barrel that stood opposite a metal dumpster. It had taken several weeks' careful watching to discover the secret that lay behind the dumpster—a small service door that led directly into the church. During the day the dumpster was kept shoved against the wall so the door couldn't be seen, but on certain nights it was pulled out just enough to permit the body of a man to slip sideways through the gap—not just one, as Nellie had eventually discovered, but eight, in a predictable sequence with five minutes' wait between each one. If everything went as usual tonight, she'd arrived approximately ten minutes ahead of the first man. Flattening herself against the barrel, she tucked her breathing into a quiet inner place, and settled down to wait.

She would never have known about the hidden door if it hadn't been for a gang of boys who'd been hired to patrol the neighborhood on the nights the men came to the church. About a month ago she'd been out rambling Snake Eye's curiously twisted streets on one of her frequent night prowls, when the gang had spotted her and shoved her around before warning her off the area. Something about the way they'd delivered the message, as if it came from the Goddess Herself, and the way they'd let her off so easily, had told Nellie they were working for someone who wanted the area kept clear and quiet. In the following weeks, she'd haunted the neighborhood. The gang had been easy enough to avoid once she'd known they were there, and she'd soon noted the shadowy men who'd turned, one by one, down the side wall of the Sanctuary of the Blessed Goddess. It had been short work to track them to the courtyard and the hidden door, and several more weeks' observation had established their meeting times—alternating every third and fourth night, one hour past midnight.

Gradually the men began to arrive. As usual they kept to a tight schedule, slipping around the far corner at five-minute intervals, glancing once around the courtyard, then heading directly toward the dumpster and the hidden door. Each man entered the courtyard wearing the same guarded posture, and their order of arrival followed an established sequence. In fact everything about the men seemed prearranged and methodical, and it was this that had originally piqued Nellie's curiosity. Fixed patterns of behavior were the norm in the Interior, but in the Outbacks they stuck out like a sore thumb. Squeezing herself deeper into the narrow space behind the barrel, she scratched at the pimples forming over several ingrown hairs on her scalp, and waited.

The first man slipped across the courtyard, then the second. Predictable as ever, they were also deadly quiet—one moment the courtyard stretched silent and empty, and the next a soundless figure was gliding past Nellie's hiding place toward the dumpster, his face clearly identifiable in the moonlight. During the past few weeks she'd passed several of these men in the street during daylight hours and they'd seemed entirely ordinary, with nothing to distinguish them from the next man. What would call them from their beds to come sneaking through the streets to the Goddess's sanctuary, night after night? And what could the Goddess possibly have to tell them one hour past midnight that She couldn't say during daylight hours? If Ivana had secrets to tell, Nellie damn well wanted to hear them. Slitting her eyes, she maintained a careful watch on the silent courtyard.

Overhead the twin moons traveled their parallel arc, pouring down a thick pearly light. The third man arrived, and the fourth. Then a long pause followed, during which Nellie massaged a cramp in her leg, stopping immediately when the sixth man appeared. Where was the fifth? Nellie counted in her head, recalling the men's individual faces. Yes, it was the fifth man who hadn't shown. Sometimes a man failed to arrive, but the order of appearance always continued unchanged. As the seventh, then eighth man slipped behind the dumpster she crouched, arguing furiously with herself. Her tentative plan had been to follow the eighth man into the church, but what if the fifth had been delayed and was just around the corner? *Don't be a wimp*, she scoffed inwardly. These guys were robots. If the fifth man hadn't shown in sequence, he was sick or out of town.

She was about to step out from the barrel when a slight sound froze her into position, just in time to escape the notice of a figure that was slinking into the courtyard. Shooting glances in every direction, it crept cautiously toward the dumpster. A hyper-alertness sang through Nellie's brain and she leaned forward, muttering under her breath. Whoever this guy was, he wasn't one of the usual eight. He was too short for one thing, and was moving with greater stealth, keeping an arm over his face. Even so, she was sure she knew him from somewhere. The figure reached the dumpster and turned, dropping its arm to sweep the courtyard with one last glance, and Nellie went rigid, recognizing Deller's narrow weasely face. Still favoring his bandaged hand, he was cradling it against his stomach. Without a sound he turned toward the dumpster and slid behind it.

Well, that settled it. Any hesitation Nellie might have had about following strange men into an unfamiliar building late at night went up in smoke as she watched Deller slip through the shadowy doorway ahead of her. No way was she sitting with her butt glued to a mundane rain barrel while that nine-fingered weasel was in there, spying on Snake Eye's inner mysteries. Easing out from behind the barrel, she was halfway across the courtyard when a sudden murmur of voices coming along the church's west wall sent her scuttling back to her hiding place. Hunched deep in the barrel's shadow, she peered out cautiously, then stared wide-eyed at the two men crossing the courtyard. One was the fifth man, out of sequence—no surprise there. But unless Lulunar was pulling one of its doubling tricks, she'd seen his companion one week ago, close to the deserted quarry. For the tenth figure currently crossing the courtyard was the driver of the burgundy van, the man who'd lifted the four children out of the back of the vehicle. Why would the fifth man bring a pain doctor, an Interior agent, to a middle-of-the-night meeting in one of the Goddess's sanctuaries?

Stifling a yelp of warning, Nellie sank further into the barrel's shadow. Vague white rooms swirled in her head, followed by a wave of nausea. *Get a grip*, she thought, hitting her stomach with both hands. *No one's going to live this life for you if you don't.*

When her nausea cleared, she peered around the barrel and saw the two men had gone in. Quickly she crossed the courtyard and slid behind the dumpster, then passed through a narrow doorway into a low-ceilinged corridor. There she waited, nostrils flared, as her eyes adjusted to the gloom. The air felt heavy, weighted with the scent of closed-in places. To her left the corridor disappeared into darkness, but a hundred feet to her right a low-watt ceiling bulb burned.

Leaving the door to the courtyard slightly ajar, Nellie turned, about to proceed along the hall when she noticed a small alcove carved into the wall directly opposite. Set into the alcove was a statue of the Goddess dressed in Her usual blue robe, hands raised in supplication and an unlit candle at Her feet. At the sight of the candle, a hiss snaked from Nellie's lips. *Sacrilege.* Any true believer would have the parish priest drawn and quartered for such disrespect. Leaning forward she kissed Ivana's feet and whispered profuse apologies, then turned and tiptoed along the narrow corridor. The walls leaned in, the air pressed close. Without tuning into the molecular field she could sense what seemed to be countless gates to other levels, their spidery seams running the walls, ceiling, and floor. A tiny wave of flux came at her, rippling the air with warning. Instinctively she stepped toward it, always ready for another shapeshifting rush, then regretfully drew back. She was here for a higher purpose, a divine purpose really—to discover the Goddess's secrets and protect Her from the ninth man, if need be. For tonight, the joys of flux would have to wait.

She reached the low-watt bulb to find the corridor forked and turned left toward an open doorway. Through it she could see rows of pews and beyond them, a faintly lit floor-to-ceiling statue of the Goddess. Creeping to the doorway, Nellie peered into the main sanctuary of the church. All around the room candles flickered in alcoves and on various tables, blossoming into a fiery field beneath the feet of the huge statue of the Goddess that dominated the front wall. Hands cupped She stood in the usual position, feet bare and eyes uplifted. Sometimes those hands held ceremonial objects that had been consecrated for a specific purpose, and several times Nellie had seen them cradle the bloody heart of a freshly sacrificed animal, but tonight they were empty.

At the front of the sanctuary she could see the shadowy outlines of the men seated in the first several pews. Facing them was the parish priest, dressed in his emerald green robe of daily office. As they spoke the men's voices blurred and overlapped, playing tricks with echoes, too quick to be made out clearly. Nellie scowled. She was going to have to move in closer if she wanted to hear anything, but that should be easy enough among the pews—just as long as she didn't bump into Deller. A quick scan of the sanctuary hadn't revealed his hiding place, and the pews were the obvious option. Dropping to her knees, she began to crawl up a side aisle. Fortunately the priest was standing in front of the center aisle, and his view of her was blocked. Unobserved, she slid into the fifth pew and flattened herself against the stone floor.

The men seemed to be discussing different suburbs of the city. "Not Waktuk," said someone quickly. "They've already met their quota."

"What about Skrenden?" asked someone else.

"You're better off in West Daven," came a third voice. "School attendance is low, and the kids are anywhere and everywhere."

"Do the West Daven police know how to handle complaints?" asked a fourth.

"No one in West Daven goes to the police," came the dry response. "But that won't make it easy—West Daven women don't cut the placenta until the tenth year."

The men shared a chuckle, and then the man who'd inquired about the police asked, "What about the churches, Father?"

"The churches are Dorniver's only adequate birth registry," said the priest. "Everyone brings their newborns to the Goddess Ivana."

There was another agreeable murmur of laughter from the men, and then the same voice—probably, Nellie realized, the Interior agent—asked, "Father, I need to know—"

A sneeze erupted at the back of the sanctuary. For one knife-edged moment Nellie froze, then erupted from her pew. There was no point in continuing to crouch on the floor, hoping to remain unobserved—the men had been alerted to the presence of someone else in the room and they would be searching everywhere. As she tore down the aisle, a shout went up behind her, and she put on a surge of speed. No need to panic, she told herself grimly, she had a good head start. But as she approached the back entrance, the drapes to a nearby confessional booth opened and Deller burst into her path. Furiously they struggled in the entranceway, clawing and shoving. In a diamond-brilliant frenzy, Nellie grabbed Deller's bandaged hand and twisted it until he fell back with a gasp. Then she was through the doorway and pounding down the narrow corridor with him at her heels.

He'd recognized her. In spite of the gloom and their mutual fear, Deller had gone bug-eyed when he'd fixed on her. But this was no time to gloat. Behind them the men seemed to be gaining, and Nellie sprinted, her feet pounding panic through her body. On either side the walls slanted inward, cold shoulders cutting off her escape. The door behind the dumpster was too far, she would never reach it in time, and when the Interior agent saw her scalp he would drag her to the floor and cut her open a second time. Dizziness flooded Nellie's knees and she staggered, whimpering.

"Oh no, you don't." A hand shoved her firmly onward and Deller hissed, "You're not screwing me up again, bitch."

The men were so close, Nellie was sure she could hear their breathing. "We can't do it," she whispered, and Deller shoved her again, hard. If only, she thought wildly, she could figure out where the closest gate to the next level was. But she couldn't actually see the gates unless she tuned into the molecular field, and she couldn't get enough focus to do that while she was pounding in absolute terror down some creepy Goddess-forsaken hallway.

Or could she? There were so many gates in this place, the air virtually throbbed with them. Even in the middle of her panic Nellie could feel them, she could *feel* them. Then, to her right, she saw a pocket of flux undulating in the wall. Stumbling to a halt, she turned and threw the full force of her fear directly at it. Immediately the wall divided cleanly, leaving a space the height and breadth of her body. With a cry Nellie sprang through the opening. Sudden darkness enveloped her and she paused, instinctively assessing the new level's molecular field. Quickly her body adjusted to its vibratory rate. Then she turned, intending to send her mind into the gate and draw it closed, but was almost knocked off her feet as Deller came hurtling through the gap.

"Out of my way!" she hissed, ducking to one side. Then she sent her mind into the faintly lit opening and drew it closed.

Chapter 6

I N PITCH DARKNESS Nellie slumped against the wall behind her and rode out the initial buzz in her brain as her body completed its adjustment to the new level's quicker vibratory rate. Through the wall she could hear two sets of footsteps fading rapidly down the hall and she tensed, realizing they must belong to her double and Deller's. A heavy pounding of men's feet followed. Would they make it? Their doubles had a better chance than she and Deller since her own double hadn't stopped to open a gate, but even if they reached the door hidden behind the dumpster the men would probably catch them in the courtyard. If not, the patrol gang awaited them in the streets. Oh well. Nellie gave a mental shrug. They were just doubles from another level, and not worth worrying about. What she needed to do now was figure out where she was, then come up with a plan to dump Deller.

The question was whether to ditch him here in this level, or take him back to their home level before losing him. A tiny grin played across Nellie's mouth as she considered the first option. Why not? It wasn't as if she'd asked Deller to follow her through the gate, and she was hardly his babysitter. If he got stuck here alone, that was his problem. So what if he ran into his double and eventually

figured things out? Without the ability to open the gates, he would
have no way of tracking her down to seek revenge, and she certainly
wasn't planning on returning to this level anytime soon. He would
be missed in their home level, of course, but everyone would assume
he was another kid who'd been picked up and shipped off to the
Interior for experiments. Best of all, the Skulls would be useless
without him. All things considered, his absence would improve
her life considerably.

Besides, thought Nellie grimly. *tit for tat.* He owed her for the
haircut. Straightening, she focused on her surroundings, probing
for information. The immediate area smelled musty and the air
was so still she could hear the slight pound of her heart in her ears.
Leaning to the left, she felt her arm brush against what seemed
to be a stack of crates. Slowly she tuned into the molecular field
and watched the quiet play of energy in the dark. Except for the
rapid pulse of Deller's body to her right, it was all low-key. The
room appeared to be a storage area, jam-packed with boxes and
crates, and she sensed nothing that would leap at her, snarling, in
the dark.

Carefully she assessed the harsh rhythm of Deller's breathing,
with its tiny whistle that meant his nose was packed with snot.
About a foot to her right he seemed to be just sitting, probably
assessing things like she was. The question was: How clued in was
he? Could she count on him being disoriented by his abrupt passage
between the levels, or at least stunned temporarily stupid? Cautiously Nellie raised herself to a crouch. All she had to do was put
some distance between them and lose him in the room's absolute
darkness, then reopen the gate, get herself through it, and shut it
again real quick. That shouldn't be too difficult. Quietly she shifted
to get a better balance. A soft swearing started beside her, but Deller
seemed to be muttering to himself. So far, so good. Edging her
right foot forward, Nellie leaned her weight onto her left, ready to
push up into a standing position, and heard her ankle joint crack
like tinder wood.

Instantly Deller was on his feet, shoving her against the wall. "Where d'you think you're going?" he hissed, his stinky weasely breath all over her face.

"Somewhere else," she hissed back. "I'm not spending another minute breathing the stink that comes off you."

"You're not moving an inch without my say-so," he replied grimly. "Sit back down until I tell you to move."

"Why should I listen to someone stupid enough to sneeze a pack of devils down on us?" Nellie grumbled, but she subsided against the wall and felt him draw back a bit ... a very little bit. Holding her breath, she listened to his nose whistle in the dark. Deller breathed the rhythm of quick narrow air, as if he was sitting on some intense private pain, holding it in, containing it. Pain had a secret hold on this boy, it clutched him from the inside out. Keeping that pain at bay—managing it—was what made him such a swift thinker.

Not that being a quick thinker made him any more difficult to handle, Nellie decided quickly. Here in this room he couldn't attack or hurt her because her screams would summon the men. Nor could he force her to go anywhere with him for the same reason. All she had to do was sit tight until he got bored and left. Then she could reopen the gate and return to their home level. The levels were great for getting rid of people who were bugging you. Eventually you could always find a way to be left alone. An inexplicable pain hooked Nellie's heart, and she listened without moving to the rasp of Deller's breathing in the dark.

Grunting softly, he shifted. "This place has a real buzz," he whispered. "Can you feel it?"

With a start, Nellie realized he was sensing the new level's vibratory rate. That was no good. If he kept thinking along these lines, he might figure things out. "You're just jumpy," she said dismissively. "That's why you're leaning all over me."

Immediately Deller pulled back. "Just making sure you don't take off," he muttered, coughing low in his throat.

"So what if I did?" she sneered. "Scared of the dark, Dellie? Scared you can't get home to Mommy?"

He snorted and a pause floated between them, waiting like that moment on the top of the warehouse fence when they'd tensed, watching each other before she'd sprung. Then Deller spoke again, struggling to pull his voice out of an airy arc of fear.

"How did you know about the secret door in the wall?" he asked.

She fought the sudden scattering of her thoughts, lacing her voice with obvious scorn. "What secret door?"

"You didn't even touch it," Deller faltered. "Just sort of *looked* at it, and it came open."

"It was already open," she scoffed. "You didn't notice. The hall was dark."

"Then how'd you get it closed?" Deller demanded, leaning toward her again.

"Just pushed," she said vaguely, fumbling for a better lie, but was spared the effort as a shout went up on the other side of the wall.

"Sssst," Deller hissed unnecessarily and they both froze, listening to the tramp of approaching feet and the terrified pleading of a fourteen-year-old boy. *So*, thought Nellie with satisfaction, *Deller's double had been caught and hers had escaped. Didn't that just tell you who could take better care when things got into a ruckus?*

"Who was that?" whispered Deller, as the pleading voice faded down the hall.

"Who was who?" mocked Nellie, her triumphant grin taking over the dark.

"Who'd they catch?" asked Deller, obviously exasperated. "I didn't see anyone hiding in the church but us."

Nellie couldn't help it, her entire body convulsed with satisfaction. "You!" she crowed and knew the game was up, the secret out, but she couldn't help it—the truth was beauty in her mouth, a moment of singing revenge for the razor and the taunts that had dug deep, deeper than she'd ever wanted to go.

"Me?" said Deller, thunderstruck. "But I'm right here, beside you."

"Your *double*," Nellie gloated and listened to his breath quicken. "Don't you know anything about traveling the levels?"

Deller's silence was so intense she could feel it like a wave, permeating the surrounding dark. "So," he said finally, his voice husky with thought. "You're a rerraren, are you, Bunny?"

Rerraren. The word hung between them, one of those fragments of the old speech that Outbackers used to shut everyone else out. "What's that?" Nellie asked suspiciously, her eyes narrowing. "You calling me crazy?"

"Maybe," Deller said slowly. "Or maybe I just figured out why they were after your brains."

She opened her mouth but there were no words, just the abyss of her mind opening endlessly down.

"So, we're somewhere else then?" Deller asked, after a pause. "Lulunar took us into another world? That's why the air's got such a buzz to it. What did you call it—a level?"

Lulunar? she thought. *Fine, let him think it's the twin moons that did it.* "Don't worry," she said casually. "We're only one level over, so it'll be easy to get back. We just have to wait until we're sure there's no one in the hall, and then I'll open the gate."

"But that's the hall in this level, isn't it?" asked Deller. "How d'you know it'll be quiet in our level?"

A grin of admiration flashed across Nellie's face. He was quick, that was for sure. "Because everything's the same in the levels," she explained. "They're copycats. If the hall's quiet here, it'll probably be quiet there too."

"Probably?" asked Deller.

"Well, they're *usually* the same," Nellie admitted. "It depends on flux, I guess. And on how much you mess things up when you travel from one level to the next."

"So what you're saying is that when this hall gets quiet, we won't have a clue about our hall—" Abruptly Deller cut off, listening, and then she heard it too—a long wavering cry, so faint it seemed to caress the air.

"That's ... me," said Deller slowly. "Isn't it?"

"Not *you*," Nellie scoffed, trying to shake her unease. "Just one of your doubles. And you can thank the Goddess for that. If we were in our level, it *would* be you."

"But it *is* me, isn't it?" said Deller. "Some kind of me, in a different place?"

"Don't be ridiculous," Nellie snapped, her unease growing. Some kind of *me*—what was he talking about? Doubles were just ... *doubles*. "Doubles are like shadows," she said quickly. "Just *ideas* of yourself. You should be glad those men are busy with your double. It makes it a zillion times easier for me to open the gate and get us back home."

Instantly Deller's hand gripped her shoulder. "We can't," he said hoarsely.

"You bet we can," Nellie hissed, trying to shake him off. "*I* can."

"They'll murder him, Bunny, don't you know that?" Deller whispered and she froze, thinking of the Interior agent and the line of listless children standing beside the burgundy van. That agent's double now had hold of Deller's double, and she knew better than Deller how much mercy the man was likely to show. But so what? This wasn't her home level, what did she care about what went on here? There were hundreds of levels—you could go crazy trying to keep track of them all.

"You're thinking too much," she said. "This place isn't *real*, not like our home level. Once we get back, it'll fade like a dream. You'll see."

Another cry wavered in the distance, and Deller's grip tightened. "We can't go," he said thickly, "until we get him out."

Fear turned cartwheels in Nellie's head. The guy was a lunatic. She had to dump him, and fast. "You go rescue him," she hissed, "and I'll wait here. That ain't my kind of foolishness."

"I can't get back without you," Deller said doggedly. "Either you come with me, or I start yelling so loud they'll find us in five seconds flat."

Nellie's brain blew itself out with shock. "You got a death wish?" she squeaked. "He's just a stupid double."

"What kind of a rerraren are you?" Deller leaned so close she could smell each word. "Don't you know what a double means, Bunny? You ever seen what happens to a person who goes on living after his soul's died?"

"But you've got hundreds of doubles," Nellie protested. She wanted to rake her fingers across his face, scratch some sense into him. "What does one matter?"

"Do I start yelling now?" Deller whispered threateningly.

Another scream stroked the air. Nellie hesitated, pondering her options. She could try slowing down the molecular field so Deller couldn't move, then speed it up again and count on his disorientation to jerk her arm free of his grip. But then what? Better to fool him into thinking she was going along with him, then make her escape when he wasn't breathing down her neck.

"I guess not," she muttered, faking passivity as he started pulling her across the room. Hissing at a bumped shin, she fumbled with her free hand, feeling her way in the dark.

"Here's the door," Deller whispered.

Nellie sent up a fervent prayer to the Goddess, hoping it was locked, but the door creaked open to reveal another shadowy hallway. Domed and narrow, its only light came from an entranceway to the right. *The sanctuary*, Nellie thought, looking at it in dread. Muffled voices could be heard through the opening—short staccato questions, interspersed with whimpering replies. Tightening his grip on her arm, Deller started down the hall. Another scream cut the air, rising as if it had wings.

"Wait a minute," Nellie muttered, fighting the ooze in her knees. "Can't you just *wait*?"

"Ssst," hissed Deller, flattening himself against the doorjamb and peering around it. "They're right over there."

Peering over his shoulder, Nellie saw the men at the front of the sanctuary, swarming beneath the floor-to-ceiling statue of the Goddess. Lit by candles and EXIT signs, the room was a dance of elongated shadows, but she could make out the priest in his green robe and the Interior agent, body tensed snakelike to strike. A space opened between the swarming men and she caught sight of Deller's double with his arms raised, trying to protect his head. The men seemed to be doing more yelling than hitting, but there was blood on the boy's face and he kept shifting his arms, as if unsure which part of himself to protect.

"We need a decoy," whispered Deller. "If I run across and lead them off, can you get him out?"

"They won't all go after you." Nellie fought the urge to claw his hand from her arm. "They'll see doubles and know it's a trick."

"Huh," Deller grunted, his eyes running restlessly across the sanctuary. Nellie had to give him credit—all he'd let go upon seeing his double was a single muttered gasp. Scanning the room, she noted the back entrance next to the confessional booth. That escape route wouldn't help this time—the gate to their own level had to be opened from the wall in the storage room. Grimly she scanned the sanctuary again. The place was a mirage of flickering candles, voices of fire crying out to the Goddess. Shadows and light danced across the tapestries on the walls, the room's molecular field pulsed like a long slow ache. At the front of the church, the Interior agent ducked forward. Deller's double gave a hoarse grunt and Nellie felt brilliant flames of pain shoot from his body—another entreaty to the Goddess, unseen and unheard.

"Fire," she hissed, her eyes skittering across the sanctuary. "We'll set this place on fire with candles."

Deller stiffened, his gaze racing from tapestry to tapestry. "You game?" he asked, darting her a glance. Heart thundering, she nodded. In the last few seconds, everything had changed. Her eyes had been opened, she'd sensed Deller's double cry out to the Goddess and now she could feel Ivana responding to his plea, filling the sanctuary with Her holy anger. This place was about to go up in a fiery prayer—anyone who'd ever suffered and cried out to the Goddess would be part of Her blazing revenge.

"I'll take the far side," said Deller. "You stick to this wall." Then he was off, stopping only to lift a lit candle from a nearby alcove before ducking along the back wall. Quickly Nellie darted to another alcove and grabbed two candles that were glowing at the base of a small blue-robed statue. Slipping behind a confessional booth, she raised one of the lit stubs to the lower edge of a tapestry. Blood pounded in her head as she watched the flame flicker against the thick border, the heavy cloth refusing to catch. Impatient, she jammed the candle against the tapestry and the flame snuffed out. Nellie's entire body convulsed with disappointment. *Moron*, she thought contemptuously, breathed deep, and brought the second candle to the tapestry's lower edge.

It caught. Slow flames licked at the border's thick weave, then mounted the tapestry's design. Fascinated, she stared, then jerked herself out of her trance and slipped from behind the confessional booth. A glance toward the front of the church showed shadowy figures continuing to swarm, focused on their prey. As Deller's double let out another cry, Nellie set the confessional booth's drapes on fire. Beside it stood a small table covered with pamphlets. Circling it in a crouch, she touched the candle flame to the various stacks of paper and the table went up in a crackling roar.

Shouts alerted her and she glanced up to see the men turning en masse toward the back of the church. Suddenly Deller came barreling past, hunched low to the floor, and she followed him up the side aisle as the group of men tore down the center of the room.

"Stay here," Deller hissed and took off toward the boy who sprawled semi-conscious, alone before the altar. Just beyond them loomed the floor-to-ceiling statue of the Goddess, a mass of prayer smouldering at her feet. Closing her eyes, Nellie wished those prayers leaping up the tapestries behind the statue, eating the walls alive. Then she opened her eyes to see a vivid line of flame meandering up the central tapestry. Beneath it she could just make out Deller's dark outline reaching down to hook his double under the arms.

All over the sanctuary men were running and shouting, flapping their shirts uselessly at flaming tapestries. Somewhere a fire alarm had gone off, and a bucket brigade was forming at the back entrance. As Nellie watched, the priest came darting through the doorway with a fire extinguisher, but to no avail—the tapestries were ancient, as old as the church itself, and ready to release their souls. With a creaking roar the entire back wall of the sanctuary erupted into flame, a century of prayer spewing ashes and smoke.

Darting forward, Nellie grabbed one of the Deller's double's arms and helped Deller pull him into the hallway. "I think he's coming to," Deller panted, one arm over his face to muffle a cough. Thick tendrils of smoke were beginning to drift into the corridor. "How do we explain this to him?"

"We don't." Yanking the boy's inert form from Deller, Nellie started lugging it down the hall for all she was worth. "We shove him out the first door we come to, and then we ditch this level and head back to our own."

"Okay, okay." Darting after her, Deller retrieved his double. "I'll handle him. You find the door."

Leaving them behind, Nellie flew down the shadowy hall, pausing only when she reached a T-intersection at the far end. To her right she saw a short stairwell, leading down to a lobby and an outside entrance. "Over here," she hissed, waving her arms madly at Deller. Then she ducked down the stairs and shoved the push-handle door so hard she was carried outside in a wide arc. Cool night air rushed her face, kissing her cheeks and neck. *The Goddess*, thought Nellie, blinking furiously. *Letting me know She loves me, even in the middle of this mess.* With a sob she turned toward the lobby and saw Deller coming down the stairs, carrying his woozy double on his back. Dragging the boy through the doorway, he propped him against the outer wall and slapped his face lightly. The boy shuddered and opened his eyes.

"Enough," Nellie hissed from the open doorway. "Come *on*."

Motionless, the boy stared at Deller. His lips parted slightly and he blinked. Leaning into his face, Deller slapped him again, harder. "Listen to me," he said urgently. "You're in big trouble. You've got to get running, fast. Quick now, go on."

The boy gawked, wide-eyed and openmouthed.

"*Now*," Deller repeated. "Run. For your life." He shoved the boy who, staggered, ran a few steps and turned back again to stare. Riveted, Deller stood staring back.

"Shit!" hissed Nellie. Grabbing Deller firmly by the hair, she yanked him through the doorway. Then they were tearing together down the hall, their hearts thundering, the breath clawing at their lungs. Ahead the entrance to the sanctuary floated, a delicate orange blossom. Smoke clogged the air, sirens wailed outside the church. Swerving through the storage room entrance, Nellie slammed the door and locked it. There was a click as Deller turned on the overhead light and the storage room took shape around them—a jumble of confessional booth drapes, boxed hymnals and crates of small blue-robed statues.

"Turn it off," said Nellie. "It has to be the same as when we came in."

The light clicked off and she stood probing the darkness with her mind. Tuning into the molecular field, she tested one gate after another but none felt familiar, their seams at the wrong height or angle. Fighting panic, she sent her mind skittering along the back wall. It had to be here; gates didn't just disappear. Was she going too fast, had she lost the knack, had the Goddess decided to keep them—

"Got it!" she exulted and sent her mind into the full length of the gate, forcing it open.

A wave of pain hit her. Instead of dead scar tissue, the gate was stunningly, screamingly alive, and Nellie felt as if she was slicing through a wall of nerves. A terrified shriek lit up the inside of her head and she reeled back against Deller.

"Hey, wrong way," he grunted and pushed her through the opening. The air swirled and sang as she stumbled into the hall and leaned against the opposite wall, adjusting to her home level's vibratory rate. Then she focused on the gate and drew it closed. Abrupt silence descended as the other level's sirens and shouts were cut off. Sighing, she closed her eyes. Coming through the gate, with that colossal freaky blast of pain, had drained her. Fortunately the men who'd been chasing them in this level appeared to have given up and gone home. Briefly Nellie wondered what the men had thought when they saw her and Deller disappear into thin air, but it didn't really matter as long as they were gone and she could rest for a bit. Just a moment of quiet, that was all she needed. Then she would get going again. Just a minute...

It was too quiet. "Deller?" she whispered, opening her eyes. To either side the hall stretched, shadowy and empty. Panic flared and she came bolt upright. Had the gate shut too quickly, sealing him into the other level? She'd been joking when she'd thought about dumping him there; she never would have actually done it. Desperately Nellie scanned the hall again, and her shoulders sagged with relief. There he was, a fuzzy outline hovering a few steps to her left. He must have been disoriented by the wave of pain that erupted from the gate and was having trouble adjusting to their home level's vibratory rate. It had happened to her a few times—a bit of a delay in the adjustment period. For a moment she'd been completely out of sync, surrounded by a vast gray blur. Nellie shivered. The first time she'd thought she'd died.

Quickly she stepped toward the blurred figure and touched it with her hand. All Deller had to do was slow his frequencies to bring himself into sync, but there was no way he could know that. Slowing her own thoughts, Nellie listened to the hum at the base of her brain, then sent her mind into Deller's molecular field. There was quite a buzz coming off him; this whole thing had him really hyped. Gradually she brought him into sync and he solidified before her, staring incredulously as his surroundings came into view.

"Bunny?" he asked, his voice trembling.

Rerraren. She could see the accusation in his eyes. It was taking a major risk, letting him know she could play with vibratory states like this. Supposedly only witches could do it, and the church adamantly forbade the practice. If the priests heard about her ability, her name would be added to the List of Undesirables and she would be banned from every parish. The Goddess would hate her. But the only option was to leave Deller in his ghostlike state, and the last thing she needed was him floating around, haunting her in her home level.

Taking off down the hall, Nellie unbolted the door behind the dumpster, then sighed with relief as the courtyard came into view. She and Deller were lucky—the priest had locked the door but hadn't yet gotten around to shoving the dumpster back against the wall. As she emerged into the pre-dawn courtyard, she saw the crescent moons descending in a parallel arc toward their final moment over the horizon. The world before her was a blurred gray thought between sleep and waking. Without hesitation she bolted alone down the alley, letting the uncertainty on Deller's face fade behind her like any other dream.

Chapter 7

NELLIE HOVERED BENEATH the surface of waking, the early evening heat a heavy arm pressed over her face. Eyes closed, she lay vibrating within shrill heartless voices as a sky of whirling stars faded from her mind. With a soft grunt she turned over and opened her gummy eyes, focusing on a small blue-robed statue that stood on the upturned crate beneath the window. Hands cradled in supplication, eyes lifted upward, the ceramic Goddess's glinted in the dim, green-shadowed light. Just looking at Her, Nellie felt wrapped in calm and wordless understanding. Finally Ivana had chosen to bless this shack directly with Her presence, finally the Mother of all mothers had descended to dwell with the loneliest of Her children.

Whispering her devotion, Nellie leaned forward and kissed the Goddess's tiny toes. Then she scratched intently at the latest bug bite on her shin, popping the inflamed blister and digging deep into the delicious combination of itch and pain. After a hurried encounter with the bucket of rainwater in the corner, she reached for the bag of buns and fruit she kept hanging from a wall hook. The buns were stale and the nevva fruits bruised, but she munched steadily, her eyes fixed on the ceramic statue. Images from the previous night kept flashing through her head—the face of the Interior agent as he came through the moonlit courtyard, the church wall splitting as she threw her mind at it, the screams of Deller's double as he was beaten in the sanctuary. Then the floor-to-ceiling statue of the Goddess standing silent and immovable as flames devoured the wall behind it, and Deller locked into a trance, staring at his double's bloodied face. Finally, their return to this level and that moment of inexplicable pain as the gate opened—a sensation so intense, just remembering it made Nellie feel as if the membranes of her brain were tearing apart.

A thick shudder ran through her and she ducked the memory, then came back to it tentatively. Why had that gate been different? Every other gate she'd opened had been nothing more than dead space. Their surrounding molecular fields had pulsed and danced with energy, but the gates themselves had been motionless hairlike seams—simply doorways to be opened, passed through and closed. Had this gate felt pain because she'd opened it so quickly? But why would speed matter to dead space? And why hadn't she felt any pain the first time she'd opened it? Like a pulsing light, the memory of the second opening kept flashing through Nellie's mind—brilliant, terrifying, a soundless scream. Trembling, she knelt before the Goddess and repeatedly kissed Her naked feet.

"Blessed Ivana, come to me," Nellie whispered, rocking on her knees. "Blessed Ivana, bless all the lonely children suffering because their mothers are gone."

She'd grabbed the blue-robed figure from an open crate in the split second before Deller had turned off the storage room's overhead light. Cold and smooth, the statue had been surprisingly heavy for its size. Ramming it under her T-shirt, she'd cradled it against her stomach all the way home, talking to it in low whispers, dedicating herself to it, promising it her love.

"Blessed Ivana," she whispered to it now, rocking desperately. "Blessed, blessed, *blessed* Ivana."

Usually the Goddess's blessing came swiftly, a formless whisper that passed through Nellie's brain, causing the tangled mess of her thoughts to relax. But today there was no release, just the statue's dull upward stare and the early evening heat crushing all hope to the ground. Again the memory of the opening gate tore at Nellie's mind, and she cried out in fear. Why did the moment keep coming at her like this? Had it taken over her mind for good? What if a similar wave of pain attacked her every time she opened a gate to another level? That would be unbearable; she would have to stop traveling the levels and live out the rest of her life stuck in the mundane like everyone else.

She had to get out of the shack into the open, where the sky would take her thoughts and scatter them like clouds in a fast-moving wind. Tying a kerchief firmly over her bristling scalp, Nellie tugged on a T-shirt and a pair of shorts and slipped out the door. The sensation of coolness was immediate and she hoisted herself into the nearest tree, crawling branch to branch until she reached the edge of the copse. Then she dropped with a quiet thud into the long blond grass and crouched silently, sniffing the air.

Nothing came to her but the sweet scent of the dreaming grass. In every direction the evening stretched, shadowing itself endlessly, blurring her sharp-edged thoughts and giving them room to move. Low over the horizon the twin moons could be seen, the tips of two ghostly thumbprints in a sepia-blue dusk. A few remnants of sleep still grumbled at the base of Nellie's brain and she leaned against a doogden tree, waiting for them to drift free of her head. A quick walk to Dorniver was what she needed. She'd taken a few dollars from her secret stash under the remembering dress and her plan was to buy something to eat, then hang around, looking for an easy pocket to pick. Today was the second day of Lulunar, when the Festival of the Twins was celebrated, and the streets would be crowded with pockets loaded for spending. Any target she chose, however, would have to be *very* easy, and in *this* level. Until she figured out what had gone wrong with the last gate, she was going to have to take the risks every pickpocket faced.

A steady lope soon brought Dorniver's outskirts onto the horizon, a hunched scattering of gas stations, hotels and stores. As the first houses began to appear, Nellie stared at their lit windows with the usual ache. Sometimes, as she watched mothers calling small children in from the streets, a raw howl went off inside and she bent double, twisting until she got herself back under control. Other times she picked up stones and flung them, small vicious thoughts, at the glowing windows. Then tears burned her eyes and breath tore at her lungs, but she always stayed to watch the mother or father who came running to survey the damage, calling for their children and scanning for danger.

Fathers—now that had taken some getting used to when she'd first arrived. Trotting through the evening streets, Nellie shook her head thoughtfully. Actually, it still did. In the Interior, there had been no such thing as marriage. Couples had dated, but all breedings had been dictated by the Suitable Births Registry. Children remained with their mothers, never even meeting their fathers. But here in the Outbacks, couples married and both parents raised their children together.

Weird, thought Nellie, stopping at a street vendor's stall to buy a sandwich and a drink.

"Hey kid, you're supposed to eat that, not breathe it," the vendor grinned but she ignored him, cramming the last few bites into her mouth. If only it *was* possible to breathe in food. Things would be so much simpler if she could live on air. Giving a loud belch, she started off down the street. Tonight's official activities would be taking place in front of City Hall. Street theatre groups, a musical festival and various fireworks displays would crowd the area with merrymakers careless of their wallets and the general contents of their pockets. Cutting through a series of alleys and backyards, Nellie made her way swiftly toward the festivities and soon began to encounter small groups gathered around jugglers, clowns and other street performers. In a parking lot she caught sight of a mime troupe performing the odyssey of the Goddess's twins, two actors enacting the sons' lifelong search for each other on a makeshift stage while two other actors, dressed as moons, perched on a scaffold and watched the drama unfold from their perspective in the afterlife.

Hovering at the edge of the parking lot, Nellie watched the actors' fluid movements and white-painted faces. The story was familiar and sang to some inner ache she didn't understand, but what had attracted her attention was a slight mid-air shimmer between the two actors playing the twin moons. That shimmer was a gate—or what most Outbackers considered to be a gate—one of the temporary kind that could fade within minutes of its appearance. These gates came and went in the air, visible only to those who could tune into them. Outbackers called them "mindjoys," naturally occurring quirks in the molecular field that could take the mind on a breathless rush through color and sound.

Having sampled them eagerly when she first discovered them, Nellie now looked upon them with a mild contempt. A lesser form of flux, a mindjoy couldn't grant the full-body rush of shapeshifting, nor did it hide any hairlike seams that could be opened onto another level. Though many Outbackers repeatedly sought out mindjoys, Nellie thought of them as flux for the stupid, flash-in-the-pan vibrations that took the imagination on a quick trip, then disappeared. How often had she seen individuals step inside the shimmery mid-air undulations, only to stand grinning insipidly until they lost all sense of time and place? It was a situation of innocent beware. Most mindjoys were relatively harmless, offering brief experiences of ecstasy and various pleasure trips, but it was tantalizingly easy to overindulge, and then the mind became muddled, unable to distinguish between mental and physical realities. Sometimes a period of abstinence allowed the mind to sort itself out, and sometimes it didn't.

Had Lulunar bestowed the mindjoy upon the theater troupe as a gesture of approval, or had the actors consciously called it into being between themselves? Nellie had heard of the secret groups

that explored the many aspects of flux. Some of them had unlocked
the deeper mysteries and were rumored to play with the vibrations
that resonated at the core of the life force, calling new forms of
energy into being and manipulating them. Speculation had it that
these groups had learned how to create their own private levels,
entire worlds that didn't fade but remained fixed and everlasting,
and could be fashioned to meet individual whims. It was said that
these groups sometimes recruited new members by disguising a gate
to one of their levels as a mindjoy, then setting it up in a public
area and waiting to see who tuned in. Nellie had always given these
groups and their blasphemies a wide berth, but today she hesitated.
What if this mindjoy hid a secret gate? Would it cry out in pain if
she attempted to open it?

Tentatively she touched her mind to the midair shimmer that
undulated between the two actors, but no explosion of pain rocked
her. Instead her head filled with rippling spirals of coloured light
and a delicate trance-like singing. Snorting with disgust, Nellie
withdrew. This mindjoy might last another twenty minutes before it
faded. Tantalizing as its images were, they led no further than this
level and its molecular field, and could be easily explored by anyone
who'd taken a dose of crva, a common street drug that allowed the
user to see energy at the molecular level but was notorious for slur-
ring physical responses and blunting consciousness.

Dismissing the mime troupe and their shimmering mindjoy,
Nellie continued through the crowded streets, her eyes absorbing
every detail. On all sides children swarmed, wearing the traditional
jester's cap that sported a leering clown face at the back of the head.
Many of the merrymakers had also donned a mirrored mask, and
everywhere she looked Nellie saw her own reflection slip-sliding
across the faces of others. Buying her own mask from a nearby
vendor, she put it on and slipped deeper into the crowd.

Something about the way Outbackers celebrated Lulunar, with
their eerie costuming and mind-teasing festivals, made her want
to simultaneously leap, shout and weep. A wild, almost angry

exuberance filled her and she took a deep breath, knowing it was time to throw off everything that laid claim, tugging at the different parts of her mind, and run. Letting her joy explode Nellie took off through the crowd, ignoring protests as she ducked under elbows and around hips. Twisting and darting, she forced herself to run faster and faster until her surroundings blurred and her body became just another quirk in the molecular field, taunting the expected and jitterbugging with the unknown. Finally she staggered to a halt, raw and gasping, and looked up to find herself not at City Hall as she'd expected, but in front of the Sanctuary of the Blessed Goddess. Aglow with the last of the evening light, the domed yellow-stone building loomed before her, peaking in the spire with the cupped brass hands. At its base a chatting gossiping crowd was filing up the front walk and in through the open doorway. A few of the children wore carnival clothes.

Of course, thought Nellie, thrilled by a sudden knowing as she watched the crowd ascend the church steps. *The Goddess is holding Her own ritual to celebrate the Festival of the Twins.* This must be the reason she'd run in this direction—the Great Mother had reached down into the hustle and bustle of heathen street festivities, picked up her lost and lonely daughter, and led her toward the holiness of divine worship. Nellie's soul had been rescued from pagan revelry, pure and simple. With a voluminous sigh, she started toward the church. She was one of the chosen ones. The Goddess loved her; She—

A hand clapped her shoulder from behind and Nellie whirled, claws up and ready to scratch.

"Thought it was you," whooped a weasely face, grinning at her from under a tangle of brown hair. *Deller.* With a hiss Nellie drew back, scanning the crowd for the rest of the Skulls.

"Hey," said Deller, stepping toward her. Instantly Nellie danced backward and he frowned in confusion. "What's the matter?" he demanded. "What—d'you think I'm after you?"

Pushing her mirror mask onto her forehead, Nellie studied him through slitted eyes. "What d'you want, then?" she asked, her voice taking careful steps up her throat. In all her pondering of last night's events, she hadn't once considered seeking out Deller to discuss them. He was a Skull, and the Skulls were vermin. Sure, he'd been halfway decent last night, but the events that had thrown them together had been chance. Being part of the Skulls wasn't. Seeing him now she felt only the danger of his knowing her secret ways, and a slight regret she hadn't dumped him in the other level when the opportunity had presented itself.

Deller's eyes drifted casually lower. "Thought I'd take another look around the place," he said, shrugging. "You?"

Crossing her arms over the blobs on her chest, Nellie scowled. What was the politest way to tell vermin to get lost? On second thought, who cared about polite? "Same, I guess," she huffed and started toward the church. Immediately Deller reached for her shoulder and she spun round, clawing his hand.

"Don't touch," she growled. "Don't you ever touch me."

"Hssst," Deller snarled in reply, sucking the cut she'd opened across the back of his good hand. "What is it with you? You after both my hands? I just wanted to know if you were going in." Tucking his fingers under his chin in the ritual prayer position, he winked. "Want to go do the Goddess thing?"

Blasphemy. Out and out sacrilege. Lunging at Deller, Nellie shoved him hard in the gut. "Don't shame the Goddess!" she yelled, pushing him repeatedly so he staggered in backward lurches across the street. "Ivana is the truest mother. Don't you *ever* take Her name in vain."

"Hey," Deller protested, lifting his bandaged hand out of range and warding her off with the other. "*You* were the one who decided to set the church on fire last night."

"That was in another level." Turning on her heel, Nellie marched toward the church. "Besides," she shot over her shoulder, "the Goddess told me to do it. She placed the vision in my mind, or I never would've thought of it."

"So you and the Goddess are good buds?" Sucking the back of his hand, Deller fell into step beside her.

"We hold frequent conversations." Pointedly Nellie gave him her back, then joined the crowd climbing the church stairs. She hoped Deller would clue into the obvious and take a hike. Why in the world had he decided to come back here anyway? It couldn't be because of his devotion to Ivana. Just one look at him would tell anyone he was a pagan. Maybe Nellie didn't attend church often—well, almost never, except for some mid-afternoon visits to small parishes when she needed to get in a good dose of official praying—but the Goddess knew she loved Her with her whole heart and was one of Her most devoted followers. Not like Deller, the *heathen*. Shooting him a contemptuous look, Nellie caught Deller smirking and whirled on him, forcing the crowd to part and go around them.

"Exactly what are you laughing at?" she demanded.

"I'm not laughing," grinned Deller, flinching in spite of himself.

"You are too," insisted Nellie, jabbing an accusing finger in his face. Someone had to protect the Goddess's holy house from vermin. "You're laughing at Ivana and the holiness of Her worship." With satisfaction, she watched the grin flee Deller's face. "Beware, heathen," she hissed, deciding some extra emphasis would do him good. "You don't know the danger you're calling down upon yourself."

Rerraren. There it was again, the unspoken flashing across Deller's face. It truly was a weasely face—narrow and long, with a wide mouth and muted green eyes—and the rest of him carried the same weasely quality, tense and restless, always sniffing for prey. Well, he had it wrong if he thought he could go after the Goddess. He was nothing but a speck of dirt on the hem of Her heavenly blue robe.

"Beware," Nellie spat again for good measure, feeling the sky come to rest approvingly on her shoulders. "Just you beware." Several older women gave her admiring glances as they passed and Nellie nodded back stiffly, then sailed up the last few stairs. Maybe she didn't have the right kind of clothes, maybe she hadn't memorized all the words to the Goddess's ritual prayers, but at least she had the proper attitude. *She* wasn't a heathen.

Entering the lobby, she was swallowed by immediate coolness and the feeling of an ancient knowing carried within the stone walls. In spite of the blasphemy she'd seen taking place here the previous night, immediate wonder leapt through her. Everywhere she looked candles glowed, sending great shadows across the domed ceiling. In the distance an organ played, slow and doleful, and the scent of incense weighted the air. Statues of the Goddess peered from wall alcoves, their tiny ceramic hands cradling offerings that had been placed within them—tightly rolled prayer scrolls, flowers, jewelry, even a child's tiny doll. Frantically Nellie searched her pockets, but she'd spent her last cent on the mirror mask. Thoughtfully she tugged at the kerchief wound around her scalp. It wasn't much, but it was something. If only she didn't need it to cover the worms. Her hand brushed the mask riding the top of her head and her face brightened. Of course! The mirror mask was like a soul—you looked into it and saw yourself. What better offering to make to Ivana! Carefully she slid the mask off her head and hung it from the nearest statue's upraised hands. Silvery and moonlike, it swung from its string, a myriad candle flames leaping across its face.

"That's right, dearie," whispered an elderly woman, patting Nellie's arm. "Give all your devilry to the Goddess and She'll cleanse you."

Turning, Nellie was about to protest, but the woman hobbled on, revealing Deller standing in her wake. At the sight of him, Nellie's anger came rushing back. She'd assumed she'd left him outside, crushed and withered, having learned proper respect.

"How dare—," she began, but he shook his head at her, touching a finger to his lips and she fell silent, her anger swallowed by the change in his expression. All signs of mockery gone, the weasely caution was back, prowling his body. Eyes narrowed, he turned from her to study the crowd.

"The men are here," he said quietly. "Have you seen them? So far I've spotted four. D'you think they'll recognize us?"

"No," said Nellie immediately. "It was too dark." She'd been spying on the eight men for over a month. Time after time she'd passed them in the street and they'd never given her a second glance.

"But you're wearing the same clothes," Deller said dubiously. "And the kerchief."

"We were at the back of the church and they were at the front," Nellie shrugged. "I couldn't tell them apart in all those shadows."

Deller shook his head. "They might've seen us in the fire."

"That was in another level," Nellie said. "With their *doubles*. Not these guys." Crossing her arms, she surveyed him scornfully. *If Deller wasn't such a heathen*, she thought, *he would know it was the Goddess who'd saved us last night*. Against the Goddess, mere men could do nothing in *any* level. But how could she expect him to understand something like that? He wasn't a chosen one. Let him worry his guts over piddling little details if he wanted to, she had more important things on her mind. Rapt, Nellie stood watching candle flames flicker and leap on a nearby prayer table, signs of the Goddess's divine presence.

"Okay then, we'll sit at the back." Deller started toward the nearest pew and Nellie stood thunderstruck, gaping after him. Where on earth had he gotten the idea she'd traded in her *brain* for an empty dried-out Skull? She wasn't about to start taking orders from *him*.

"You sit at the back," she sniffed and sailed past him. "I'm sitting at the front."

Most of the congregation were now seated, and she moved quickly up the nearly empty aisle toward a seat that gaped at the end of the second pew. Slipping into it she knelt on the prayer bench, locked her fingers under her chin and began to whisper fervently. A knee bumped her shoulder and she looked up to see Deller slide into the empty spot on the pew. Annoyance twisted her lips and she prayed more desperately, trying to shut him out. Why did the pagan have to keep following her around? Hadn't she made herself abundantly clear?

Abruptly the prayer bench rocked beneath her knees, and she felt Deller's shoulder press against her own as he knelt beside her.

"This church has a real buzz," he hissed.

"I am *praying*," she hissed back, keeping her eyes squeezed shut.

"Can't you feel it?" he whispered nervously, his breath tickling her ear.

Glaring through narrowed slits, Nellie said slowly, "That *buzz* is the presence of the Goddess. Only a pagan wouldn't know that."

Deller's face twitched, and then he said slowly, "You're really into this stuff."

"The Goddess," Nellie sighed dramatically, "is the morning star that watches over all missing mothers and children."

Deller blinked, his face unreadable. "Sure," he said. "No prob. But I don't get a buzz every time I pass one of Her statues. This church is freaky."

He was right, of course. Tonight the Sanctuary of the Blessed Goddess shifted and sighed with flux. The air was dense with it, the molecular field quivering with unusual vibrations.

"Is this the same buzz you felt last night?" Nellie asked suspiciously.

"No," he said quickly. "Different. Thicker."

So he was truly feeling it. Nellie studied him with new eyes. Suddenly she realized she hadn't the faintest idea why he'd been at the church the previous night, spying on the eight men. "Hey," she whispered, elbowing him for emphasis. "What were you doing here last night, anyway?"

He shook his head. "Not here." His eyes darted to the front of the church, and Nellie followed his gaze to see last night's green-robed priest step out from behind the floor-to-ceiling statue of the Goddess, followed by several white-robed priestesses. Immediately preceding them were two small boys, chanting and carrying incense balls on chains. All across the sanctuary, pews groaned as the congregation rose and reached for their prayerbooks. Unsure of the procedure, Deller glanced to see what Nellie was doing, then got to his feet beside her. Little did he know, she thought grimly, that he probably had more experience at this than she did.

Cautiously she glanced at the open prayerbook held by the woman on her other side, then flipped to the correct page in her own and tried to follow along. A sideways peek at Deller showed him slit-eyed and weasel-tense, looking as pagan as ever. Burying her nose in her prayerbook, Nellie pretended she'd never seen him before. On all sides the voices of the congregation rose and fell in murmured waves, repeating phrases back to the priest. They had everything memorized, Nellie realized in amazement. Even when she squinted, she couldn't read the prayerbook's tiny script in the flickering candlelight.

Finally the priest left off chanting and bowing, and the congregation sank into the pews. The priestesses stepped back into the shadows and the two boys walked solemnly down the center aisle, swinging their incense balls. Turning to the altar, the priest began lighting various candles. Arms crossed over her chest, Nellie watched him narrowly. She was beginning to feel a bit fed up with all these fancy goings-on. What did any of it have to do with the Goddess and the suffering of mothers and children? When she'd first entered the church, she'd thought she sensed the deep shadowy thud of the Goddess's mother-heart, but all this chanting and swinging of incense balls had long since chased the feeling away. Now she couldn't feel Ivana anywhere.

"Shove over," she hissed at Deller. "I'm leaving."

Incredulous, he gaped. "Don't be an idiot," he said. "The priest'll recognize you for sure."

She shouldered him impatiently and he shouldered her back.

"Wait until it's over," he said quietly. "Then I'll tell you why I was here last night. Just keep your eyes open and see what you can pick up."

Muttering savagely, Nellie subsided against the back of the pew and watched the priest move about the altar, bowing in one direction then another, lighting candles and making ritual gestures with his hands. Her eyes narrowed to thinking slits and she turned in the pew, sliding her gaze across the congregation. Why were they sitting there like a pack of dolts, watching this nonsense? Couldn't they tell the Goddess had already left out of sheer boredom?

From the back of the room came the creaking of chains as the two boys filed back up the center aisle, swinging their incense balls. The organ swelled into another mournful dirge and the congregation rose, opening their hymnals. Standing on tiptoe, Nellie peered sullenly over the shoulder of a woman in the first pew, keeping her eyes fixed on the priest. If she was stuck here, she might as well keep an eye on him—he might have everyone else fooled, but she could tell he was up to no good.

Without warning the priest disappeared. Turning toward the floor-to-ceiling statue of the Goddess, he bowed three times, stepped deeper into the shadows at its base, and vanished. Glancing around, Nellie waited for gasps of stunned astonishment, but everyone continued to stare blankly at their hymnals. Even Deller gave no response. *Maybe they think he just slipped around the back of the statue*, Nellie thought wildly, *the way he came in.* But he hadn't, she knew he hadn't. The shadows at the base of the statue were so dense, she hadn't actually seen the priest disappear, but she'd felt it with her mind—a ripple in the molecular field as a gate opened and the priest stepped through to some other place. Leaning toward Deller she whispered, "Did you see?"

"See what?" he whispered back.

"The priest," she said, almost fearfully.

"What about him?" Deller asked. "There he is."

And indeed there came the priest, stepping out of the shadows at the statue's base and returning to the altar. Once again he circled it, bowing and chanting, followed by the priestesses and the boys who were swinging their incense balls wildly. Finally the priest turned to face the congregation and made a downward gesture with his hands. As people around her sank into the pews Nellie remained standing, her arms crossed as she glared fiercely at the green-robed figure. *Hypocrite*, she thought at him savagely. *Charlatan. Moron.*

The priest's gaze zeroed in on her and in that moment his face shifted, the features blurring. Suddenly a new face surfaced where his had been, composed of such brilliant light Nellie couldn't look directly at it. *A doubling*, she thought, flinching under a vivid kick of fear. *Here in the Goddess's sanctuary, in the Goddess's servant.* Rooted to the spot, she stood motionless as the thing that had taken over the priest scanned her face, then began moving inward, jabbing fiercely at her mind. With a gasp she jerked back, and its hold was lost. Darkness spun in her head, her brain felt as if it had been split in two. Slowly she forced her eyes open and back onto the priest's face.

The man's gaze flicked across her own, bland and indifferent, and then he turned once again to bow to the altar. Whatever had temporarily claimed him was now gone, the doubling ended. As she sank into her seat, Nellie realized she could probably walk up to the priest and he would give her the same generic smile he distributed to everyone. This was the way it was with most people—flux came and went like the blink of an eye, a newspaper blowing down the street. Few tuned into its comings and goings. Even fewer remembered.

But a doubling here, in one of the Goddess's priests?

The woman seated beside Nellie shifted impatiently as the congregation began filing out of the pews and up the aisles to the front of the church. Kneeling in a long row, adults and children waited as the priest moved along the line, placing his hands on their heads and reciting a few words.

"I've seen enough of this," Deller hissed into her ear. "You going up there to get blessed by the priest?"

"Uh-uh," Nellie responded vehemently.

Slipping from the pew, Deller ducked into the crowd, pushing his way against the stream that was flowing toward the pulpit, Nellie at his heels and clutching the back of his T-shirt with both hands.

Chapter 8

COMING THROUGH THE church entrance, Nellie felt the evening open before her like a deep-scented susurra blossom. For a moment she stood on the top step breathing it in, releasing the thick weight of incense and candlesmoke and the pressure of closed-in places. Then she was tearing down the stairs behind Deller, hesitating as he veered to the left, but he turned and beckoned so she followed, sprinting along the sidewalk. The Sanctuary of the Blessed Goddess disappeared behind a row of doogden trees, and she was filled with a desire to leap, scissor-kicking, into the air, to spin and shriek like a mad woman. Instead she pursued Deller's quick darting form through a series of back alleys, keeping pace, sensing the test in it, the wordless challenge. As they neared downtown, the festival crowd grew and they were forced to slow their pace. Coming around a corner she almost ran into him, leaning against a corner store, eyes closed and chest heaving. Slumped next to him, Nellie bent double and sucked her own raw air.

"Did you see the men guarding the doors to the rest of the church?" Deller wheezed. "Sure didn't want anyone wandering off to use the cans."

With a start Nellie realized she'd been so caught up with gawking at candles and shadows, she'd probably missed half the things the Goddess had intended to show her. Instead it had all been revealed to the pagan Deller. Flushing, she turned toward the crowd and pretended to study it. "They were probably just standing around," she said dismissively. "No big deal."

"They were blocking the doorways," Deller insisted hoarsely. "It was the same men we saw last night. I saw them turn an old lady back. I think she wanted to use the can."

"Was the Interior agent with them?" Too late, Nellie realized what she'd said. Weasely and intent, Deller's eyes honed in on her.

"What agent?" he asked slowly.

She shrugged, ducking his gaze. "That extra guy that came to the meeting last night."

"How d'you know he's from the Interior?" demanded Deller.

"Just do," she said lamely, letting her gaze settle on a middle-aged woman standing several feet away, engrossed in a mindjoy. The crowd parted as it passed, paying her no more attention than a fire hydrant.

"You're an odd one, aren't you, Bunny?" Deller's voice was speculative, thinking its way word to word. "With scars like that on your head you should be dead, or at least half-crazy. You think and run like a boy, but you're always by yourself, messy and dirty, and you smell like you think water's your worst enemy."

"I had a bath a couple of days ago." Nellie scowled defensively. What was she supposed to do when she lived in a shack that smelled like a fart? Without thinking she rubbed at an itch in her nose, then began to slide her finger into her left nostril. Realizing what she was doing, she yanked it out and shot Deller a glance. His mouth twitched, but his eyes kept their weasely look, studying her.

"How'd you learn to get into other levels like that?" he asked abruptly.

"Just did." Shrugging, Nellie let a calculated boredom slacken her face.

"And I suppose that's how you learned to pull me from thin air back into my body too?" Deller said wryly.

Nellie shrugged again. If he didn't shut up about this soon, she was taking off. Some things were private. Besides, she didn't answer nosy parker questions.

"Okay," Deller sighed. "So it's your secret. But at least tell me this much. What were you doing out in the middle of the night, spying on the denerren?"

"The what?" Nellie grimaced at the unfamiliar term.

Deller turned and spat deliberately, then pulled a package of oolaga candy from his pocket and offered it to her. "Denerren," he repeated, and spat again. "Traitors born of our blood, but sold out to the Elfadden."

"The what?" repeated Nellie. Warily she took a piece of candy and unwrapped it.

"Kids disappearing," Deller continued, ignoring her interruption. "Their mothers frantic. Men found dead with the Mark of Silence on their foreheads, and everyone watching their backs, wondering who's going to get it next. Not knowing where it'll come from, now that our own are beginning to turn."

"The Mark of Silence?" Suddenly Nellie remembered the body of a man she'd come across in an alley several months back. The man's throat had been slit, and on his forehead there had been an odd smudged mark. Quickly she sketched it on her own and Deller nodded.

"How'd you know that?" he asked tersely.

Nellie scowled, twisting her entire body vigorously. More nosy parker questions. "What are you saying?" she demanded. "Those men in the church are stealing kids from Dorniver and sending them to the Interior?"

"You heard them talking." Deller's eyes fixed on her, clamping her to the wall. "They're planning to hit West Daven next. I guess they're finished with Glover Heights. Mothers there are getting so paranoid, they won't leave their kids with the neighbors."

Images of the birdlike machines and the four children she'd seen near the quarry kept flashing through Nellie's mind. Had those children come from Glover Heights or some other Dorniver suburb? For some reason she'd assumed they were from the Interior. "What's all this got to do with you?" she asked cautiously. "Why were you spying on them?"

"They got my brother." The words twisted out of Deller, a corkscrew sound. "About half a year back. He went to bed like normal, but he wasn't there in the morning. Must've gone out for some reason, maybe to play a joke on someone, and they grabbed him. He was a year younger than me and except for our eyes, we looked so alike people used to mix us up. I've been looking and looking for him. Started hanging around the hospital ..." Deller's voice faltered. "... and the morgue. When I joined the Jinnet, they got me spying on the priests. That's why I was there last night."

"The Jinnet?" Nellie was hit with a memory of eating supper with her mother while pictures of unshaven men flashed across their TV set. The Jinnet had received frequent coverage on Interior news broadcasts. One of several underground resistance movements, they sometimes managed to blow up an important building or assassinate a politician. Nellie's brain hummed with admiration and she looked at Deller with new eyes.

"But I don't need them anymore," he continued, again ignoring her interruption. "Not now I've got you. You're ten times better than the Jinnet, all on your own." He stared at her, his weasely eyes fierce, almost exultant. *Rerraren*. Nellie felt the thought pass through his body like a prayer, and took a cautious step back. Involuntarily, Deller jerked forward.

"Your brother's gone now," she said gruffly, putting up a hand to ward him off. "He's dead, or they took him to the Interior for some kind of experiment." Again, the memory of the birdlike machines flashed through her head. "I can't do nothing about that."

She watched hope flutter and die in Deller's face. His mouth opened in a soundless stammer, and then the usual weaseliness returned, tightening his expression. "Okay," he muttered, his shoulders slumping. "If that's the way you want it, Bunny."

A wail took over the inside of Nellie's head. "I don't get nothing the way I *want* it," she hissed. As she turned away, she felt Deller's hand grip her arm. Enraged, she swung round, but he saw her claws coming and pulled back.

"Wait," he stammered. The weaseliness was gone again, and a kind of helplessness twisted his face. "Can't you just stick around a while? Hey, you could come to the clubhouse, or—"

"For what?" Nellie snapped, taking another step back. "So you can put your mark on me? I'm not going to your clubhouse, Mr. Skull. I'm not stupid. I read magazines. I know what you do to *bunnies*."

Heat reddened Deller's face. "That was just something to call you," he mumbled. "You were just another girl then. Just some …girl."

"Yeah, well I'm still a girl," Nellie said grimly. "A girl that's got to go. See ya."

"When?" The word shot from Deller like a physical force.

Nellie turned to stare back at him. "When what?"

"When … D'you want …?" He looked baffled, as if trying to speak an entirely new language. "Well, like, d'you want to meet somewhere?"

She could feel it rising within her like a hand, desperate to grab what was being offered and never let go. Someone wanted her, someone actually wanted to see her, maybe tomorrow, maybe even the day after that.

Turning, she ducked into the crowd and ran like a scream.

HIGH ABOVE THE SHACK the crescent moons rode the sky, a pearly whisper calling her home—home to be with her mother, reunited and traveling eternity where no one chased her down streets or bugged her about missing brothers, looking like a busted heart when she said no. Nellie's feet scuffed the dusty grass and her shoulders drooped as a voice in her head lectured her sternly, telling her she'd done wrong, she'd done mean.

"What do I care about his brother?" she muttered, kicking at a shadowy clump of weeds. "We've all got someone missing. No one's coming back. What makes him think he's so special?"

The drone of an approaching vehicle sent her ducking into the undergrowth where she crouched, watching several trucks with dimmed headlights pass by. In this area night convoys were frequent, traveling the dirt roads that angled everywhere through the bush. Last week she would have written them off as smugglers and land pirates to be avoided and otherwise ignored, but now Nellie watched them with new eyes. What if these trucks carried stolen children from West Daven or Glover Heights? What if it wasn't smugglers driving them but denerren, double agents for the Interior?

With a low growl she crept onto the empty road and knelt, her palms pressed to the packed dirt, but no images of children came to her, just the usual jumble of cartons and crates. So the trucks belonged to smugglers, as she'd thought. All this talk of Deller's was making her jumpy, causing her to see missing children everywhere. Coming back from Dorniver tonight she'd been skittish as a cat, certain that Interior agents were about to ooze out of every shadow. Like that one over there between the trees, ducking down so as not to be noticed. Freezing in her tracks Nellie stared, then hissed and relaxed. Just a stupid bush, playing games with the wind. First chance she got she was trading in her brain for something more useful, like an extra bladder.

Still she felt *something*, kind of creepy and close by—a darkness within a darkness, waiting. Turning uneasily, she stared in every direction but saw only the calm easy shift of bush and tree. What was it? What *was* it? Abruptly she broke into a trot, refusing to look back. As she neared the shack she veered into the shrub, picking her way carefully until she reached the copse, then swung herself up into the familiar route of branches. Reaching the shack, she was about to drop to the ground, when a shadowy outline jutting from the front wall caught her eyes and she froze.

The door was open. Fear pounded in Nellie's mouth, solid and tasting of blood. She *always* wedged the door shut with a large rock, then tied the handle to a bent nail with a piece of rope. From where she was crouched she could see the rope, lit faintly by the twin moons, hanging loosely from the door handle. Cautiously she listened, but no sounds came from within the shack. Probably the intruder had been nothing more than a wild dog, come and gone. But what if it was something bigger, like a bear? No, the bottom of the door was jammed open as far as it would go in the uneven ground, and that left only a narrow gap. Even Nellie had to suck in her gut and slide sideways through the opening. Whatever had entered the shack tonight had to be as thin or thinner than she was.

Striking the closest wall with her fist, Nellie listened and heard nothing. She pounded a second time, harder. Again there was no response. Relieved, she dropped to the ground and peeked through the doorway. Still no sound came to her, but the smell wasn't right and the air seemed uneasy, muttering as if something unwelcome had passed through it. Slipping into the shack, she lit the black candle stub and looked around. Everything seemed to be in place—the crate in front of the window, her nest of blankets, the tea towels. The tea towels ...

With a cry she leapt across the shack and yanked at the towels, scattering them. A patch of bare earth stared up at her, blank as the sudden nothingness of her brain. Wordless sounds crawled up Nellie's throat and she bent double, disbelieving. The remembering dress was gone, and with it all the money she'd stored for a rainy day. *The remembering dress gone. The remembering dress, the remembering.* She always wore that dress to remember. Without it, the few memories she had of her mother were sure to disappear.

Who would want to steal her memories? There could be no other reason to take that specific dress. Who but she, Nellie Joan Kinnan, would have any interest in a dirt-stained, oversized, gold-brocaded remembering dress?

Hands pressed to the dirt floor, Nellie focused, but the only vibrations that came back to her were her own. Defeated, she curled into the space the remembering dress had occupied, and rested within the throb of her own emptiness. *Gone, gone—past and present, everything gone.* Common sense told her to seek safer shelter, but her body had filled with a leaden heaviness and she couldn't move. The shack and the remembering dress were her last link to her mother. It was here and here alone that she'd slipped into that glimmering gold fabric and called out in a voice of utter loneliness, and her mother had always come to her, each time she'd risen from beyond the grave and reached out in infinite love. Nellie wasn't kidding herself, she knew a ghost when she saw one. Her mother was definitely dead, but still filled with enough love to reach all the way from the underworld and touch her daughter's face when she called. How would her mother be able to find her if Nellie wasn't wearing the goldspun dress of angel light? Without it she would be only one among thousands, every one of them calling out for the love that had gone missing in their lives.

With a snaking hiss, the candle gutted. Utterly alone, Nellie lay at the heart of a darkness that deepened into itself until she could feel all its levels, all her doubles within those levels hugging themselves and listening to the empty thud of their hearts. How long was she supposed to go on pretending loneliness was just a different kind of friend?

Nellie's face slackened into a deeper emptiness, and she slept.

SHE WOKE FROM A DREAM so vivid that for a moment it felt as if the stars she'd seen singing deep in space were actually the neurons of her brain calling to one another. They'd been shifting again, realigning along some new axis, and Nellie felt herself tilt and retilt as her mind adjusted to its waking state. She was cold. Hard earth pressed against her hip and she moaned, trying to find a more comfortable position in the dark. *The remembering dress is gone, someone's stolen the remembering dress.* The thought came at her like pain, and she rolled onto her other side, feeling about for something to cover herself with.

And saw it. Several feet to her left an open gate hovered midair, clearly outlined by light that spilled through it from the next level. Frozen in a half-crouch, Nellie stared, terrified something was about to step through. Was she awake or dreaming? But she had to be awake—she could feel the ground, cold and hard beneath her, and when she shifted the stiffness in her hip was a crystal-brilliant pain.

Rising slowly to her feet, she hugged herself and stared at the well-lit gate. Though she tuned into the shack's molecular field on a regular basis, she'd made a point of never opening any of the hairline seams she'd seen there. The shack's molecular field often heaved with flux and when flux was around, opening a gate could mean coming into contact with anything. Far better not to know what pressed close, one level away, she'd decided, while she slept and dreamed. Better to keep the levels firmly separated in the shack, her one true sanctuary.

The gate that hovered before her, however, did not belong to the shack's molecular field, and the vibrations it emitted were faster than the frequencies of any level she'd yet encountered—so much so they could only be sensed, not felt. Hugging herself, Nellie continued to stare at the open gate. Had it been sent by the Goddess to console her for the loss of the remembering dress? Could this be a doorway onto the world of the dead and the arms of her waiting mother?

With a hoarse cry she lurched forward, but the gate danced back, out of reach. Stumbling to a halt, she stared at it. Was it possible this was an erva-induced hallucination? She'd filched a cold drink from a vendor's stall on her way home. Some of the vendors were known to spike their drinks, but she hadn't noticed any side effects before falling asleep. Now as she stood watching the gate, her thoughts felt clear. No, this wasn't erva. Tentatively she took a step forward.

Mom, she thought. Again the gate flickered backward. Despair surged through Nellie. Grabbing whatever was within reach, she flung it at the shimmering opening, but the objects merely flew through the apparition and crashed against the shack's far wall. Panting, she stared as the gate continued to hover, unperturbed, in mid-air.

"What is this?" she whispered. "Some kind of doorway to Lulu-land?"

As if in answer, the gate opened wider. Then, without seeming to move, it was suddenly all around her, its vibrations pulsing through her skin, deep into her body. With a gasp Nellie braced herself, but there was no pain. Her right foot lifted, taking her through the opening, and the gate shut behind her, closing off the shack and her home level. Habit took over and she focused on riding out the first few seconds as her body adjusted to the vibration rate of the new molecular field.

Flux was certainly playing games with the levels tonight. Looking around, Nellie could see no sign of the shack. Ceiling, walls, floor—everything gleamed, a radiant white. Ahead stretched a row of doors, all of them closed except for one halfway down a long hallway, which stood ajar. Tiptoeing toward it, she hesitated just outside. All that could be heard from within was a steady electronic hum. Cautiously she peered around the doorjamb.

The room was well lit. Cupboards and medical equipment lined the walls, and a large computer dominated the far end, but what drew Nellie's attention was a line of cubicles that ran through the center of the room. Covered by a plastic dome, each cubicle was the length and breadth of an average adult body. Nellie's breath caught in her throat and she froze. Everything about the room—its whiteness, the quietly beeping machines, the cubicles' sleepy blinking

lights—was familiar. The gate she'd woken to see hovering midair in the shack seemed to have opened directly into one of her
memories. Without approaching the cubicles, she knew what she
would find lying inside. The question pounding the blood through
her veins was not what, but whom? Would it be a stranger or one
of her own doubles, her head cut open and wires running directly
into her brain?

Entering the room, Nellie approached the nearest cubicle. From
the doorway the dome had been opaque, but as she leaned over
the lid, it became transparent, revealing the child that lay within.
Eyes closed, she was about four years old. Her chest rose and fell
in a regular sleeping rhythm and she was naked, wearing only a
helmet. When Nellie saw the nightmare tangle of wires and tubes
that ran in and out of various places in the girl's skin, she bent
double and rode out a rush of hot and cold. As it faded, she found
her body pivoting toward the room's open door. *Run, run*, her legs
screamed, but she forced herself to move toward the next cubicle
and the next, studying the face of the child in each one. Even if
she hadn't yet come across one of her own doubles, there had to be
a reason the Goddess had brought her here. She could leave now
and never understand, or she could move on to the next cubicle in
the hope of discovering the meaning of this place.

The boy she found there looked so like Deller that, except for the
slant to his eyes, he could have been his twin. Like the other children she'd seen, a helmet rode his head, and a shock of wires ran in
and out of small openings in his skin. Shyly her eyes flicked across
his naked penis and the wires that were taped even there. Above
his head, a small green light pulsed in the rhythm of his heartbeat.
Urgently Nellie pressed against the cubicle, her hands scrabbling
across the surface. If she could get it open, she could wake the boy
and take him back to Deller. But there didn't seem to be any buttons or levers. The cubicle felt completely smooth.

Inside the cubicle, the boy's eyes opened. Slanted and weasely,
they stared up at her. Above his head the light flashed more quickly

as he started to speak. Pressed against the cubicle, Nellie moaned in frustration. Nothing could be heard through the dome, and the dark-colored plastic made it difficult to see the boy's lips clearly.

In the distance an alarm went off, and footsteps could be heard running down the hall. With a gasp, Nellie pushed off the cubicle and dashed through the open doorway. To her left, she could see several lab-coated figures coming toward her. A shout went up as she turned to the right and took off. The gate was still there—she could see a hairline crack superimposed over the wall at the hall's far end. Would it open for her, or was this some kind of a set-up, a grim inter-level joke?

The gate opened before she reached it. Throwing herself through the gap, she felt it vanish before she landed and turned back to the place it had been, midair in the shack's early morning gloom.

Chapter 9

S HE HEADED DIRECTLY INTO the pre-dawn gloom to find
Deller, pausing only to pack the blue-robed statue of the
Goddess into her knapsack. Outside, the early morning air
breathed in sleepy gusts and the sky drowsed, sluggish and heavy-
lidded, above the trees. Just over the horizon hovered two ghostly
smudges, the twin moons. Nellie trudged quickly toward them,
passing bushes that hunched deep in shadow and the occasional
wickawoo's waking cheep. Wet grass flicked her bare legs, and she
brushed furiously at insects hitching a ride on her arms, trying to
ignore the strange trembling that kept sweeping her body.

It was just that it was too big, the whole thing gone wild-crazy,
over the edge, and she no longer knew how to fit everything into a
recognizable pattern. Before last night, she'd never thought much
about the relationship between the levels. She'd traveled enough to
know they weren't stacked next to each other like a deck of cards,
and she couldn't expect to find them organized spatially like doors
in a hallway. Levels were more like notes in a song, she'd eventually
decided, as long as you understood that when flux was active both
the singer and the song could change with each note. But until last
night, those notes had all been reasonably familiar, even when flux

was playing its tricks. Sure, she had to keep on her toes for small changes, like a double with a knife, but no mysterious gate had ever appeared out of thin air and opened onto a room of children with wires running into their bodies, *white rooms filled with children being held hostage for experiments...*

The strange trembling swept her again and Nellie bent over, gagging until her body gave up trying to eject the nothingness of an empty stomach. Straightening, she wiped her mouth and leaned shakily against a doogden tree. She was cold, her skin rippling with goosebumps. Why had that gate appeared to her? Had Ivana sent it, or was it simply one of those flukes that happened during the month of Lulunar? She'd only been traveling for seven months, and so had no previous experience with the month of the twins and the chaos it could spawn among the levels. A year ago she hadn't even believed the levels existed, dismissing them as erva-spawned conjecture and fantasy.

Tightening her knapsack straps, she trudged on toward Dorniver. This early, traffic was infrequent and she felt safe sticking to the main road. A dog barked from a nearby shack, running the full length of its chain, and she glanced speculatively at the next few houses she passed. They seemed quiet, their curtains drawn, with no dogs prowling the yard. Hunger bellowed in her gut and she paused, pondering a raid on a backyard garden, but the rattling of an unseen dog chain convinced her otherwise. Tightening her stomach, she slapped it a few times to quell its queasy growl, then broke into a trot that soon brought the city into view, stroked with the easy pastel light of dawn.

She didn't know where Deller lived, if he had a family, or if he fended for himself in the streets. There was little chance he attended school and he could be anywhere in the city, running with the Skulls or trying to sniff out his brother's dead-cold trail. If only, Nellie thought, cursing her stupidity, she'd thought to ask his last name.

Heading toward the river, she soon found the deserted warehouse that housed the Skulls' headquarters. Located in an area that had been slotted for demolition, the warehouse squatted on a long street of ramshackle buildings. A few doors down a small factory seemed to be in operation, but the buildings to either side were obviously empty, their windows smashed and graffiti festooning their walls. The warehouse had several entrances, but Nellie remembered exiting through an alcove on the west side, next to a lopsided black skull that had been spray-painted on the wall. Approaching the building, she found the skull leering ominously in the gloom. The small entranceway was in shadow, but she immediately spotted a large padlock hanging above the doorknob. With a groan she slumped against the wall and took a disgusted swing at the lock. Creaking, it gave. So the padlock was a disguise, just like most of the Skulls' blustering.

Tentatively she removed the padlock and pushed open the door. Warnings tiptoed along her skin and breathed down the back of her neck. Careful, she had to be *careful*. No one could catch her inside this place, not even Deller. Her plan was to locate a suitable hiding spot nearby, head Deller off when she saw him coming, and tell him about his brother. And then? Nellie shrugged off the thought. Then she would be alone with what she'd seen, and so would he.

But first she had to see this place on her own terms and beat the ugly hold it had on her thoughts. Peering through the open doorway, she scanned the small shadowy room with its sagging table and three-legged chairs. Cobwebs draped everywhere, and a scurry of mice and spiders greeted her entrance. The place had probably been a lunchroom once, or some kind of an office. Cupboards lined one wall, and a dusty sink stood under the cardboard-covered window. On the table splayed several magazines, some half-eaten doughnuts, and a jelly sandwich minus a large bite. Without hesitation Nellie wolfed the food, then chugged the remains of a bottle of nevva juice. Gradually the roar in her stomach abated, her shivering stopped, and the steady kick of fear at the base of her brain let up. Slumping to the floor, she wrapped her arms around her knees and stared dully at the sliver of light cutting through the two pieces of cardboard taped over the window.

So the sun was up and another day had officially begun. What would tonight bring, what was she going to do when the sun went down and the twin moons took over the sky? She couldn't go back to the shack, not after her experience with the strange new gate. If it had opened there once it could open again, and who knew what other gates it might attract? Only an utter madman would continue living in such a place. And, Nellie thought, fighting off a yawn, there was always the chance the thief who'd stolen her remembering dress and money would return, intending to take up permanent residence.

She snapped out of a murky doze to hear footsteps approaching the door. Scrambling to her feet, she scanned frantically for a hiding place. The bathroom was the obvious option, but any advantage she might gain there was lost to the open outer door—a dead giveaway to her presence. Backed against the wall, she watched a shadow ooze across the entrance. A shoulder edged the doorjamb and feet shuffled nervously.

"What d'you want?" she yelled, hurling her terror at the door in loud angry sound.

A thin face topped in a tangle of black hair peeked around the doorjamb, and Snakebite began an agitated dance in and out of the entrance. "What d'*you* want?" he whined, openmouthed.

"I want Deller!" Nellie bellowed. "Get him now, or I'll blow the whole street with my brains. Like this." With a crazy-man leer, she leaned forward and snapped her fingers.

Instantly Snakebite withdrew, and she listened to the thud of his feet racing down the sidewalk. Edging to the doorway, she peered into the street. It appeared deserted, with only Snakebite's rapidly retreating butt in sight. Who knew if he actually intended to carry out her order, but regardless, she wasn't fool enough to get caught in the same trap twice. Scouting out the back of the building, she found the rusty frame of an old truck parked against the wall. A grunting jump took her from the top of the cab onto the warehouse roof. From here she had a clear view of the city rooftops and the brass hands that crowned every church spire, reaching toward the heavens. Quickly she sent a prayer toward them, her heart beating like wickawoo's wings. Then she squatted in the shadow of a heating vent, fixed her eyes in the direction Snakebite had taken, and waited.

It was mid-morning before she saw Deller, several of the Skulls in his wake as he came striding down the street toward the warehouse. Two paces ahead, Snakebite flickered like a nervous insect across his path, running backward and talking in an eager high-pitched voice. Hunched behind the heating vent, Nellie observed the approaching group through narrowed eyes. Now that she was consciously studying them, it was obvious none of them lived wild, fending for themselves in the streets. Each was too well dressed, his hair recently washed. Even at this distance she could smell the scent of shampoo and laundry soap pouring off them. It was the smell of a mother, and the thought sent an electric knife singing through Nellie's heart. All of the boys coming toward her saw the sun rise and set in a mother's face every day, and didn't even notice it.

Pullo was the tallest and probably the strongest, but even at a distance, Deller's command of the group was evident, his head turning to one boy then another as they clamored for his attention. Coming to a halt outside the warehouse, he nodded tersely to one of Pullo's remarks, then cut off Snakebite's yapping with a wave of his good hand. Overnight he'd discarded the tensor bandage from his other hand, and the absence of his third finger was marked by a beige bandage that curved over the stump.

"I wanna touch her scars." Snakebite danced about, babbling eagerly. "Let's get her down and touch her scars."

"Go get her then," Deller said, his face expressionless. "I'll wait here and see if she blows your brains out."

"She wouldn't." Pullo scratched nervously at his neck. "Not if she sent Snakebite to fetch you."

Deller shrugged, then watched the rest of the group sidle into the entrance. Fierce whispering drifted out of the alcove. "You go first. No, you." A tiny grin played across Deller's lips as the Skulls finally stumbled, a congealed mass of arms and legs, into their headquarters. Silence descended onto the street, the overheated air shimmering like a raw nerve. Nellie shifted, her butt cooking on the warehouse roof. Hooding his eyes with his good hand, Deller turned to scan the rooftops. His gaze paused on the heating vent and he came quickly toward it, stopping directly opposite.

"Bunny?" he called softly, his voice carrying clearly in the stillness of the street.

Slowly she crawled out from behind the vent and sat looking down at him. "How'd you guess?" she asked finally.

"Not dumb enough to wait inside, are you?" he shrugged.

The warehouse roof reverberated slightly as Snakebite came ricocheting through the entrance, bumping into the doorjamb. "She's not here!" he shouted, rubbing his shoulder. "She took off."

"Did you check the can?" asked Deller.

"Yeah," grimaced Snakebite.

"Check again," said Deller, "you might've missed her," and the other boy darted back inside. A butterfly fluttered around Deller's head, then landed on his wrist. He cupped it with his hand.

"I saw your brother," Nellie said, her heart suddenly pounding. "Last night." She watched Deller's head snap up, the sunlight smashing against his face, splintering like glass. Slowly his hand lifted, releasing the butterfly. "Come up and I'll tell you," she croaked, hugging herself and rocking. "There's a truck out back."

"I know," said Deller, and vanished around the side of the building. A moment later the roof quivered slightly and she turned to see him working his way quietly toward her. "Wait," he said, settling beside her. "Until they've gone."

As if in response, the rest of the Skulls poured through the entrance. For several minutes they spilled about the street, shouting for Deller and arguing among themselves. Then without once looking up they headed off, still wrangling, in the direction they'd come. Hunched against the vent Nellie stared after them, running after them in her head. Why was she here? She didn't want to be here, didn't want to say what she was going to have to say. Deller was so close, she could feel the heat humming in his body. Chancing a glance in his direction, she saw the fierce press of his lips as he pulled a nevva fruit from his pocket and skinned it, tossing the peel into the street. If she hadn't known to look for it, she would have missed the slight shake in his hands as he split the peeled fruit and handed her half.

The sweet scent came at her like a punch to the gut. Without a word she inhaled the nevva fruit, spitting the seeds over her knees and watching them bounce off the edge of the roof. Silently Deller handed her the other half and she forced herself to slow down, eating it piece by piece. Her eyes kept darting toward Deller's left knee, angled casually one inch from her own. It had been a year and a half since she'd let anyone come this close.

"It was another gate," she said finally.

Deller's face shot round and he stared. "He's in another level?"

"I think so," Nellie said slowly. "It was a different kind of gate, not like I'm used to."

"How d'you know it wasn't his double?" Deller asked cautiously.

"There were no doubles." She said it with surprise, realizing she hadn't seen her own double anywhere, in the hallway or any of the cubicles. "I think the gate came out of Lulunar. It wasn't like any level I've seen. Nothing was the way it should've been."

Quickly she explained, watching tiny flickers come and go in Deller's face. "I couldn't get him out," she said fervently when she finished. "I looked and looked for a switch to open it, but there wasn't one, I swear."

Deller nodded, blew out a gulping sigh, and buried his face in his knees. Silence descended, the late-morning heat hovering on heavy wings. A fly settled on Nellie's arm and she shook it off. From her position on the warehouse roof, the sun appeared to be resting in the hands that sat atop the downtown spire of the Goddess's largest and wealthiest church, the Temple of the Blessed Heart. Again the fly landed on her arm, and again she shook it off. Beside her Deller continued to sit motionless, his face buried in his knees. Uneasily she picked up a piece of discarded nevva peel and tore it to shreds.

"Can you get through the gate again?" Deller asked abruptly, his voice muffled by his knees.

"I don't know." She'd expected this question and had practiced various refusals, but now none of them seemed to fit her mouth. "I've never seen a gate like that. I didn't go looking for it. It just showed up, already open."

"Then it was looking for you." Raising his head, Deller stared across the city. Knee prints reddened his forehead. "It'll come back," he said grimly, "looking for you again. And this time, I'll be there to help you."

Fear undulated through Nellie. "Maybe it was just Lulunar," she said quickly. "You know—the two-moon craziness thing?"

"D'you really think that?" Deller stared at her, a tear sliding down one cheek. He blinked and another followed. Nellie swallowed, feeling her own sadness pour through her like a river.

"I guess not," she said helplessly, and stared determinedly at the brass hands rising from the Temple of the Blessed Heart. If she didn't look at Deller, he would stop crying. He would get it together and go back to being the tough leader of the Skulls. Then the hole that was threatening to tear open the inside of her head would fade away and leave her alone. She wasn't going to think about her mother, she wasn't going to think about what they must have done to her before she died, she wasn't …

"Is it far?" asked Deller. "We'll get my bike and I'll double-ride you there. Then we'll wait for the gate."

"It might not come." If she brought Deller to the shack, she would be well and truly homeless. Once the Skulls knew about her secret place, her sanctuary, she would never be able to live there again. But after the mysterious gate and the stolen remembering dress, she couldn't live there anyway. The fine lines holding Nellie's mind together finally broke, and her head sank to her chest. "It's not like it's got a name and comes when you call it," she mumbled.

"I'm not asking you to call it," said Deller, and she lifted her head to find him looking at her, really looking—as if he saw *her*, more than just a ghost of hunger and need. "You already put yourself out for me," he said softly. "It's not *your* brother. If the gate shows up again, I'll go through it by myself. You can wait for me in this level. If I don't come back ... " He shrugged. "Close it, I guess."

Nellie nodded, ducking the warm search of his eyes. She'd forgotten eyes could do this, open the places she kept shut tight inside and make them ooze together in a sad-happy mix. "Let's go then," she said gruffly, scrambling to her feet. "Before it gets hotter than it already is."

THE BIKE WAS STORED in a shed behind Deller's house, a gloomy three-story clapboard with peeling gray paint that leaned slightly, as if following the wind. Wheeling the bike along a weedy walkway, Deller propped it against the sagging front porch, then ducked inside and emerged a minute later with a hastily slapped-together cheese sandwich.

"Here," he said sheepishly, handing it to Nellie; then he grabbed the bike and wheeled it to the curb. She stood riveted, staring at the sandwich in her hand, an oddness resonating through her head. Since her mother had disappeared, she'd rarely been offered food and had had to steal almost every bite she'd swallowed. A shaky breath lifted through her and she glanced carefully at the boy sitting on his bike and staring fixedly down the street.

Don't think this is going to make me love you, she thought at him fiercely. *Just don't think anyone's going to make me love them ever again.*

Biting savagely into the sandwich, Nellie swung onto the bike behind him and gripped the back of the seat with one hand while she ate from the other. As Deller pulled out awkwardly from the curb, she settled her right foot onto the chain guard and concentrated on keeping her balance. She would not, she told herself furiously, she definitely would *not* hold onto Deller. She'd seen the magazines he read, she knew what kind of thoughts filled his head. Munching the dry cheese sandwich, she rode out the bike's wobbly movements and watched the city go by. Occasionally she jabbed a finger over Deller's shoulder, delivering a terse set of directions, but otherwise they stuck to a mutual silence, traveling a tangled route of back alleys to the edge of the city, then taking the main road to the quarry. Except for the odd honk of a car horn no one bothered them, and gradually Nellie began to enjoy the warm breeze, the quiet whir of the bike, and the blur of passing shrubbery. This sure beat walking. Maybe she could figure out how to filch a bike. Nothing brand new—just a dumpy-looking one like Deller's, so no one would think of filching it off her. Across the road, a barking dog lunged the full length of its chain and she stuck her tongue out at it. In a minute they would arrive at her regular turn-off point.

"Here," she shouted at the back of Deller's head. "Turn right."

He veered into the tall blond grass and Nellie dismounted, grunting at the ache in her butt. "You can leave your bike there," she said, pointing to a bush. "No one comes out here much, except me."

As he slid the bike into the foliage, she turned toward a small hill that sat a short ways off, hiding the shack and the copse that surrounded it. Usually she waited until she'd passed the hill to turn in toward the copse, but after last night's events she wanted to get a fix on the shack before she got too close. Somewhere high up, looking down on it would be best. Dashing up the hill, Nellie tore through the whiplash of dengleberry bushes, the sensation of riding the bike still with her. "C'mon," she called, but Deller had already caught up to her and was pulling slightly ahead.

"You live out here?" he asked, throwing her a confused look, his thoughts written all over his face: *What are your parents, moonshine derelicts? You some trash barrel kid they dumped at the side of the road?* Lightning shame forked through Nellie. Putting on a burst of speed, she crested the hill ahead of him.

She saw, gave a hoarse cry, and fell to her knees.

"What is it, Bunny? What—?" Pulling up beside her, Deller went abruptly quiet. Earthquakes of silence filled the air, deep soundless apocalypses. No birds sang, the wind had gone utterly still. From the highway came the hum of a single car passing. Huddled against the ground, Nellie pulled up handful after handful of long blond grass, ripping the quiet to shreds.

"Was that your house, Bunny?" asked Deller in a bewildered voice. "Is that where you lived?"

She opened the absolute soundlessness that was her mouth, and nodded. For a long moment Deller's face seemed about to slide into separate pieces, and then he turned to stare again at the wreck of the place that had housed her shack. Where the copse had stood that morning there was now only a large gash, torn deep in the ground. Trees lay every which way, some flung as far as fifty feet. A thick scent of burning hung in the air, and the trees and surrounding grass had been badly singed, but there was no sign of the shack, not even a charred board or shingle. The site looked as if a fist of fire had erupted from the ground, uprooting everything in its path.

"That was your house?" Deller asked again, as if he couldn't make sense of what he was seeing. "That's where the gate showed itself to you?"

"Yeah," Nellie finally managed, the effort exhausting her.

Deller stood shuddering in the silence, being eaten by small gusts of wind. "What about your mom and dad?" he asked finally.

"It was just me," she mumbled, and they remained as they were a while longer, staring at the ravaged pocket of earth.

"Well," said Deller heavily, "I guess we should get going then."

"Yeah," said Nellie. "Okay." Staggering to her feet, she followed him down the side of the hill.

Part 2

Chapter 10

LATER, NELLIE REMEMBERED the ride back to Dorniver as taking place within a long invisible tunnel. Beyond this tunnel the world went on as it normally did—the wind riding the doogden trees, passing trucks rippling the road beneath the bike, dogs barking and running the full length of their chains—but all of it without sound, as if each object suddenly lacked the specific noise that gave it meaning. Clinging to the bike seat, she stared past Deller's back and rode out the soundless transparent corridor that remained with her even after their arrival in Dorniver. Cars passed, people talked and laughed on street corners, and she heard none of it. No thought came to her about where they might be headed, although she felt no surprise when they turned down a familiar street and pulled up before a dilapidated clapboard house. Levering himself awkwardly off the bike, Deller gestured for her to do the same, but the tunnel of meaninglessness was still with her. Blank and uncomprehending, all she could do was stare at his face and wonder why he kept moving his mouth if he didn't have anything to say.

Hands gripped the numb post of her left leg and heaved it over the bike's crossbar, then led her across a mangy lawn toward a sagging porch. There she sat, watching a noiseless wind play with the scraggly leaves of a nevva bush until Deller's face appeared before her again. His lips moved emphatically and when she didn't respond he reached for her, pulling her insistently to her feet. Briefly the world spun round, and then she was stumbling through an open doorway into a cool shadowy place. Across the room stood a worn couch with several throw cushions. Hands guided her to it, something warm slid over her, darkness rushed her brain and she slept.

NELLIE WOKE TO THE smell of cooking, the hiss of a frying pan, and the blurred murmur of voices. Muttering dozily, she nuzzled deeper into the musty throw cushion beneath her head, but the bellow of her empty stomach pulled her firmly awake. Eyes slitted, she scanned her surroundings. Nothing was familiar, not the slightly rank smell of the couch she was lying on, the green and orange afghan that covered her, or the framed photograph of a man with slightly slanted eyes on the mantel across the room. So this wasn't a dream of one of the apartments she'd shared with her mother, though she could smell food—yummy food, the kind a mother cooked on a stove, then dished onto a plate all hot and steamy while you squirmed onto a kitchen chair that stood waiting just for you. But, Nellie thought, bewildered, staring around herself, there no longer was a chair waiting just for her, nor was there a mother cooking her supper, and how in the world had she gotten onto this ramshackle couch under the world's ugliest afghan, while painfully delicious smells invaded her nose? What was this, one of Lulunar's nastier tricks?

"Hey!" grinned Deller, coming through a nearby doorway. "You finally woke up. I thought maybe you were going to sleep until next week."

Shock fisted Nellie's throat and she started to her feet, staring around herself in renewed fear. *Where was she, how had she gotten here, were the Skulls—?* Glancing at her clothes, she assessed them quickly but they seemed undisturbed, all the buttons and zippers properly done up. So, no magazine stuff had happened while she slept. Tightening the kerchief around her head, she crossed her arms over the blobs on her chest. Snatches of memory were coming back to her—something about the shack, a huge gash in the ground, and burnt popsicle-stick trees. But how had she gotten from there to here? And why was Deller looking at her as if they shared some kind of meaning, something no one else knew? Again Nellie glanced at her clothes, but nothing was askew. She tightened her arms across her chest.

"Um, I'm sorry if I've been bothering you," she said gruffly, ransacking her memory for something nice to say. Being in a house was different than goofing off in the street—you had to mind your manners and speak properly. "Well, I guess I'll be leaving now," she added politely, avoiding his gaze. "I do so thank you for your warm hospitality."

Deller's face twisted in disbelief. "You're leaving? But what about supper? Mom made extra hamburgers for you."

Hunger undulated savagely in Nellie's gut. "Hamburgers?" she said faintly. "I guess maybe I could take one with me."

"Take one with—?" Quickly Deller turned and hollered, "Mom, c'mere, would you? She's awake, but she says she's leaving."

Footsteps rushed the kitchen door and Nellie looked up to see a broad plump figure coming toward her, dressed in an aproned sweatsuit and carrying the heady scent of hand soap and tobacco. A soundless cry passed through Nellie, her eyes dropped and she stared fixedly down. Once upon a time there had been a different woman, shorter and slighter but also dressed in a rumpled sweatshirt, who'd come flying toward her on invisible wings of hand soap and perfume.

A finger slid under Nellie's chin, tilting up her face. "There now," said a husky voice, roughened by years of smoking cigarettes. "You look like you could be kind of hungry. C'mon into the kitchen and get yourself something to eat."

With a wide, almost pleading grin, Deller gestured emphatically toward the open doorway. Nellie slitted her eyes at him

suspiciously. All this being nice made him look like an idiot, but
then it didn't exactly come natural to him. Turning from his over-
done grin, she followed his mother into a kitchen that was dense
with the smell of food. A chair was pulled out for her and she
sat down tentatively, certain it was about to dissolve beneath her.
Still beaming like an idiot, Deller dropped into the chair opposite
and tilted it back against the wall. Cautiously Nellie hunched in
her seat and slid a fingertip carefully over the susurra-patterned
tablecloth. It was yellow, her favorite color. So were the chairs and
the walls. She wobbled her chair slightly to make sure it was still
there. Sixteen months had passed since she'd sat on a chair in front
of a table and the scene felt unreal, as if she'd entered a movie of
someone else's life.

A steaming hamburger was set before her. "You want mustard or
relish?" asked Deller, pushing several condiment containers toward
her, but the roar that erupted in Nellie's head shut everything else
out. Slapping the hamburger together, she rammed it into her
mouth, chewing and swallowing, rushing it toward the rage of
her stomach. *Hey kid, you're supposed to eat that, not breathe it*, she
remembered, but when a second hamburger appeared on her plate
she attacked it with equal ferocity.

"Now," said Deller's mother, plunking a glass of milk in front
of her. "Drink this. And while you do, Deller can tell me your
name."

Glass halfway to her lips, Nellie glanced at Deller in time to
see panic grab his face. Shifting in his seat, he took on a decided
wariness.

"Name?" he said carefully. "I, uh, I guess I don't really know
her name."

"Don't know her name?" demanded his mother, settling into
an empty chair at the end of the table. This close, the scent of
tobacco came off her in waves, and Nellie could see the thinking
green of her eyes. "But you said she was your friend, she'd gone
looking for Fen."

"Yeah, well..." Deller's eyes darted toward Nellie, as if trying to read her name on her forehead. A tiny grin crept across Nellie's mouth and she drank her milk, letting him sweat.

"A while ago," muttered Deller. "Well..." He stalled with a long breath. "Well, a while ago Pullo nicknamed her Bunny, and the name kind of stuck."

Instantly his mother stiffened. "Bunny?" she roared. Surging to her feet, she leaned across the table and slapped him soundly on the face. "Is this the way I raised you to behave?" she boomed. "Running with a pack of hooligans, scaring young girls, mocking them and stealing their dignity? Is this why I gave you breath?"

Flinching back in her chair, Nellie stared at Deller's mother in stunned amazement. Rigid, the woman stood waiting for a reply, her anger coming off her in dense tobacco-scented waves. With her short thick hair, slitted green eyes and narrow face, she sure looked like Deller. But not weasely, Nellie thought. More like the way Deller could look if he smartened up. A *lot*.

Across the table Deller was a headless figure, hunched between his shoulders. "No," he mumbled.

"Ssssst," hissed his mother, lighting a cigarette and inhaling. "You know I don't have no call with that kind of ugliness, boy."

"It was way before I *knew* her," Deller protested to the half-eaten hamburger on his plate. "*Before* she went looking for Fen. Anyway, it was Pullo's idea, not mine."

"Last time I looked, your brain belonged to you," snapped his mother. "Now, I'm going to give you a few minutes to apologize to this young lady and find out her *decent* name, while I fetch some dengleberry preserves from the basement."

With another disgusted hiss, she pushed back her chair and strode from the room, leaving Nellie and Deller staring with enormous intensity at their plates. Somewhere nearby a door creaked, and emphatic footsteps descended a rickety staircase. Then there was only silence looming over the kitchen table and pressing down between them until it felt almost solid.

"Look," Deller mumbled finally, still talking to his plate. "Everything I did to you ... well, you would've done the same to me if you could've."

Nellie considered, staring at her milk glass, then nodded. "Except for the Bunny stuff," she said. "I wouldn't have done that."

Some of Deller's stiffness left him, and his head ascended slowly out of his shoulders. "It is a dumb name," he agreed, shooting her a glance, "but we didn't know your real one." Again his eyes darted across her face, then away. "So, uh, what is your name, Bu–? I mean, well, what is it?"

Nellie scratched and fidgeted. A cough claimed her throat and a sniff took over her nose. "Nellie," she whispered finally. No one had called her that since ... She wasn't going to think about it, she wasn't going to think about it *right now.*

"Hey," said Deller in a startled voice. "You're not crying, are you?"

"No," Nellie lied, but he'd already launched himself from the table, disappearing through a doorway to reappear seconds later with a thick wad of toilet paper. Gratefully she accepted it and blew ferociously. A lot of gunk came out. She mopped it up carefully.

"Nellie's a nice name," Deller said with forced cheerfulness. "Sort of like mine, really, except for the beginning and the end." He fidgeted, playing with his fork as footsteps began to mount the basement stairs. "I expect," he said carefully, a very weasely look crossing his face, "next we're going to have to tell her about your hair."

Nellie's eyes shot toward him in absolute panic.

"Don't worry," Deller said wearily. "She won't go after you." He paused, then added, "And I shouldn't have done it. But I didn't *know* you then. Didn't know you were living on your own in the bush, making do. You were just some girl ... " He trailed off as his mother entered the room, carrying a jar that caught the light in deep rich purples.

"So, Deller," she said brusquely, setting the jar on the counter and turning toward them. "How about you introduce us properly?"

"It's Nellie," Deller said quickly, rising from his seat. "Her name's Nellie. Um, could you sit down please, Mom? We've got something else to tell you."

His mother's eyes narrowed apprehensively, and she scanned his face over a long drag from her cigarette. Then she nodded and settled into the chair at the end of the table. Standing, Deller skirted the back of her chair and came to a halt behind Nellie. Instinctively Nellie ducked, lifting an arm to shield herself.

"There there," said Deller's mother, taking her hand and squeezing it. "You're in my house now, and no one's going to hurt you."

"Mom, she's from the Interior." Ignoring the interruption, Deller spoke in a breathless rush. "They did an operation on her there. I, uh … well, we sort of cut off her hair for a trick, and you can see the scars on her scalp."

As he spoke, his hands fumbled with Nellie's handkerchief, lifting it from her head. Instantly air and light swooped in on her scalp, exposing her secret ugliness. *The worms.* Closing her eyes, Nellie rocked fiercely. *This wasn't happening; she wasn't here and no one was touching her; she was going to climb onto the swing inside her head and swing herself out of her body, up into the clouds where it was safe …*

But someone was touching her. Two hands made of more than clouds and air were gently tracing the scars on her scalp. "Oh sweet Goddess," clucked a voice wrecked by decades of cigarettes. "Sweet blessed Goddess. You said it was you that cut her hair, Deller?"

"Yeah," came Deller's glum voice.

"We'll be having a talk about that later, won't we, dear? Sweet, sweet Goddess."

Then Nellie felt herself gathered together like a heap of loose clothing and lifted into a warm fleshy lap. The smell of tobacco and hand soap enveloped her, and a hand guided her head onto a plump shoulder. "There there," a voice murmured, stroking the frightened bristle on her scalp. "There now, there."

Nuzzling into the softness, Nellie shuddered and shuddered. Great cracks opened within her, cracks she hadn't known were there, and as they opened they released waves of sadness, long raw waves of loneliness and bewilderment. How had all of this happened to her, why had her mother been taken away, leaving her alone? "There there," soothed the voice above her head, but the cracks kept opening, the sadness passing from her body into the one that held her until it faded quietly away.

"No more tonight," Deller's mother murmured. "The Goddess knows I want to hear about Fen, but we'll just give her a bath and put her to bed. She's too worn down. Then you and me got some talking to do, don't we, son?"

When she slid into the water's silky warmth, Nellie began to sob helplessly and didn't let up until Deller's mother had finished scrubbing the lice from her scalp and left her alone to get dressed. Lying in the water, surrounded by dead floating bugs, she felt the sobs gradually die off, her grief retreating into the place she usually kept it hidden. She shouldn't have cried like that, she thought shakily, wouldn't have, but it had been so long since she'd been surrounded by softness and warmth. Weakness had caught her unaware. She was going to have to watch herself more closely, toughen up those crybaby cracks. Clambering out of the tub, Nellie fought off a fresh wave of tears as she reached for the voluminous nightgown Deller's mother had draped over a chair. She was so tired she was staggering, her brain a dead weight. Fumbling with the door, she opened it to find Deller's mother waiting in the hall.

"This way," said the woman, taking her by the hand and leading her to a small bedroom at the back of the second floor. "You just go to sleep now. Deller and I will be here in the morning, and then we'll talk some more."

Nellie had never snuggled into such softness. Every part of her had been scrubbed clean, her skin gave off a fresh soap scent, she'd been washed down to the soft raw hoping of her heart. Alone in the darkened room, she lay listening to the gentle thump in her chest.

She'd never felt this close to it, it was as if she could take one step into her skin and there it would be—the sad-happiness that lived at the core of her being. With a sigh she turned over, nuzzling deeper into the pillow, the movement brushing the sheets and nightgown gently against her skin. And suddenly it was too much, too much kindness and goodness touching her everywhere—any more and she would break into a thousand pieces, flying every which way. So she froze, locking her body into a single position until the ache of her arm went numb beneath her, then sank into sleep.

MUTTERING AND TOSSING, Nellie kicked against the unfamiliar weight that held her down, the warmth that clutched at her and fenced her in. What was grabbing at her, why was she so hot? With an emphatic kick, she sent the weight flying and came abruptly awake. Immediately she froze, staring at the strange room, its lumpy shadowy outlines and single arrow of brilliant moonlight that sailed through a crack in the window curtains and lay in suspended flight across the floor. Turning, she saw the blankets she'd kicked off dangling from the foot of the bed. Ah yes, now she was beginning to remember. This was Deller's house, a bedroom at the back of the second floor. His mother had tucked her into this bed just like the made-up mother in her mind had been tucking her into an imaginary bed for the past sixteen months. *And this is just the same*, Nellie told herself sternly. *Just made-up friendliness. Once you tell them what you know about Fen, their niceness will be over and done with.*

Sitting up, she felt the warmth of the bed slip away. She'd come awake as cleanly as if the arrow of moonlight had pierced her brain, but something continued to nag at her, teasing the edge of her thoughts. Stars, she'd been dreaming about stars again. A familiar slide started up in her head, tilting to the right, and the room's molecular field came into focus, the energy of each molecule flickering quietly in the dark. And then she saw them, the hairline seams that ran the walls and ceiling, and hovered midair. Gates.

Turning to her left, Nellie scanned the rest of the room and let out a gasp. In the space between the bedroom's open door and the wall behind it, and directly in line with the arrow of moonlight that lay across the floor, lurked a shadow too deep to be shadow, a darkness that could only be an opened gate.

She could tell immediately that this gate differed from the one that had materialized in the shack. No light shone through it, and the vibrations it emitted were only slightly quicker than those given off by her home level. Tuning out of the molecular field, she crossed the room and closed the bedroom door, then faced the open gate. Hovering inches from the wall, the shadowy opening would have been easy to miss if she hadn't known it was there. Beyond it she could see the blur that would solidify into a copycat version of her home level once she stepped through and adjusted to its vibratory rate.

Reaching toward the gate, Nellie ran her fingers along the opened seam and was relieved to feel no wave of pain coming at her, no terrified scream lighting up the inside of her head. So the gate in the Sanctuary of the Blessed Goddess had been a fluke, nothing more. Relieved, she ran her fingers along the opened seam again. Who would have left a gate standing open like this? Had the traveler been intending to return and failed? The gate obviously hadn't been used in a while, and this presumably eliminated Deller and his mother. Anyway, wouldn't Deller have told her if he was able to travel the levels? Nellie shrugged. Maybe, maybe not.

She picked up the hem of her nightgown and knotted it at her waist, then stepped through the gate. Immediately she adjusted to the new level's vibratory rate and found herself standing flat up against the bedroom wall. Turning, she discovered what she'd expected—a mirror image of the room she'd just left, with the same arrow of moonlight along the floor, same furniture, and an oblivious snoring double on the bed. Directly in front of her hovered the gate that would take her back to her home level, and superimposed over it was a second one, also open and vibrating at a slightly quicker rate. Adjusting her own vibrations to meet those of the new gate, Nellie stepped through it and turned to see a scene exactly like the one that preceded it—another silent bedroom, sleeping double, and superimposed gate. The third gate led to yet another bedroom and open gate, where a fourth gate opened onto a fifth identical scenario. Rarely had Nellie traveled so many levels in sequence and she kept count, not wanting to get lost. Unfamiliar vibrations were fine for a while, but levels were like mindjoys in one respect—if you stayed in them too long, you got queasy and muddled. She always looked forward to the moment she could cross back into her home level and get the uneasy buzz out of her head.

Nothing changed. Nellie went on and on, stepping through what seemed a series of endless open gates, darkened bedrooms, and snoring doubles. Then without warning, she edged through a gate to find herself in a dark closed-in place. Adjusting her vibratory rate, she scanned the area but found no sign of a bedroom or her double. Cautiously she stepped forward and bumped into some kind of barrier. When she pressed her hands against it, she could sense vibrations—very faint, but readable.

The image that surfaced into her mind was sharp and unavoidable—a boy with a thin weasely face stepping through a gate into a bedroom exactly like the ones she'd just passed through, except the double sleeping on the bed belonged to him. Nellie blinked and squinted, but there was no doubt about it—the boy was obviously the same one she'd seen last night in the cubicle. Now that he was standing, she could see he was slightly shorter than Deller but had the same brown hair and green eyes, though unlike Deller's, his were slightly slanted. Staring about himself, he muttered, "This is just like taking a morning crap. Same stuff coming out every time."

Suddenly the air at the center of the bedroom rippled violently and a brilliant seam of light appeared, opening outward. As the boy stared, two lab-coated men stepped through the gate. Beyond them Nellie could see only a blur, but when she probed it with her mind she recognized the rapid vibratory rate of the gate that had appeared in her shack. Crying out, she shrank back. As she did, the images began to fade and she forced herself to return to them, just in time to see one of the men grab the boy, upend him over his shoulder, and duck back through the gate.

Just before he passed through the gate, the second man turned back to the bedroom and raised a handheld device. Instantly the place filled with a blinding flash and Nellie felt a scream go up as the molecular field was destroyed. Shakily she withdrew her hands from the charred wall before her. So this was how Deller's brother had been taken. Somewhere on the other side of this charred barrier Fen was alive, trapped inside a cubicle, his every neuron wired to a machine for some incomprehensible purpose. And he was a traveler. He knew how to walk the levels as she did.

With trembling hands, Nellie traced the scars on her scalp. Once the men had taken Fen, they'd destroyed the gate and its immediate surroundings just as her shack had been destroyed. Both of these gates had led her to Fen, and both shared the same rapid vibratory rate. Nellie tasted fear, remembering the lab-coated men who'd pursued her down the hall until she'd made it back to her shack. What if the room with the cubicles was right on the other side of this wall? Would the lab-coated men be able to sense her here, as they'd sensed Fen?

Panicking, she blundered back to the previous level and shut the gate. Then she stood in the darkness, listening to the soft snory rhythm of her double's breathing, its whispery question of sound. Why was it, she wondered shakily, that wherever she went her doubles were always sleeping or staring at her in stunned surprise? Except for the one in the corner store, of course, but even she hadn't tried to follow Nellie back through the gate. Why didn't any of them travel like she did? What made her so different, even from her own doubles?

In utter loneliness Nellie made her way through the sequence of gates, listening to the dream-breathing of each double as she closed the corresponding gate. Back in her home level she sat on the edge of the bed and stared at the arrow of moonlight that was now angled up the far wall. Was she safe here, far from the place Fen had been taken, or could the lab-coated men track her vibratory trail to this level? Maybe it would be best to steal some of Deller's clothes and take off for the hills beyond the quarry where only rumors and wild animals lived. But she was tired, so tired, and who knew what really lived in those hills, what kinds of gates could open there?

Slipping into bed, she sank into dreams and waited for morning to find her.

Chapter 11

"**Y**ou mean Fen—?" Deller's mother stopped and pressed her fingertips to her temples, as if fighting off a stab of pain. "You're telling me my son could step... *can* step," she corrected herself softly, "into other levels?"

"Yeah." Nellie nodded emphatically, trying to dislodge the sadness she saw in the woman's eyes. "I saw him in the vibrations the wrecked level was giving off. It was very clear."

"You're sure it wasn't a dream?" Deller's mother assessed her narrowly. "You weren't asleep and making it up?"

Nellie stiffened indignantly. "I can tell the difference between asleep and awake," she sniffed, and the woman nodded, then gave a long sigh.

"She can do a lot of things, Mom," said Deller, leaning forward anxiously. "If she says it happened, I believe her."

"I do too," his mother said softly. "I don't want to, but I do."

They were sitting at the kitchen table, the remains of breakfast spread around them, listening to the house walls creak in a rising wind. Outside the window deep clouds grumbled across the sky, and the rooms above Nellie's head whispered with doubt and misgivings. How many gates had Fen opened in this house? she wondered silently. What had he seen before he was taken?

"I don't really understand it," she said quickly. "I've never gone that far into the levels before. Usually I go just one, to get what I want, and then I come back. When I was first learning about them, I'd go four or five levels to see if anything changed but it never did much, so I stopped. The two gates that led to Fen … " She paused, screwing up her face as she thought. "Well, their vibrations were way quicker than anything I've seen. Usually the vibrations of the next level are a bit quicker, but not like that." She paused again. "It's like something from far away, from a place where the vibrations are a lot faster, moved in close to us. That's probably why it's different, not a copycat level of this one."

"How far did Fen go?" Deller asked hoarsely.

"Ten levels," said Nellie. "But the men who came through and grabbed him—they weren't coming from the eleventh level or the twelfth. Their vibrations were way too fast." She looked at them, expecting to see understanding open their faces, but Deller and his mother continued to stare blankly at her. Then Deller turned to his mother.

"It makes sense, doesn't it?" he said eagerly. "The way he'd go to his room, and then we'd go looking for him and he'd be gone. And we never heard him leaving his room or coming down the hall. I tried to get it out of him, how he pulled his vanishing act, but he'd just look at me and grin."

"When did he start vanishing?" asked Nellie.

Deller frowned, thinking. "Not long. Couple of months, maybe."

His mother poked at a fried egg on her plate. "Can anyone learn to do this?" she asked, not looking up. "Could you teach me?"

Nellie darted her an assessing look. "Maybe," she said dubiously. "But I don't think it's like other things, like cooking or driving a car." Seeing the woman grimace, she added hastily, "Or using a computer or flying an airplane. It has something to do with the way you see and hear." She stumbled over her words, thinking. "Like seeing sound or hearing light. You can't teach someone that, not really."

She wasn't going to reveal anything further—nothing about the energy that danced at the core of every molecule, or the way humans showed up as figures of living light in the molecular field. That was hers.

"Fen talked about something like that once." Deller leaned forward excitedly. "We were listening to the radio, and he said he could see the radio waves moving through the air. Zillions of them, he said. All in different colors. I tried to get him to say more, but he shut up, like he'd let out some kind of secret."

"Your father was like that too," Deller's mother said, gazing out the window. "Saw things the rest of us couldn't. Heard things. Fen must've gotten it from him."

Deller nodded. "Like his eyes." As he spoke, his gaze drifted across Nellie's face.

"What about my eyes?" she asked, instinctively ducking her head.

Deller shrugged. "It's their shape," he said. "People with eyes like that are called 'sarpa' in the old speech. It means 'knower of secrets'."

"What secrets?" demanded Nellie.

"How should I know?" shrugged Deller. "I don't know them."

"You have the kind of eyes my husband had," added his mother quietly, and Nellie thought of the picture of the man on the living room mantel. "We used to say he was descended from one of the Goddess's five other children."

"Five other children?" demanded Nellie, astounded. She hadn't known the Goddess had children other than the twin sons.

"Here in the Outbacks there's a story that the Goddess actually had seven children," said Deller's mother. "The two twins that died, and five others that went on to live normal lives. Their children married and had children, and their children had children, and all of them had the same curious slant to their eyes."

"But I'm not one of the Goddess's children," said Nellie, her hands lifting to touch her eyes.

"It's just a story," Deller said quickly. "Probably made up to go along with the Constellation of the Five Children."

"The what?" gaped Nellie. Never, in all her classes in the Interior, had she heard of a star sign that had to do with children.

"Never mind," said Deller impatiently. "I'll show you some-time."

"Oh," said Nellie. "Yeah. Well." She hesitated, then blurted, "What's a rerarren?"

A hooded glance passed between Deller and his mother, and then she said, "'Walker between worlds.' Very few have that power, even among the sarpas. My husband couldn't, though if you say Fen can, perhaps he could too and just never said. Perhaps that's why ... " Another glance passed between mother and son, and then a long silence fell upon the three while the upstairs rooms whispered over their heads. With a shuddery sigh, Deller's mother got to her feet. "I want you to take me there," she said, stubbing out her cigarette. "To the place they stole my son."

Nellie shifted and scratched nervously. This was exactly what she'd feared would happen if she talked about the levels—others wanting to hone in on what she knew, steal her private world. "I can't," she said, her face twisting. "Those men we saw will notice if too many start traveling the levels. I know what I'm doing and how to keep quiet, but someone new at it ... " She fell silent, watching their faces hook onto her last words. *Someone new at it.* Fen.

Deller's mother stood staring down at her hands. "So there's no way through?" she asked hoarsely. "They've destroyed the way to Fen?"

"It's all closed over," said Nellie. "A big burn scar."

"Just like the place you used to live," Deller added.

"And even if it wasn't," said Nellie, "the gates that lead to Fen are different. They aren't ordinary gates to ordinary levels." She paused. "Maybe Lulunar brought them in."

Deller's mother moaned and leaned heavily on the table. Outside, the wind came at the house in a rush, sending a long creaky sigh through the walls.

"Well, I have to go to work," she said. "But I'll be back around five to make us some supper. We'll talk more then."

Taking a quick breath, Nellie surged to her feet. "I think I'll be going too," she said rapidly, staring intensely at a spot on the opposite wall. "I can come back later and talk if you like, but there are things I've got to be seeing to." She'd lain awake for hours before she'd gotten up, pondering her way through this short speech. Last night had been foolish, letting a great raw wound come open so others could see it. She couldn't go around blubbering and playing at hope like that. From now on she would keep her mind fixed firmly on reality. Family meant herself and her dead mother. And the Goddess, of course.

It was Fen they wanted, not her.

"Thank you for supper and breakfast," she added politely to the stunned faces staring at her. "Have a good day." She stepped back from the table.

The front legs of Deller's chair hit the floor with a crash. "What are you talking about?" he demanded, jumping up. "Where are you going to go?"

"That's my business." Nellie's eyes slitted dangerously. "I can take care of myself."

Deller's mother took a step toward her and Nellie danced backward. An odd look crossed the woman's face, a mix of dismay and interest. Then she crossed her arms and put on a firm motherly expression. Warnings ran softly up and down the back of Nellie's neck.

"Now Nellie," she said. "You're not going anywhere, d'you hear? You're a young girl, a mere scrap of a thing, and the world out there is too big for any one of us on our own. We've got an extra bed and enough food to keep you. You'll stay here with us." Plucking her purse from the top of the fridge, she continued, "Now I expect both of you to be in your chairs for supper at five sharp, no excuses. Deller, I've got a few things at the front door I need carried to the car." Without another look at Nellie she walked out of the kitchen, Deller trailing uncertainly in her wake.

A hot sad breath gusted through Nellie and she sagged against the table, listening to their footsteps cross the living room floor. It had been a good act, she thought admiringly. Most adults ranted and threatened to hit, but Deller's mother had just gone real quiet and given her speech as if she actually believed it. Of course she didn't, not really. No adult thought they could actually *make* a kid do something. What Nellie couldn't figure out was why an adult never *asked* a kid to do something. If Deller's mother had looked her in the eye and *asked* her to stick around, well, that would have been a different situation entirely.

She was wearing a pair of pants and a T-shirt that probably belonged to Fen. Slipping through the back door, she stood listening as a car started up at the front curb. The wind came at her in a twisting whine, splattering her with a gust of rain. For a moment she considered filching Deller's bike, then decided against it. Ducking her head, she took off down the alley, carried along on a long moan of wind.

NELLIE HEADED TOWARD the river and the deserted warehouse that housed the Skulls' headquarters. Though she'd decided not to continue living in Deller's home, there was something in her that couldn't quite give him up, not yet. Images of his face kept flashing through her head, tense with excitement as he'd talked about Fen's disappearing act, or tracked with tears when she'd first told him about the cubicle. What would it be like to have a brother waiting for you like that, hoping and dreaming after you? There had never been anyone but a mother in Nellie's life, her face tense and strained, peering through a series of endless windows. Had her mother ever cried for her? The question dropped through Nellie's mind like a pebble through water, her thoughts rippling into silence. She couldn't remember. She couldn't remember ever seeing her mother cry.

The gusting wind and rain were herding most people indoors. Now and then someone rushed past, hidden beneath an opened newspaper or umbrella. Days like this meant food was more difficult to come by, the weather forcing street vendors to take time off. Turning into a back alley, Nellie spied a delivery truck idling with its back door open as the driver darted into a store's service entrance, carrying a load of bread. Without hesitating, she scrambled into the truck and snatched several packages of baked goods, then hit the ground running. Shouts erupted behind her, but she veered onto the nearest street without looking back. No one ever caught her. Most adults were too fat, and none of them knew the back alley network like she did. Give her two backyard fences, and she could lose anyone.

Tucking the baked goods under her T-shirt, she took off at a steady lope and reached the Skulls' headquarters within ten minutes. Halfway down the block, a lone truck was pulling out of the only factory still in operation, and she ducked behind an office building as it drove past. By now the rain was pelting down. Lifting her T-shirt, Nellie checked the top package of doughnuts. Damp, but not soaked. If she managed to get out of this rain soon, she'd have more than mush for lunch.

Most of the office building's first floor windows had been smashed. Draping a moldy tarp over a windowsill to cover the broken glass, Nellie heaved herself through the gap, then hauled in the tarp. In the dim light all she could see was dust, broken by rodent tracks and the odd vague footprint left by previous tenants come to spend a few nights like herself, but nothing appeared to be recent. Slowly she walked through empty rooms so thick with gloom, it was like moving through the inside of a headache. Climbing a staircase to the second floor, she settled in a bare room with a row of windows that overlooked the Skulls' headquarters. Here she would be able to watch Deller come and go, and feel out her thoughts about him from a distance. Getting close to people complicated things and messed up her brain so she couldn't think straight.

Gusts of wind came through a broken side window, but the ones facing the street were undamaged. Rain swilled the glass, clearing away the dirt. Right here, thought Nellie, touching the sill. Here would make a good place to set the statue of Ivana that she'd found in the Sanctuary of the Blessed Goddess's storage room.

The groan that took her then almost sent her to her knees. The statue was gone. Clear as anything she could remember placing it inside her knapsack yesterday morning before leaving the shack, then setting the knapsack on the bedroom dresser in her room last night. And she recalled, just as clearly, the sensation of slipping out of the house this morning without any knapsack on her back. In her rush to escape she'd forgotten the Goddess, pure and simple. Ivana would never forgive her for leaving Her holy image in a pagan house like that.

For it had been a very pagan house. Nowhere had Nellie seen a statue of the Goddess, not over a doorway or in a single window, and no altar had graced the living room or kitchen. And that talk about the Constellation of the Five Children—probably blasphemy, all of it. Made-up nonsense. Otherwise how was it possible she'd never studied the sarpas in her classes or heard the priests mention them? Her eyes were weird, that was all there was to it.

Fuming, Nellie paced the row of windows and stared down at the Skulls' headquarters. What would Deller do when he found the statue in her knapsack? Desecrate it by drawing a beard on its face? Or something worse? She shook her head. People who lived in houses were just fooling themselves with their furniture and hot water and hamburgers and such. All of it was emptiness without the Goddess. Only She could turn a house into a home. Everything outside of Her love was illusion, and she—Nellie Joan Kinnan— had just about fallen prey to that illusion herself.

Illusion. Nellie played the word over her tongue. It was a slippy-slidey word, sounding just like what it meant. And it sure described the way her life had been since her mother's death. Everything—the city around her, the people coming and going on its streets—had felt like pictures on a wall, a thin surface loneliness, until she'd learned to tune into the molecular field and see the Goddess's love at the core of things. That ability had come to her one night as she'd been sitting cold and alone in a deserted rusty old truck, thinking about dying and how it would reunite her with her mother. It had been one of her deepest darkest moments, but in the middle of it her mind had suddenly tilted to the right and the molecular field had appeared all around her, glowing like love. That was the moment she'd first felt the Goddess reach out to her, and began to understand who She truly was. *Rerarren. Sarpa.* Nellie clucked and shook her head. The only knower of secrets was Ivana, no one else.

Whispering an incantation to the Goddess, she let her mind tilt and watched the room's molecular field ooze into focus. A quick scan showed her two gates snaking the east wall, several that hovered midair, and another that ran along the floor. Idly, she studied the closest midair gate. It looked as if it hadn't been used in ages. Would it give off a flash of pain if she tried to open it? None of the gates in Deller's house had shown any signs of pain. The one at the Sanctuary of the Blessed Goddess must have been a fluke. Or maybe... Nellie's heart quickened. Maybe it had been a lesson sent by the Goddess to teach her reverence for a holy place—a kind of "Keep Out" sign. After all, the Goddess must have loads of divine secrets in Her holy house, secrets She wouldn't want just anyone stumbling across, certainly not that pagan Deller.

An eager grin took over Nellie's face. This place wasn't holy. No one would take a hissy-fit if she opened gates in this dump. Probing the midair gate, she felt it open without the slightest twinge of pain. Almost giddy with relief, she stepped through the gate and adjusted to the new level's vibratory rate, grinning at her astonished double who was sitting in a corner cramming doughnuts into her mouth. "Don't mind me," she singsonged grandly, sending her mind into the molecular field and slowing it down, her grin growing as her dumbfounded double froze into position. It was such fun to play this trick and watch her doubles become speechless zombies. "Sweet dreams," Nellie sang to her double, then returned the molecular field to its normal vibratory rate, opened another of the midair gates and stepped through.

She was on a roll now, back in her element as she chose from the various gates in each level, repeating the prank time after time. *Man, are you dumb*, she thought, staring at the seventh double she'd frozen into position. *So dumb you deserve to be easy prey*. With a grin she reversed the slowdown process. Then before her dozed-out double could react, she reached into a box of pastries and smeared a mustache of whipping cream across the girl's upper lip—just so the double would know this had all been real, not a dream, when she finally got her head back together.

"See?" Nellie gloated, staring directly into her double's astonished eyes. "I am real. I am here. You're just too dumb to know about it."

Standing, she approached one of the midair gates, about to move on to another level, when a sudden thought hit her and she swivelled back to stare at her gaping double. At every level she'd entered in this office building, she'd found everything as she'd expected—one broken window on the far side, a thick layer of dust undisturbed except for her double's footprints, and her double, caught in the throes of stuffing a soggy doughnut into her ravenous mouth. Traveling the levels was always like this—every level contained a double of herself and anyone who'd been in the immediate vicinity when she'd exited her home level.

So where had Fen's doubles been last night? In the ten levels she'd passed through, the only doubles she'd encountered had been her own. Had the lab-coated men come back through the levels after they'd kidnaped Fen, hunting down his doubles, or had the doubles automatically vanished when he was taken through the last gate?

Swallowing, Nellie stared at the gate in front of her. How many levels had she passed through today? Was she close to the tenth? Hastily she headed back the way she'd come, sealing each gate behind her. At the last two levels she paused and snatched the top box of pastries from her double's lap before moving on. Why should she go hungry tomorrow if there was so much food around, begging to be eaten? So what if a few of her doubles went without supper? They were way too fat and needed to go on a diet anyway.

With a grim smile, Nellie stepped through to her home level and sealed the gate. She had five boxes of pastry, a dry place to sleep, and as far as she knew, no one currently on her tail. Things could be worse. Taking up a position by the window, she munched her way through a soggy cream doughnut, and waited for Deller to put on an appearance.

FROM HER POSITION BY the window, Nellie watched Deller and his mother. The rain had let up an hour ago and the sun was out, riding a brilliant bank of clouds. Up and down the street puddles glittered and threw out light, and the air sang with a fresh clean scent, but the two figures standing in front of the Skulls' headquarters were oblivious. Hunched in the entranceway, Deller stared at his feet while his mother gazed down the empty street, a magazine tucked under one arm and repeatedly calling Nellie's name. Behind her the black skull leered in lopsided spray-painted fashion on the wall. Before entering the warehouse she'd given it a single disgusted glance, and had emerged with the magazine tucked under her arm. From the ramrod shape of her shoulders, Nellie had the feeling the woman had never before seen the warehouse or known of its existence. Deller would definitely be up for another little chat when they got home.

Dense and merciless, the sun beat down. Heaviness dragged at Nellie's brain and her tongue was a pulpy mass in her mouth. It had been hours since she'd had anything to drink and her body was whimpering for water. Pressing her cheek against the windowframe, she sucked her phlegmy tongue and watched.

"Nellie, Nellie." The calls came clearly through the broken window at the room's far end, the sound slightly delayed so it didn't quite match the movement of Deller's mother's mouth. Abruptly the woman left off calling and began arguing with her son, waving the magazine in his face. Ducking to avoid a swat, Deller turned slightly and Nellie let out a gasp. There on his back she could clearly see her knapsack, the tip of the statue's blue-robed head poking through a gap at the top. Greedily her eyes followed his every fidget and shuffle as he gave his mother monosyllabic replies. Here before her eyes was the sign she'd been waiting for, proof of the Goddess's great love for Her lost and lonely daughter. How it must have pained Ivana to stoop to using a heathen such as Deller to deliver Her divine message. And how obvious that She was asking Nellie to rescue the statue, the sooner the better. Softly Nellie began to bump her head against the window frame, keeping time with her thoughts. *It's mine, the Goddess gave it to me. You've got your own mother, it's mine, it's mine.* The sun pressed its great weight through the windowpane, the air spread its heated wings and beat against her lungs. She had to get the statue back, she had to.

With a final wave of the magazine, Deller's mother turned and walked down the street. For a moment Deller stood watching her leave, then ducked into the Skulls' headquarters. Rising to tiptoe Nellie peered out eagerly, whimpering as she tried to stare through the cardboard that covered the Skulls' single window. Jitters claimed her arms and legs, and she forced herself to calm down, narrowing herself into the slits of her eyes. This could be her last chance to get the Goddess back. Soon the rest of the Skulls would converge on their headquarters, and who knew what would happen to the statue then? She had to get it back, she had to get it back *now*.

Slipping through a broken window on the first floor, she crept around the back of the building and peered out into the street, but nothing moved. Quickly she darted through the dazzling slash of heat that ran the middle of the road, then snuck into the alcove that led to the Skulls' headquarters. A listless fly buzzed her ear and she waved it away. No sound came from inside the warehouse—no pacing, fidgeting or creaking of chairs. What was Deller doing? Waiting, of course. For her.

Head up, Nellie let out a scream and rocketed through the open doorway. The sudden darkness was blinding, but she'd prepared for it, holding her hands over her eyes and counting to thirty before she'd dashed. Two blinks and the room came into focus, the statue poised on the table and Deller tilted back in a three-legged chair beside it, his weasely eyes fixed on her.

"Give it to me," Nellie hissed.

"Come and get it," Deller replied.

Fury exploded through her. As she lunged, Deller's chair came crashing down and he sprang. For a second the statue teetered on the edge of the table, now in his grip, now hers. Breath tore at their lungs, they clawed and scratched as it slipped between their sweaty hands. Suddenly Deller wrenched the blue-robed figure from her grasp. Swinging it above his head, he brought it in a magnificent crash against the edge of the table. Instinctively Nellie raised an arm to her face as shards of ceramic flew everywhere and the air filled with a thick sweet-smelling powder. Coughing and choking, she staggered backward. By the wall it was better, the air clearer, and she could watch the dusty cloud above the table drift aimlessly about the room.

Huddled against the opposite wall, Deller peered over his own arm. Wordless, the two watched each other through the swirling drifting cloud. Forget the missing finger, Nellie thought coldly, her rage clear and clean within her. When the dust settled, she was going to claw the eyes from his head, then hone in on his brain. For the Goddess was gone, of this there was no doubt. In the moment the statue had shattered against the tabletop Nellie had felt a divine presence lift, agonized and desecrated, from the splinters, and flutter through the crack in the cardboard that covered the window. And Ivana wasn't coming back. She'd been betrayed twice, once through the loss of the remembering dress, and now through the destruction of the statue. Goddesses didn't hang around, giving Their devotees endless chances at showing respect. This was Lulunar, month of the twins. Nellie had been given two chances, she'd blown them both, and the Blessed Mother had just given her her walking papers.

"It was just a stupid statue," Deller muttered, staring at Nellie over his arm. "Not like my *brother.*"

She stared back, unblinking. She was going to kill him, no question. Given enough time, she would figure out how and when.

"There was something in it." Deller shifted uneasily under her gaze. "Did you notice?"

She said nothing, continuing to stare. What did she care about what he thought had been inside the statue? The *Goddess* had been inside it. *How*—she was thinking about how and when.

Most of the powder had settled, leaving a fine haze in the air. Pulling his T-shirt over his nose, Deller crossed to the table and ran his finger through the white film that covered it. With a muffled oath he yanked down his T-shirt, lifted his finger to his mouth, and tasted the powder. Incredulity crossed his face. Glancing at Nellie, he said, "It's erva."

"What?" she snapped. All thoughts of his pending death vanished. Lowering her arm, she sniffed the air. It did smell like the drug. Automatically, out of habit, she shrugged. "You're lying," she scoffed.

"You ever done it?" asked Deller.

"Course I done it," Nellie jeered, rubbing her runny nose on her sleeve. In the initial weeks following her mother's disappearance, she'd accepted small doses of erva from several men. The multi-colored mind trips had entranced her until she'd seen other girls her age, working just to get their daily dose. Magazine stuff.

She wasn't a magazine girl.

"Come over here and taste it," Deller said impatiently. "Just a bit, so you don't spin out."

Approaching the table, Nellie touched her finger to the powdery film and licked it. Carefully she hid her shock. Deller was right. The powder did have the sweet high-singing taste of erva. "So?" she shrugged again, keeping her face deliberately bored.

Deller gaped. "So it came out of the statue you got from the Sanctuary of the Blessed Goddess. It looks like that priest has more than one career going. He baptizes babies and registers their births for the Interior by day, then reports to the Elfadden by night, and pushes erva on the side."

"No," protested Nellie, her mind balking at the enormity of it. "He serves the Goddess. She'd strike him dead before She let him desecrate Her holy house."

Deller let out a twisted howl. "She didn't strike him dead when he was kicking and punching my double."

"That was in another level," Nellie said defensively.

Deller rolled his eyes. "How many crates of those statues did you see in that storage room?"

"I dunno." Taking a step back, Nellie crossed her arms. She didn't want to think about things going wrong in the Goddess's house of worship. She just didn't *want* to.

"Well, I saw lots," Deller said hoarsely. "The room was stuffed with them. Y'know how much erva that makes?"

"You don't know they were all full of erva!" Nellie shouted angrily. "The door was unlocked. Anyone could've snuck into that room and put erva into one of those statues—the janitor, or some crazy case off the street."

"The room was locked," Deller said flatly. "I unlocked it from the inside before opening it. Then I left it unlocked when we went out so we could get back in."

Wordless, Nellie watched the erva haze settle onto his clothes.

"Okay," Deller sighed. "We'll go back and see. You and me, in *this* level. We'll check the other statues in the crates and see if they're loaded too."

A last desperate possibility exploded through Nellie's mind. "It was you!" she blurted. "You took the statue and filled it with erva before you brought it here today, just so you could make me stop believing in the Goddess. Well it won't work, pagan. Nothing will ever make me stop believing in Her."

Deller's face disintegrated into absolute shock. "You are *nuts!*" he shouted. "Out of your lulu mind." He made the doubling sign, spinning his fingers against both of his temples.

Finally Nellie gave in to the knowing that rose through her like a deep-sea swimmer surfacing for air. Deller was right. The erva in the statue was connected directly to the middle-of-the-night meetings that were being held in the Sanctuary of the Blessed Goddess. She'd known all along that something ugly was going on there—that was why she'd started spying on the men in the first place. So why was she fighting the truth now?

"Okay," she said gruffly. "We'll go back." She had to, she knew that. The message from the Goddess was clear—She wanted Her devotee Nellie Joan Kinnan to return to Her divine sanctuary and clear Her holy name.

Deller's shoulders collapsed so suddenly that Nellie flinched. "Really?" he asked, his voice skyrocketing. "You will?"

She could see his lower lip begin to tremble. Sharp tears pricked her own eyes and she glanced away. "And I'll help you look for Fen," she mumbled. "Until we find him, or know what…happened to him."

Deller ducked his head and took a long shuddery breath. "Let's go tell my mom," he said.

Slowly she followed him through the doorway.

Chapter 12

NELLIE WOKE IN THE BEDROOM at the back of the second story, her eyes fixed on the arrow of moonlight that lay suspended along the floor. This time there was no ooze of confusion, she knew immediately where she was and why she'd come awake. Slipping out of the bed's warmth, she stepped onto the arrow of light and followed its trajectory across the floor. At the closed bedroom door she tuned into the molecular field and the gate to the next level came into view, a dark hairline seam woven through the dance of energy that surrounded it. Sending her mind into the gate, she drew it open. No flash of pain accompanied this gesture, and she stepped through the gate to find the next level as it had appeared the previous night—shadowy and quiet, with only her double's breathing disturbing the stillness. Without pausing Nellie opened the next gate and passed through it, repeating the process until she'd progressed several more levels. Then she opened the bedroom door and stepped out into the hall that led to the rest of the house.

Deller's bedroom was two doors down and to the right. She'd caught glimpses of it as she'd passed, enough to leave a hazy impression of model airplanes suspended from the ceiling, grubby sports equipment and scattered clothing. Since their return to the house earlier that evening, they hadn't had a chance to talk privately. As they'd come up the front walk, his mother had descended upon them and the evening had been engulfed by her questions: *How did Fen look? You said he had an electrode here, on the right side of his head? How many doctors were there? Where did the hallway lead? Did you look through a window to get an outside view?*

There had been some discussion about a meeting with the Jinnet the following night, and then Deller had muttered something about phones being tapped and left the house. Seated at the kitchen table, his mother had chain-smoked her way through question after question. Only after Nellie was consumed by four consecutive yawns did she relent, handing her another voluminous nightgown and sending her up the narrow staircase to take a bath. Nellie had skipped the bath. It had been only twenty-four hours since her last one, and she figured civilization wouldn't come crashing down if she waited a week or so for the next.

The door to Deller's bedroom—Deller's *double's* bedroom, Nellie reminded herself—stood ajar. No arrow of moonlight slanted through the windows on this side of the house, but the curtains stood completely open, and the room was a well-defined series of grays. Suspended and motionless, the planes took on eerie silver outlines. Beneath them lay Deller's double, splayed on his back in a T-shirt and cotton pyjama pants, his bandaged hand cradled on his chest. Gone was the usual weasely look. A lock of hair fell lazily across his forehead and suddenly, bewilderingly, Nellie wanted to take it into the softness of her fingertips and brush it off his sleeping face.

Transfixed, she stood in the silver-gray silence, listening to him breathe. What were the thoughts that blew across his brain, what made him from the inside out? And how could she get at it without showing too much of herself? Tonight before she'd fallen asleep a longing had come to her, a thin heated twisting desire to get past her own claws and Deller's weaseliness and just talk, as if the real reason for talking lay in the talking itself, words opening like hands and touching whatever came to them.

The solution had come to her as she'd lain in bed, watching sleep settle into corners of the room. What if she talked to one of Deller's doubles, and asked him the questions she wanted to ask Deller? His doubles must think the same as he did, and there was always the chance they wouldn't be quite as weasely. Sure, it was going behind his back, almost like mind reading, but what did it matter if he didn't know about it? Talking to a double was like talking to an idea of a person, sort of like imagining a conversation.

She'd decided to go several levels in case anything leaked back to Deller, like a conversation heard through a wall. Fortunately the door to his mother's bedroom was shut, but even so Nellie leaned carefully against Deller's double's door as she closed it behind herself, begging it not to creak. Then she turned to whisper his name, letting out a hiss when she found the boy in the bed already awake and watching her, his eyes steady in the silver-gray light.

"D'you really think we can get Fen back?" he asked, his voice thick with sleep.

"I dunno." Hunching her shoulders, Nellie retreated behind a scowl. Lying in bed pretending to be asleep, and all the while secretly watching her—this double was weasely, maybe even more weasely than Deller.

"Why did you come home with me today?" Motionless, the boy lay on his back, studying her face.

"I dunno," Nellie repeated, trying to calm the wingbeat of fear in her head.

"You don't know much, do you?" the double said quietly.

"No," she replied.

"That makes two of us." Sitting up, he swivelled and placed his back to the wall. "Your hair's starting to look better. It's growing a bit."

Nellie's hands zoomed to her bristly scalp. She'd forgotten her kerchief. How was she supposed to hold a conversation of significant meaning, looking like a shaved rat? "How's your finger?" she asked, patting down the stubble on her head.

"Gone," shrugged Deller's double.

"Can I see?" she asked, thinking it would be polite to show more than a passing interest.

"No," he grunted, and an awkward pause stiffened them both. "But you can sit down if you want," he added after a moment.

The space at the end of the bed loomed ominously. Nellie's eyes darted around the room. To her left stood a small desk and chair. Hitching the hem of her voluminous nightie, she straddled the chair back to front and faced the bed. "Just so you know," she said, clearing her throat delicately. "I didn't come here for any magazine stuff." This had to be absolutely clear.

Deller's double shrugged and his mouth quirked. "Better keep it down then," he advised. "You'll wake Mom. Believe me, she doesn't want any magazine stuff either."

Nellie sniffed and rubbed at an itch in her nose. Deller's double was getting weaselier and weaselier. Oh well. It was what came natural to him. "I want to ask you about something," she said, clearing her throat delicately a second time. "Well, a bunch of things."

"Sure," said Deller's double, crossing his arms. "Shoot."

Suddenly Nellie was breathing hot scattered breaths, her heart thundering, thundering. "Why don't you believe in the Goddess?" she blurted, leaning forward.

Deller's double looked startled. Then his eyes hooded and a very weasely expression snuck across his face. "I never said I didn't believe in Her," he said carefully. "I don't believe in priests or any of that church crap, but I don't know what I think about *Her*. Maybe She's real. I just haven't seen anything to prove it."

"But She has to be real," Nellie protested. "I feel Her like my heart beating inside me. I just know She's real."

Deller's double scanned her face, his eyes still hooded. "Maybe you're right," he said. "But I don't feel Her. And I'll never believe that ooly-gooly church stuff."

Nellie scowled and stared up at the planes, hanging midair like thick gray thoughts. "But don't you believe you'll be a star when you die and go to live with the Goddess?" She paused significantly, then added, "And your father?" It was a calculated guess and she saw it hit home.

"Maybe," Deller's double said gruffly, avoiding her gaze. "As long as I don't have to be one of those moons. I'm not into all this death stuff the priests are always going on about. It's as if they think you can only be happy after you die. twin moons," he said scathingly. "*Dead* moons."

"But don't you think you'll be happy when you die and get to see your father again?" Nellie asked.

"Why can't we be happy here?" asked the boy in the bed.

For a long moment Nellie stared at him, and then her suspicion unrolled like a ball of string. So Deller wasn't a complete pagan. Even if he did have some odd thoughts about the twin moons, he did sort of believe in the Goddess. All he needed, really, was a little faith, some proof Ivana existed. It shouldn't be too difficult to come up with something as simple as that. "I don't actually go to church much," she confessed eagerly. "Just sometimes in the afternoons. There aren't any priests or priestesses around then—just a pack of old ladies praying."

Deller's double grinned. "And you."

"And the Goddess," she said firmly.

"Okay," he shrugged. "Now I get to ask you a question."

Nellie tensed, slitting her eyes. "Oh yeah?" she said guardedly.

"How'd you get out of the Interior?"

The question came at her like an acid-tipped arrow of moonlight. "With my mom," she said carefully.

The double's eyes narrowed and he straightened. "What happened to her?" he asked quietly.

Nellie shrugged and focused with elaborate intensity on the planes above her head.

"Well?" said Deller's double in a waiting kind of voice.

Nellie shrugged again. A slow fist pounded, deep in her gut. If he didn't stop asking this question soon, she was going to throw up all over the place.

"Okay," said Deller's double after a pause. "I guess it's your turn."

Nellie hugged the back of her chair, waiting for the fist to let up in her gut. "What d'you know about the levels?" she asked finally.

"What levels?" Deller's double frowned slightly.

"Never mind." Nellie paused, thinking rapidly. Why didn't Deller's doubles know about the levels if he did? But then she knew about them, and most of her doubles didn't seem to. "Have you ever seen anyone who ... looks exactly like you?" she asked cagily.

"My brother Fen," Deller's double said promptly, then paused. "Well, not exactly. Sometimes people think we're twins, if they don't look at his eyes."

"No," said Nellie. "I mean, like ... well, like a *double*."

"A doubling?" Deller's double's frown deepened. "I ain't got devils coming through me, if that's what you're asking. Just because I don't believe in the Godd—"

"What happened after the men heard you cough at the church?" Nellie interrupted hoarsely.

Deller's double stared. "You were there," he said. "We ran out. One of the men grabbed me in the courtyard. You threw a brick at him. He let me go and we got away. Why are you asking me?"

She shrugged, her thoughts scrambling. So events didn't always turn out exactly the same in the levels. Things could happen differently in each one.

"I had a weird dream about it later, though," Deller's double continued slowly. "In the dream, the whole thing happened differently. Instead of me getting away, the men grabbed me and dragged me back. Then they beat me up." His face twisted. "Real bad. I could feel it. I think I must've passed out because the next thing I knew, I was being dragged down a hall. There were sirens, as if there was a fire, and alarms. And then—"

"Yeah?" Nellie leaned forward eagerly.

Deller's double spoke slowly, his face incredulous. "This guy shoved me out of the church door. He looked just like me, but he wasn't Fen. Fen's shorter than me, and like I said, his eyes are different and his face a bit wider. This guy was *exactly* like me. 'You've got to run,' he said, slapping my face. Then he ran back into the church. I've had that dream three times now, and it's always the same. Why would I keep dreaming the same dream?"

Nellie sank back with a sigh. So even if they didn't know about the levels, doubles could *dream* about each other. She had to be very careful here tonight, in case the real Deller dreamed about this conversation and remembered it tomorrow morning. But what would it matter? she thought, suddenly gleeful. He would be dreaming the thoughts of a double who didn't know about the levels. So even if Deller did dream about this conversation, he would never figure out what was really going on.

"What were you going to do to me after you shaved my head?" she asked suddenly.

A weasely look crept across Deller's double's face, and his eyes hooded heavily. "I dunno," he shrugged.

"Yes, you do," she challenged.

"Not what you're thinking," he said quickly.

Nellie's eyes slitted. "What am I think–?"

"Shh," hissed the double, raising a hand. Soft footsteps could be heard coming across the hall. "Quick," he hissed. "Under the bed."

Flattening herself to the floor, Nellie slithered under the bed, straight into a mound of dustballs. Nose buried in her elbow, she listened as bedsprings jounced and creaked above her head. Deller's double quieted, then abruptly rolled over, jostling the springs and muttering. *A nightmare*, Nellie thought admiringly. *He thinks quick in a fix.*

A light tap sounded on the door. "Deller?" came a muffled voice.

Deller's double stopped shifting. "Whaaaa–?" he mumbled, as if coming awake.

The door opened. "You all right?" asked his mother. Pressed to the floor, Nellie watched a pair of slippers approach the bed. "I heard you talking in your sleep," the woman continued. "Lucky you didn't wake Nellie. I checked and she's sound asleep. That girl sleeps like a log."

The springs above Nellie's head went deadly quiet, the boy in the bed suddenly still.

"You're sure you're all right then?" his mother asked again.

"Yeah, just a weird dream," muttered Deller's double.

"All right. See you in the morning." The slippers padded back across the floor, the door closed and soft sounds retreated across the hall. Rigid and breathing only the tiniest of breaths, Nellie lay in the absolute stillness that followed, trying to read the mind of the boy that lay above her. Pressing her hands against the bottom of the mattress, she was about to scan his vibrations when he began bouncing frantically and she had to plaster herself to the floor to avoid getting flattened.

"So, what the hell are you?" he hissed as she came slithering out from under the bed. "A double? A *doubling*?"

"Course not," Nellie snapped, scrambling to her feet. *Her, a double?* Brushing dustballs from her nightgown, she started backing toward the door.

"What would happen if I went down the hall right now and looked in on Nellie?" asked the boy on the bed, his eyes glinting. "Would I find someone who looks exactly like you?"

"Why would you want to do that?" Thoughts racing, Nellie fumbled with the doorknob. She'd left the gate to this level standing open in her double's bedroom. That meant all she had to do was take off down the hall and—

"Where d'you think you're going?" With a savage creak of bedsprings Deller's double launched himself from the bed, and Nellie tore open the door and raced down the shadowy hallway. Dashing into the bedroom at the far end, she caught sight of her double in the bed, snoring loudly. Figured. Without hesitation, Nellie stepped through the waiting gate and sealed it behind her. There—easy as that, her troubles were over. Quickly she passed through the next several levels, sealing each gate, and finally reached her home level. There she stood a moment, eyes closed, breathing in the silence of the empty room. That had been way too close. But at least she'd learned one thing—Deller's doubles were even more weasely than he was.

Opening her eyes, Nellie turned toward the bed and saw the girl. Seated cross-legged with her back to the wall, she was playing quietly with a pocketknife, spinning it on her palm. During Nellie's absence the arrow of moonlight had shifted from its position on the floor, slanting up the bed so its tip now rested on the girl's face. In its pearly light there was no denying she looked exactly like Nellie, down to the odd slant of her eyes and the frightened angry stubble on her head. The only difference was the gold-brocaded dress that ballooned about her in heavy shimmering folds.

"That's my dress," Nellie said hoarsely, taking a step forward. "You stole it from my shack."

"Uh-uh," said the girl, giving the knife a cool silver flick in the moonlight. "*My* money in the store—*you* stole that. The dress is payback."

"I'll get you some more," Nellie said quickly. "Just give me back the dress, and I promise—"

Her double leaned over the foot of the bed and spat with venomous precision on the floor. "Your promises mean shit," she said. "I've been watching you pass back and forth through the skins as if they're nothing, just bits of air. And laughing at your possibilities, rubbing doughnut goop in their faces."

"Possibilities!" Nellie gaped, dumbfounded. "They're just stupid doubles, so stupid they don't even know they're doubles. Besides, I never hurt none of them."

The girl on the bed watched her silently, walking the closed knife over the back of her fingers. Nellie stared back, her eyes slitting as she pondered the situation. This double was obviously smarter than the rest of them, and unpredictable. She looked as if she wouldn't think twice about causing a ruckus. All in all, she looked kind of weasely.

"I need that dress to remember my mother," Nellie said stiffly. "She's dead."

"So's mine," said the girl on the bed.

"But you have a dress like that in your own level," Nellie snapped.

"Maybe I want two," sneered the girl. "For Lulunar."

Nellie's eyes slitted further. She decided to change tactics. "Do you love your mother?" she asked softly.

The girl's eyes narrowed and she said nothing.

"Then you know how much I miss mine," Nellie continued, ignoring her silence. "When I found that dress on that laundry line, I just knew—"

"I found it," said the double.

"No, you found it because I found it," argued Nellie. "What happens to you happens because I do it first. The rest of you are like ... echoes."

"I'm not your echo," scoffed the other girl. "Do you carry a knife?"

Nellie's eyes flicked to the pocketknife and she shrugged.

"*I* found the dress and *you* copied," said Nellie's double. "I was ready to rob a store and you moved in on me. I was living in my own turf, respecting the skins, but you invaded, so now you're paying the price. One little dress isn't much!"

"But it's my remembering dress," whispered Nellie.

"Mine too," smirked her double.

Nellie fought the urge to fly at her and claw her eyes out. "What did you call the levels?" she asked slowly. "Skins?"

"Levels?" said the girl. "What are they?"

"What are skins?" countered Nellie.

"What you come through," said her double with a look of surprise. "From there to here. The skins are all around us, they're what keeps you from me. Most of the possibilities don't know the skins exist. They think they're all there is. Just a few of us can come through the skins and walk around in someone else's turf." She gave Nellie a sly grin.

"Tell you what," said Nellie, chewing her lip. "You're right. I shouldn't have taken your money, so you can keep the dress. I'll find another one. Why don't we make a deal? You stay on your turf and I'll stay on mine. I won't ever cross into your skin to bug you, and you'll stay in your skin and leave me alone."

Her double gave a thinking hiss, flicking the knife blade in and out of its pocket. "No one tells me where I can go," she said finally. "Why should I stay out of your skin if I feel like coming here? There's no way *you'd* keep your promise if you didn't feel like it. And you need someone watching you. You've got a few lessons to learn about respecting other people's skins."

In a swish and shimmer of gold brocade, the double eased off the bed and turned toward the window. "Keep an eye out for me," she said to Nellie over her shoulder. "I'll be wearing your remembering dress and showing up when you least expect it. Just think of me as your guardian angel."

Suddenly she disappeared. No gate opened, there was only a brief intense humming in the air, and then the other girl was no longer in the room. With a cry Nellie rushed forward, her hands raised, trying to read her double's vibrations, but all she sensed were her own. Tuning into the molecular field, she scanned wildly but could find no gate in the place her double had vanished.

Crawling into bed, Nellie curled into a frightened shell. How could this be, a double that came and went into nothingness? If a double could do that, what else could suddenly step out of thin air? Whimpering, she tried to escape her thoughts by diving into sleep, but the arrow of moonlight was resting serenely on her face. With a sob she turned and squished herself into the crack between the bed and the wall, until all she could see was the darkness in front of her face.

Chapter 13

THOUGH NELLIE WATCHED Deller suspiciously at breakfast, he showed no sign that her conversation with his double had leaked through to his dreams. In fact, he seemed to have forgotten her existence entirely. Eyes riveted to his breakfast, he shoveled eggs and toast non-stop into his mouth, managing only a few monosyllabic grunts at his mother before launching himself from the table and out the door. The screen door whirred back on its hinges and slammed shut, there was the thud of running feet, and finally a long drawn-out sigh as the house relaxed into quiet.

"Where's he going?" Nellie scowled down at her own eggs and toast. It wasn't that she *wanted* Deller nearby, but she'd assumed he would be around, bugging her every minute of the entire day.

"Gone off to his part-time job," said his mother, standing up to clear the table. "He'll be back for lunch, just before I leave for my afternoon shift. He works as a courier two mornings a week, delivering messages on his bike."

"That old thing?" asked Nellie.

"It gets him around," said his mother, carrying a stack of dishes to the sink. "And we've got our own work to do, you and I. C'mon

over here and help me with the dishes, and then there's something
I want to show you. C'mon now."

Reluctantly Nellie shuffled to the sink and stood watching the
dishwater rise in the basin. It had been a long time since she'd washed
dishes, almost a year and a half. Tentatively, she held her hands over
the soapsuds, letting them break softly against her palms.

"Go on now, the water won't bite," said Deller's mother.

Nellie eased her hands into the water and felt the warmth nuzzle
her skin. An early morning breeze wafted through the window
above the sink, rippling the curtains, and she breathed in its sweet
outside scent. Small trickling sounds came off each dish and cup as
she lifted them out of the water. She concentrated, scrubbing each
object carefully before handing it to Deller's mother for drying. It
had been so long since she'd washed dishes that she felt as if she was
reaching back through time, scrubbing plates she and her mother
might have used in the Interior. Being in a house again was doing
strange things to her head. The last time she'd turned to hand
Deller's mother a freshly washed saucer, she'd actually seen her own
mother standing there, smiling and reaching toward her ...

With a cry, Nellie let go of the saucer she was holding. Hitting
the floor, it bounced and rolled a few feet, then tilted and spun on
its rim.

"Never you mind," said Deller's mother, stooping for the saucer
and dropping it back into the soapy water. "It landed on the rug.
Nothing broken, not even a chip. Why, what's the matter with you,
child? You've gone white as a ghost."

"Nothing." Scowling, Nellie buried her arms in the dishwater
and watched the soap bubbles rise above her elbows. For a moment
she'd thought ... she'd seen her mother standing in the living room
doorway, holding a gun. Why, would she be holding a gun? Her
mother had been a schoolteacher, not a soldier. Frantically Nellie
swished her arms in the dishwater, trying to wash the scene from
her memory. Water sloshed onto her T-shirt, over the counter, and
onto the floor.

"You've got some cleaning up to do," commented Deller's mother comfortably. "But that's all right. The floor can use the wash, and I can wait with what I've got to show you upstairs until you get every inch of it spic and span."

Nellie stopped sloshing and wiped up the mess. As she did, the image of her mother holding the gun faded slowly from her thoughts until it hung like a gauze curtain, there and not there, waiting at the back of her mind. Thoughts did this to her—came at her, tore open her brain and disappeared again as if they'd never existed. By the time the dishes were finished, the memory of her mother and the gun had vanished, and she clomped noisily out of the kitchen after Deller's mother, following her up the stairs and into a bedroom with deep blue susurra flowers on the curtains and an ugly pink and lime afghan on the bed. Sliding open a dresser drawer, Deller's mother pulled a measuring tape from a sewing basket.

"Now, Nellie," she said, a lit cigarette dangling from her lips. "It's time for what we call a rite of passage."

"A right of what?" Slitting her eyes, Nellie took a step back.

"A rite of passage is something everyone experiences as they pass through life," said Deller's mother, smoothing the measuring tape between her fingers. "It's a special moment that tells you that you're growing up, getting older."

"Oh yeah." Nellie glared suspiciously at the measuring tape. She'd read about rites of passage in school—stories about virgins being offered to the gods, and young men sleeping naked on mountaintops in sub-zero temperatures. None of them had involved a tape measure from a sewing basket.

"This particular rite of passage is just for girls." Deller's mother seemed to be fighting off an enormous grin. "I went through it too—a long time ago, of course. As each girl grows up she develops breasts, just as you're doing, and that means she needs to start wearing a bra."

Nellie's arms glued themselves to her chest and she took another step back. "Actually, I've decided not to have breasts," she said flatly.

"I've been sleeping on my stomach to squish them back inside. And I already tried one of them bra things. It didn't work."

Deller's mother went into an abrupt fit of coughing and turned toward the dresser. "Why didn't it work?" she asked in a muffled voice.

"It stuck out of me like two mountaintops," Nellie complained. "Way out to here." Ungluing an arm, she waved a hand helplessly in front of her chest, then glued the arm back again.

"Looks like you probably got a bra that was meant for me," said Deller's mother. "Bras come in different sizes. That's why I need to measure you."

Nellie took a flying leap backward and tightened her arms across her chest. Damn blobs. From the first moment she'd felt them growing, she knew they would be nothing but trouble.

"C'mon now," said Deller's mother. "I'll do it over your shirt. That way no one'll see your breasts except you. A girl needs her privacy."

Hesitantly Nellie slid her a sidelong glance, then looked away again. "You won't tell Deller?" she asked in a carefully bored tone.

"Deller's not a girl," said his mother firmly. "Only girls get to share this particular rite of passage."

Nellie slid her another sidelong glance. "Will it stop them from jiggling?"

"That's exactly what a bra is for," reassured Deller's mother. "Now if you'll just straighten your T-shirt, I'll measure you so I can pick out the right size for you at the store."

Slowly Nellie unglued her arms, tugged stiffly at her T-shirt, then hung her arms rigidly at her sides.

"It's easier if you hold your arms out a little." The scent of tobacco descended upon Nellie, shutting out the rest of the world. Closing her eyes she stopped breathing, stopped thinking, stopped everything.

"That's better," said the voice above her head. "Now I'll just slip it around your back and fit it snug across your front like this."

The tape tightened gently around Nellie's chest. Suddenly she was struggling for breath, fighting the scream that surged up her throat. White rooms, she could see doctors in white lab coats leaning over her, some kind of medical instruments in their hands...

The measuring tape loosened and withdrew. Shuddering with relief, Nellie stepped back and crossed her arms again.

"Congratulations, Nellie, that rite of passage is over. Now that wasn't too bad, was it?" A hand touched Nellie's kerchiefed head. She flinched, and the hand withdrew into a moment of silence. "Hmmm," said Deller's mother. "My guess is you didn't have a bath last night."

"Yeah," said Nellie immediately. "Sure I did."

"Nellie, that smells like a lie," frowned Deller's mother. "I don't like that smell in my house."

"Okay." Nellie heaved an enormous sigh and fidgeted her feet. "I just don't *need* a bath every single night. I usually take one every three or four days in the brook, and mostly I don't even need soap, so—"

"Off you go, straight to the tub this minute, young lady." Deller's mother pointed firmly to the door. "There will be a bath for you every night this week, no discussion. After that, we can start talking about every second or third night, d'you hear?"

Nellie's mouth opened and she gaped soundlessly. This was something she'd forgotten about mothers. They took themselves very seriously and when they glared like that, there was no getting around them. This was definitely going to be one wasted morning. Slumping her shoulders, she slouched disconsolately toward the door.

HALFWAY THROUGH A sandwich and a bowl of soup, Nellie sat across from Deller and watched his mother pause in the kitchen doorway before heading out for her afternoon shift. "Now, Deller," the woman said, stubbing her cigarette into an ashtray on top of the fridge. "There's yard work that needs to be done and the back fence to paint. Supper's in the oven. Just heat it up and it'll be ready to eat. When I get back, you tell me what went on at the Jinnet."

"Yeah, Mom." Deller tilted back his chair and grinned at Nellie. He looked wind-blown, weasely and full of sun. Whatever had been bugging him at breakfast seemed to have passed, and his morning had obviously gone much better than hers. Scowling down at her sandwich, Nellie gave it a good poke.

"You remember what we talked about, son," added his mother, picking up her purse. Deller's grin vanished. His eyes hooded, looking inward, and he nodded. "See you later, Nellie," she added, and then her footsteps crossed the living room floor, the screen door creaked open, and more footsteps clicked down the front porch stairs. Nellie listened to them fade into the hot blue afternoon, where the world was full of running and yelling places and no one telling her what to do.

"I'm not doing yard work," she said, picking up her sandwich and chomping into it fiercely. "I've got significant things to do."

"Me too," said Deller. Shooting him a glance, Nellie found him hunched over his soup and watching her with hooded eyes. The hand with the missing finger rested beside his bowl, a bit of dried blood edging the bandage. "Take me through the gate," he said abruptly. "To where they took Fen. I want to see it."

Reluctance twisted Nellie's face. It wasn't right, taking someone else through a gate. If you weren't a natural traveler, you didn't belong in another level. It was just the way things were—the levels decided for themselves what they would reveal and to whom.

"Please," said Deller, leaning forward. "I'll make it up to you, I promise."

Avoiding his eyes, she shook her head. The place he was asking to see was one gate away from the lab-coated men. They might be on the lookout for travelers, could even be lying in wait.

Deller's face collapsed, and she watched him suck at a tremble in his mouth. "Please," he said again. "I never got to say goodbye. He was just gone. All this time, I've been looking and looking. If I could just see the place they took him ... "

Nellie took a ragged pulsing breath. She knew about this kind of pain. If someone came up to her and said, *I've seen your mother. She's alive. I can take you to her...*

"I'll do whatever you say," Deller added quickly, crooking his index finger. "Jinnet's honor."

Nellie assessed him through slitted eyes. Just for a moment she'd almost liked him, but now he was back to his normal weasely self. Scowling, she said, "If something happens and I say we have to come back before we get all the way there, will you listen?"

Deller's face leapt. "You're the boss." A sheen of light slid down his bangs, into the muted green of his eyes, and Nellie felt a soft shuddering warmth pass through her. Jumping up, she bumped her knee against the table.

"If you're ready, let's go," she said gruffly and headed for the stairs. Without further ado they passed into the thick upstairs heat of the house, Nellie leading, Deller following, the only sound the rustle of leaves at bedroom windows and the creaking of the floor beneath their feet. Nellie walked quickly down the hall, fighting the unease she always felt when someone was at her back. Stepping into her bedroom, she pointed to the bed and said, "Sit over there while I figure things out."

For this was going to take careful thinking. She'd never deliberately taken anyone into another level. Crossing to the gate behind the bedroom door, Nellie stared at it. Her own passage between the levels was no problem, of course—by now she adjusted automatically to each level's vibratory rate—but what about Deller? What if he got stuck out of sync again? And there was also his weasely doubles to think about. Screwing up her face, Nellie pondered. She could freeze each new level as she entered it, just to show everyone she was boss and they'd better not cause a ruckus, but then she would have to unfreeze it again, and the whole process was more complicated with Deller along. She took a long thinking breath. The best thing was probably just to wing it, and hope Deller could handle any trouble his doubles might kick up.

Sending her mind into the gate, she drew it open. "Can you see it?" she asked, looking at Deller.

"See what?" he demanded, squinting from the bed. So it was as she'd thought—the gate was so close to the wall even Deller couldn't identify it when looking directly at it. Hopefully his doubles would be as clued out as he was.

"Watch me," she said and stepped through the gate, then turned back to face the opening. In an instant Deller was there, peering through at her.

"I can see you," he said. "Short and skinny with hatchet hair, like always. But everything behind you is a blur."

Nellie wanted to slug him. "That's because I'm still tuned to the level you're in," she said frostily. "Every level vibrates at different rates and you can only see the one you're tuned to. Watch." She adjusted her vibratory rate to the surrounding molecular field. Instantly Deller and their home level were transformed into an indistinct blur and the new level came into focus, their doubles standing across the room.

"Hey, where'd you go?" Deller's words came to her as if through a wall, muffled and indistinct. With a giggle Nellie readjusted to their home level's vibratory level and pulled him through the gate. For a brief blurred moment there was nothing, and then their bodies adjusted to the new vibratory rate and the bedroom came into view.

"Whoa!" Deller hissed. "What a rush." His eyes traveled around the room and fell on their doubles, standing near the window. "What's with them?" he whispered.

Nellie shrugged. She hadn't given the doubles a second thought. As usual they were doing their own thing, which was pretty much a copycat version of her thing, or what she would have been doing if she wasn't traveling the levels. From the tone of their voices she guessed they were quarreling, but what else was new for her and Deller? Fortunately Deller's double had his back to them and her own was standing, arms crossed and head down, refusing to look up. All she and Deller had to do was make a run for it. Giving him a poke, she turned toward the gate but was stopped by the frown on his face.

"Dirty bugger," he muttered.

"What?" hissed Nellie.

"I don't like him," whispered Deller. "I can tell what he's thinking, and I don't like him."

"I don't like my doubles either," Nellie snapped. "So I don't waste time thinking about them." Opening the gate to the next level, she stepped through it and stood waiting with her arms crossed. She would give Deller twenty seconds, and then she was sealing the gate. He'd promised to do what she said and here he was, already giving her trouble. It would serve him right, getting stuck in another level with two crotchety dou—

His face appeared in the opening and Nellie blew out a sigh of relief. With a last glance over his shoulder, Deller stepped through the gap and she sealed it. By the time she'd finished, their bodies had adjusted to the new vibratory rate and she found Deller staring angrily at the next set of doubles. Still on the other side of the room, the two were doing a strange kind of dance, Deller's double taking a step forward, Nellie's whimpering and ducking back.

"C'mon," Deller's double said pleadingly. "Just once."

"No," whined Nellie's double, twisting her arms tighter around herself. "Leave me alone."

"I just want to feel them," said Deller's double. "You won't get pregnant. Lift your shirt so I can see."

Magazine stuff. Nellie snorted quietly. She should have known, after the pictures she'd seen in the Skulls' headquarters. Why didn't her double just kick the jerk where he needed it?

With another whimper her double backed into the wall, and Deller took a deep hissing breath. "I'm going to punch him in the gut," he said.

Grabbing his arm, Nellie focused and took him out of sync with the surrounding vibratory rate. He was looking too weasely, as if he was about to cause a whole lot of ruckus, and she wasn't having it. Who knew if the lab-coated men were watching for travelers, and which level they might be focusing on?

"Hey!" came Deller's muffled voice, his hazy transparent figure turning this way and that, trying to see through the blur that now surrounded him. With a tiny satisfied grunt, Nellie crossed her arms and waited. Let him sweat it out for a minute, and then she would bring him back into sync. That would teach him to *listen* when she told him to.

But Deller's hazy figure wasn't standing submissively, waiting for her to show mercy. Taking off across the room, he slid to a halt at the place he'd last seen his double, then raised his fists and began swinging wildly. Grimly Nellie altered her vibratory rate to match his and started toward him.

"Get lost!" Deller shouted, now clearly visible to her as he shadowboxed with the air. "Leave her be, you lousy shit. She's just a kid, all alone, with no one to help her. You're thinking screwed, you don't know what you're doing. You've got to wake up, wake up!"

"Cut it out!" Nellie hissed, grabbing his arm. "Stop it right now or I'll go back to our level and leave you here to rot forever, d'you hear?"

Deller stopped swinging and stood breathing heavily. "Yeah, okay," he said finally.

"They can't hear you when you're out of sync anyway." Nellie could barely speak, her fury thudding through her like blood. "Now, you listen to me, Mr. Big Shot Skull, and you listen good. If you're going to travel the levels, you've just got to learn that another level isn't *your* life. What goes on there goes on, but it has nothing to do with you. We've got seven more levels to go this afternoon. Are you going to try to solve every problem you see in each one?"

Deller shrugged without looking up. "Maybe."

Nellie let out a long hissing breath.

"Okay." Deller slanted her a glance. "But it isn't easy when it's me I'm watching, pulling that kind of shit."

"It isn't you," snapped Nellie. "Just one of your thoughts."

"I don't like that thought," Deller said grimly.

Nellie shrugged and turned toward the gate. "Get over it," she said, touching his arm and bringing them back into sync. Immediately Deller glanced toward their doubles. Following his gaze, Nellie saw them standing with stunned expressions, staring at each other.

"You didn't have to call me a shit," said Deller's double, stepping back. "All I wanted was a lousy feel. That doesn't make me a pervert."

Nellie's double gaped at him, wordless.

"I'm not a pervert," repeated the boy, still staring at her. Abruptly he turned and left the room.

A look of glee crossed Deller's face. "They did hear me!" he crowed. "You said they couldn't, but you were wrong."

Across the room, Nellie's double looked up and saw them. Starting back, she cried out in fear.

"Don't mind us," Nellie told her airily, waving a hand. "We're just passing through." Turning from the girl she opened the gate to the next level, dragged Deller through, and sealed it behind them. Then she stood in the surrounding blur, deliberately keeping them out of sync with the new vibratory rate. Anyone would need a breather after the pack of nonsense she'd just been through.

"Why could they hear me?" demanded Deller, staring around himself. "I can't hear you when you're vibrating differently than me."

Nellie shrugged. "Things leak through sometimes, I guess."

"Funny thing is," said Deller, looking more and more pleased. "My double thought it was your double saying those things. I think maybe she did too."

Nellie sighed. "I'm going to bring us into sync now. Then we're going straight to the place they took Fen without any more nonsense."

"Okay," said Deller, sobering. She touched his arm and the room came into focus, empty of anyone but themselves. "Hey, what happened to them?" Deller demanded, staring bug-eyed.

"Took off, I guess," said Nellie, opening the next gate. "Good thing too."

"That's because my double got the message," Deller said eagerly. "I can be pretty dense, but if you yell loud enough, I usually get it."

"That was in the last level," Nellie said dismissively.

"Nellie," said Deller, touching her arm. "They're all *me*. Why wouldn't they all get it, whatever level they happen to be in?"

She stared at him. This was only his second time traveling the levels, but there were already things he understood that she didn't. It bugged her.

"Whatever," she said, shrugging off her irritation. Images of her doubles running down a narrow staircase, through a doorway and into the street flickered through her mind, but she brushed them away. Who cared what they were doing? If they'd taken off, they would find somewhere else to live, or get over their fear and return to the house. And the fact that they were no longer in the bedroom was going to make it much simpler to progress through the next six levels.

Quickly she stepped through the gate. An initial glance showed the room to be empty, but a closer look revealed a ghostlike blur shimmering on the bed. Hazy and indistinct, the figure was vibrating at a different rate than the surrounding molecular field, but Nellie was still able to catch the vague glimmer of a gold-brocaded dress and the familiar all-knowing smirk.

"What's the matter?" asked Deller, coming up behind her.

"Nothing." Slitting her eyes ominously at the figure on the bed, Nellie opened the gate to the next level. What was important was that she act as if nothing unusual was going on. Under no circumstances could Deller or his mother ever meet her knife-carrying double. Deller was already muddled enough, confusing himself with his doubles. Just imagine what he would think of her if he met that gold-brocaded freak?

"Let's keep moving," she said to Deller. Immediately the figure on the bed rose to its feet and stood as if waiting. Sending it a malevolent glance, Nellie stepped through the gate. "C'mon," she hissed at Deller. "Hurry up."

He followed and she sealed the gate behind them. For a moment she stood watching, but no ghostlike blur oozed through the closed seam. With a sigh of relief she glanced around the room and saw the hazy outline of her double in the gold-brocaded dress, standing beside the bed. Swallowing hard, Nellie beat back a wave of panic. How had her double gotten here so fast? There was no gate near the bed, and no other way for her to have passed so quickly from the last level to this one. Hissing, she turned toward the next gate and opened it. Without waiting for Deller, she stepped through and adjusted to the new vibratory rate. There, as she expected, she found the hazy figure of her silently waiting double. Giving it her back, Nellie watched Deller come through the gate.

"Three more levels to go," he said, looking around. "Why d'you think Fen came this far? What was he looking for?"

This is just like taking a morning crap. Same stuff coming out every time, Nellie remembered. "To see if anything would change," she shrugged. Without another glance at the hazy figure by the bed, she opened the next gate and stepped through it. At least her double wasn't trying to make contact with Deller. If she had nothing better to do than follow them around playing mind games, then let her. Grimly Nellie progressed through the next level, Deller muttering along in her wake.

"This is the ninth level," he said. "It's the next one, isn't it?"

Nellie nodded. As she sent her mind into the closed seam before her, she sensed nothing unusual, nothing that would indicate the presence of the lab-coated men. Taking a deep breath, she drew it open. There before her stood the black charred barrier. "C'mon," she said to Deller, and stepped through. As she did, the hazy figure of her double appeared to her left, also facing the singed wall.

"So this is it," said Deller, coming up beside her and staring at the scorched space.

"This used to be another bedroom," said Nellie. "Exactly like all the others. It had the same gates. When they took out the bedroom, the gates went too."

"Level ten," mused Deller. Stepping forward, he ran a tentative hand along the charred wall. With a gasp, he stepped back. "It feels like—"

"Like what?" asked Nellie, surprised. She'd also pressed her hands to the barrier to get a reading on Fen. It hadn't given her the ooly-goolies.

"Like burnt flesh," Deller whispered.

Skin, came the thought, as if spoken directly into Nellie's mind. Whirling, she stared at her double, certain the ghostlike figure hadn't spoken aloud. Then as she watched, her double stepped forward, passing directly into the charred wall. A dense humming started up, her double vanished, and the humming cut off.

Nellie let out an astonished cry. She'd felt the moment her double had passed into the wall as if it had happened directly to herself—a sensation like a million tiny needlepricks of sound passing through her body. And there had been no gate, she was sure of it. Her double had simply stepped through the barrier that separated this level from the next without opening a gate, without even looking for one.

Chapter 14

THEY WERE SITTING at the kitchen table, waiting for a casserole to warm up in the oven. A dense silence hunched over the room, broken only by an odd pinging noise the oven made as it heated. Tilted back in his chair Deller sat with his eyes closed, running a fingertip repeatedly over the bandage on his wounded hand. Slouched opposite, Nellie watched the tense line of his jaw, the twist of his lips as thoughts surfaced onto his face. Fidgets kept jumping out all over her skin. She wanted to reach across the table and touch the soft heat of his arm; she wanted to take off pell-mell in the opposite direction.

"You think he's already dead?" Deller asked abruptly, opening his eyes. "Kids die in those experiments, don't they?"

"I dunno," Nellie said reluctantly. "I don't remember much about that stuff."

Deller watched her through the muted green of his eyes. "So you really don't know what they did to your brain."

She shrugged, glancing away. "I know it somewhere inside me. I can feel it hidden, like a secret, something I'm not supposed to know. It's like a heavy..." Her face scrunched up as she thought. "... *blob* sitting in my brain. Sometimes I get blurry pictures of what happened.

Doctors in lab coats. White rooms full of machines. Other kids." A thick shudder oozed through her, and she trailed off.

"What were they doing to the other kids?" Deller asked quickly.

"They were in machines. They weren't dead. I don't remember anyone being dead." Nellie's eyes darted in and out of his gaze. "No blood, or anything like that."

"Just machines?" Deller said hopefully. "That's the way you saw Fen, right? In a machine?"

"Yeah, and he wasn't dead," Nellie said emphatically. "I didn't see any blood, not even bruises."

Deller watched her steadily, checking her face for lies. She stared back, feeling the desperate need of the moment, trying to carry its weight without a fidget or cough. Finally he lowered his chair and placed his bandaged hand on the table. Peeling back one edge of the bandage, he lifted it off. Quietly Nellie sucked in her breath. The stub of his missing finger was swollen, the flesh jagged and purplish-red, straining against the stitches that held it together.

"I hated you when this happened." Deller stared down at his hand, shifting the remaining fingers, letting them rise and fall. "I thought, 'What did I do to her? Why didn't she just come down when I told her to? Why'd she have to jump me and jam my hand into the fence?'—"

"I didn't jam your hand into the fence!" Nellie exploded.

"I said that's what I *thought*," Deller said carefully, without looking at her. "That's what I made up in my head so I wouldn't have to think about what really happened, how we were ganging up on some girl we didn't know, who just happened to be alone… So I didn't have to think about what might've happened if we'd caught you." His face contorted briefly, and he stared intently at his hand. Lifting it into the air, he spread his fingers and looked at Nellie through the gap. "This missing finger," he said broodingly, "this *empty space* holds what could've happened to you. What I might've done."

Their eyes locked and Nellie found herself staring into the raw fear of his knowing.

"I'm glad it's empty," he said hoarsely. "I'm just so glad there's nothing there." His mouth trembled and he hesitated. "Mom and me had a long talk last night," he said finally. "About the Skulls and magazine stuff. We looked … at a magazine. She talked about girls, about how they need to be happy. 'It's important for girls to be happy,' she said. 'Girls have secret private things hidden inside them that have to do with the keeping of life. With the making of life and the carrying of it. It's a sacred thing,' she said, 'and you can't fool with it. When girls are happy, everything is happy. The sky is happy, the earth is happy, you can feel the dirt smiling beneath your feet. When girls are happy, *you*'ll be happy, son,' she said."

Taking a wobbly breath, Deller tilted his chair against the wall and stared at the ceiling. "When Fen disappeared I went kind of snake, I guess. I've been an incredible shit, but last night my mom did me the biggest favor of my life. Maybe now I'll finally get things right. Skulls," he said bitterly. "*Numb*skulls."

Nellie was shaking, deep quivery shudders. Happiness—Deller and his mother had actually sat and talked about *her* happiness. "It's still bleeding," she whispered. "Where your finger was."

"I was putting the bandage on real tight." Deller grimaced. "To punish myself, I guess."

"Maybe now you can stop." Nellie's eyes darted across his, then ran away to the corners of the room. "Because you didn't do anything to me, Deller, not really. Except cut my hair, and that'll grow back. And this afternoon you stopped your double from hurting my double, so that sort of makes up for it, doesn't it? Anyway, the Goddess wouldn't want you to punish yourself. She'd want you to be happy too. She'd forgive you, I know She would."

"The Goddess." Deller gave a ragged laugh. "I should've known She'd show up sooner or later."

Their eyes snuck across each other's faces, and they gave each other tentative smiles.

"Hungry?" asked Deller.

"Um?" Nellie fidgeted, her nervousness running through her like a live thing. "D'you think maybe we could fix your finger first?"

"That's all right," said Deller, staring at it. "I'll put another bandage on it."

"No," said Nellie gruffly. "You do it too tight."

Time stretched as Deller stared at the wound in his hand. Finally he rose without speaking and left the room. When he returned he was carrying a tube of ointment, a cotton swab and a box of bandages. Silently he sat down and held out his hand. As she leaned toward him, Nellie was visited with a memory of her mother standing over her, gently smearing a sharp-smelling ointment onto a scrape on her arm. Taking a careful breath, she squeezed some ointment onto the cotton swab and touched it to Deller's wound. He hissed and she whispered an apology, then he apologized for hissing. Slowly she peeled open a bandage, her mind like a freshly washed window, singing with light. Laying the bandage over the wound, she pressed it softly into place. A long breath lifted through her. She could feel the ointment sending itself into the wound in smooth easy wishes.

"Feels better already," said Deller.

Nellie patted the tube of ointment, cotton swab and bandages into a careful pile. The silence in the kitchen was so excruciating, she was almost afraid to move. Then without warning, her stomach let loose with a raging bellow.

A thorough grin took Deller's face. Leaning forward, he said, "I'm hungrier."

"Betcha," Nellie challenged.

"You're on," Deller agreed.

THEY LEFT FOR THE meeting soon after eating, double-riding Deller's bike through back alleys until they crossed the river and passed into the West Haven district. There, Deller locked his bike outside a corner store and gestured to Nellie to follow. As they came around the back of the building, she found herself suddenly facing a group of young toughs wearing black caps low over their eyes. Without a word Deller stepped back and they closed in, soundless beyond the thundering of her heart.

Rigid, Nellie stood, her fingers curled and ready to scratch. What was this, why hadn't Deller warned her, she hadn't expected any kind of handing over, a roughing up. Behind her someone stomped his foot, and she jerked in white-hot fear. Someone else snickered.

"That's right, girlie," said the man facing her. "You'd best be real scared. We're the welcoming committee for where you're going. You've got to get past us before you see them."

Nellie's eyes slitted and her heart slowed its thundering, giving her thinking room. So this was just a scare tactic. Probably the best thing was to look dumb and stupid—that usually kept bullies happy. "What d'you want?" she whimpered, raising an arm protectively to her face.

"C'mere," said the man facing her. Dressed in jeans and a black vest, he kept running one hand across the sweaty skin of his chest. Reluctantly Nellie took a step toward him and he leered, "Take off the headgear, cutie."

She removed the kerchief. Off to one side she could see Deller shuffling his feet and slanting sideways glances at the group. When this was over, she was going to grab that hand of his and twist it tight as a tourniquet, she was—

"Closer," said Mr. Bare Chest, and she stepped dead into the reek of sweat and aftershave. As fingers prodded the quarter-inch bristle of hair on her head, she tried to keep her shoulders from crawling up her neck. "I see three," said Mr. Bare Chest, glancing at Deller. "I thought you said four."

"There's one down the back," Deller said quickly. "I can show you."

With a grunt, the man grabbed Nellie's shoulders and spun her around. The world swirled dizzily, fingers poked at the back of her

Beth Goobie

head, and she was given a small shove. "Okay," said Mr. Bare Chest. "Her brains are toast, like you said. Take her in."

Abruptly the circle of toughs swooped toward Nellie and howled like wild dogs. Cowering, she counted heartbeats as they backed away snickering, then took off. A deep bruised silence settled into the alley, into Nellie's breathing, her skin. Cautious footsteps approached and she looked up to see Deller peering at her, his face pinched and anxious. She felt exhausted, a pile of dust waiting for any breeze to come along and blow her away.

"They did that to me too," Deller said quietly. "They do it to everyone, just so you know to keep your mouth shut."

"Could've warned me." Shakily Nellie retied her kerchief around her head.

"Those guys know fear," Deller said. "It's their specialty. It had to be real, or things would've gotten worse until it was. C'mon."

He set off toward the street and Nellie stared after him, realizing this was all she was going to get—he wasn't about to play hero for her, offer her any blood. Slouching in his wake she kicked savagely at pebbles, jettisoning her hurt bit by bit into the gutter. After several blocks it lifted, and she noticed the crowd gathered in small groups along the sidewalk. It was the fifth day of Lulunar and though no major celebrations were scheduled, small booths dotted the streets and people remained in a festive mood. Several children ran past wearing mirrored masks, and Nellie spotted a sign outside a striped tent in a small park that advertised a mindjoy artist. Everywhere she looked shop windows displayed statues of the Goddess, and most of the cars parked along the street also sported a blue-robed figure dangling from the rear-view mirror. Stopping in front of a booth with a sky-blue covering, she pondered a large display of Goddess jewelry. What she wanted right now was a set of Goddess knuckle rings, so she could punch out that bare-chested moron behind the corner store. One knock-out Goddess punch straight between the eyes, Nellie thought moodily, to send him on a quick trip all the way to the other end of Lulunar.

"C'mon," hissed Deller, tugging at her sleeve. "It's in here."

Jerking her arm free she scuffed grumpily after him, then halted as he turned into a restaurant. Puzzled, she stepped back and scanned the building. Shoved between a pawn shop and a second-hand furniture store, the narrow restaurant looked like a gloomy afterthought. Sagging curtains obscured the windows and a dust-covered statue of the Goddess stood on the sill. Inside, the only customers were two old men drinking coffee at opposite ends of the room.

"Two pieces of dengleberry pie with no whipped cream, please," Deller said to the woman at the counter. Glancing at him she nodded, but made no move toward the pie sitting in the display case. "Are there any washrooms?" Deller asked, scratching the back of his neck. Again the woman nodded, then placed two forks in a cross on the counter. This time Deller nodded and turned to Nellie. "You said you had to use the can, right?" he asked.

"Yeah, sure," she stammered, her mind racing to keep up.

"C'mon then." As Deller started toward the back of the restaurant, Nellie saw the old man in the right corner glance toward them, then write something in a notebook. The other man coughed, and the air blinked a horde of invisible hooded eyes. Uneasily she followed Deller down a short hallway, past a door marked 'Women' and another marked 'Men'. At a third door Deller stopped and knocked quietly—four short taps and three long. The door opened and a man in a black cap gave them a cursory glance.

"Three knives to the Elfadden," he said.

"Eye, throat and belly," Deller replied.

The man beckoned them through. Descending a flight of stairs, they entered a musty basement lit by a bare bulb and piled with crates. "Through here," said Deller, opening a door onto a second room, also crowded with crates. At the back of this room, a third door opened onto a narrow tunnel. "The Jinnet bought the businesses on this side of the block, then dug a common room off the basements for meetings," Deller said tersely as he led the way along the tunnel. "You can get to it from several of the stores. Saves anyone noticing the traffic."

As they approached the door that stood at the tunnel's far end, Nellie felt a familiar shift deep in her brain and a sudden panorama of stars erupted across the inside of her head. Singing in shrill eerie voices, they swirled without discernible alignment or pattern. Dimly she heard Deller give another coded knock and stood, waiting it out as the stars faded from her mind. When they'd cleared she found herself facing an open doorway, Deller standing beyond it, looking back at her from a crowded room. Cautiously she peered past him, the memory of the stars' shrill voices reverberating through her brain. She'd just been given a warning, she was sure of it. Waiting for her in this large dimly lit room was some kind of flux.

She stepped through the doorway and immediately recognized the shadowy figures that stood about, jam-packing the place. Dressed in long-suffering clothes and rundown shoes, they were Dorniver's street vendors and factory workers, mechanics and waitresses, the odd witch and healer. Here and there she recognized a face, but the rest she understood simply by the careful hunch of their shoulders and the weasely set of their faces. There were no priests in this gathering, no factory owners or City Hall administrators. Ahead of her someone shifted, and a break in the crowd allowed her a glimpse of a podium that had been set up at the room's far end. Behind it stood a table with several seated figures. Instantly Nellie zeroed in on them. Obviously these were the big shots. Big shots always found a way of setting themselves apart, and in this room they'd chosen to sit while everyone else stood.

The only thing Deller had told her was that the Jinnet would ask her to explain her ability to travel the levels and describe her encounter with Fen. After hinting they might also ask for a demonstration, he'd left the rest to her imagination. Uneasily Nellie glanced at the hunched figures surrounding her. What would they think if they saw her open a gate and step through it to another level? Probably get all uptight and start calling her a sarpa or rer-raren. Filled with misgivings she turned toward Deller, but he was standing with his back to her, engrossed in a conversation with a man who smelled as if he made his living selling fish. If she was going to check this place out, it looked as if she was going to have to do it on her own. Tugging at her kerchief to make sure it was firmly tied, Nellie began to push her way through the throng of hunched shoulders and careful voices that separated her from the big shots seated at the front of the room.

Suddenly her brain tilted dangerously, swinging so deep into the shrill singing of stars she thought she might pass out. When the sensation faded she tuned into the molecular field, scanning it for signs of flux but could find no shimmering undulations, not a single gate running the walls, ceiling or floor. Confused, she checked midair and again found nothing. For a long stretched moment Nellie dragged her gaze once more across the room, searching for a hairline crack, any shadowy seam in the molecular play of energy. About her people pulsated as figures of light. Excess energy rose wing like from their bodies, and she could almost see the thoughts throbbing in their brains.

Then ahead of her, a single narrow seam came into focus. Quickly Nellie tuned out of the molecular field, eager to discover the gate's exact location, and found herself staring directly at a woman who was seated behind the table at the front of the room. Unable to believe her eyes, Nellie tuned back into the molecular field and the gate came into focus, but though she gazed intently she could find no sign of the woman's presence. The gate seemed to be hovering midair, unattached to anything in the surrounding dance of energy.

Bewildered, she tuned out of the molecular field and stood staring at the woman. How was it possible for someone to exist as a solid reality, but not as energy? Biting her lip, Nellie tuned into the molecular field one last time and probed the area around the gate with her mind. An immediate sensation of deadness hit her, a heaviness that latched onto her thoughts and dragged them downward. Frantically she tuned out of the molecular field and took several steps back. As she'd thought, the gate was running directly through the woman's body, but it appeared to be a body without a soul.

Instinctively she made the sign of the Goddess and began backing toward the door. Never in all her days had she encountered a gate within a person's body, nor had she seen someone who didn't show up in the molecular field. Obviously this woman was doubled. Nellie had no idea what lived on the other side of this particular gate and she had no intention of finding out. Too bad if Deller had staked his reputation on her cooperation, she hadn't agreed to cooperate with a doubling. True, most doublings came and went like a sneeze, just a quick sense of something there and gone. The odd one stuck around longer—a few hours, maybe a week—and during this time the person who'd been doubled could exhibit strange behaviors, sometimes merely quixotic, sometimes dangerous and unearthly. But at some point the doubling ended and the person returned to normal. Most left no side effects beyond temporary dizziness or headaches, and some healers and witches were rumored to seek them out.

This doubling was different. The woman seated behind the table looked normal enough—plump and middle-aged, hair in a bright orange perm and chatting animatedly—but her molecular field...her *body*...had been permanently breached end to end, and her soul stolen.

Whimpering, Nellie wormed her way through the crowd. Since her arrival the gathering had grown and now stood packed shoulder to shoulder. From the front of the room came the ringing of a bell. Voices stilled as people turned from individual conversations toward the sound. Several feet from the door, Nellie continued to squeeze determinedly between bodies. She could hear someone addressing the crowd, and the ripple of laughter that came in response. Almost at the exit, she paused and observed the man in the black cap who was standing guard. Eyes fixed on the front of the room, he seemed caught up in the speaker's words. Carefully she eased behind him and gripped the doorknob. *Easy now, just a quick turn to the right—*

"Where d'you think you're going?" Turning swiftly, the guard grabbed her wrist. Nellie kicked savagely at his shin, but the burly man simply wrapped his arms around her and lifted her off her feet. Suddenly she was walking air, her arms pinned, with nothing to bite or scratch as she was lugged through the crowd to the front of the room.

"What's happening, Millen?" asked a male voice as she was dumped onto her feet before the table.

"She was trying to get out." The guard grabbed Nellie by the back of the neck and forced her head downward, keeping her at arm's length so she couldn't scratch or bite. "Going off to report, probably."

An ugly murmur rose from the crowd and all Nellie could think of was her butt flying high, ripe for kicking. Then Deller's voice threw itself above the noise, shouting to be heard.

"No!" he called frantically. "She's the girl I brought to tell you about Fen. She's here to help us." Scuffling and panting erupted behind Nellie's butt and then she saw a pair of runners appear to her left. "Let her go," Deller said to Millen. "C'mon, what's she going to do?"

"She was trying to get out," Millen repeated, giving Nellie's head another downward thrust. Pain shot through her neck and she grunted under her breath.

"She was probably looking for me," Deller said quickly, poking Nellie's shoulder. "Right, Nellie? You couldn't find me and you got scared, right?"

"Yeah," Nellie croaked to the floor, and the vice-like grip slowly released her neck. She straightened, swaying slightly.

"Put her over to the side, Millen," said a bearded man seated at the center of the table. A quick glance told Nellie she'd seen him

before, probably working the docks by the river. The man's eyes
passed carelessly over her and he said, "We'll deal with a few things
while her head clears."

A throat coughed to his left, and someone else said, "Perhaps we
should question the girl before we discuss anything in front of her."

A murmur of assent rose from the crowd and Nellie's eyes shot
toward the second speaker. For a moment she stood blinking,
unable to connect the narrow blue eyes, sharp nose and wide thin
mouth with the warning that snapped awake in her head. Then she
remembered the man she'd seen stepping out of a moment of flux
in the corner store wall. Interior Police.

The bearded man nodded to the Interior agent. "Agreed," he said,
glancing at Nellie. "What's your name then?"

Eyes slitted, Nellie stared back at him. Did he know the guy
seated two chairs to his right was Interior Police? Maybe he did,
maybe all five big shots seated behind the table had secret connections to the Interior. Or maybe only the narrow blue-eyed man did,
and no one else realized the Jinnet had been infiltrated. But if she
took the risk of identifying the Interior agent, would anyone but
Deller believe her? Would Deller?

"Come on," hissed Deller, elbowing her. "Answer him."

Slouching her shoulders, Nellie stepped away from him. "Bunny,"
she muttered to her feet. "My name's Bunny."

The bearded man glanced quickly at Deller. "I thought you said
her name was Nellie?" he said sharply.

Deller darted a look at Nellie, his face flushed and weasely-
looking. *Make that weasely-shit-scared -looking*, Nellie thought.

"It *is* Nellie," Deller stammered.

The bearded man looked back at Nellie and she shrugged. "Bunny's my nickname," she allowed reluctantly.

The man's eyebrows rose. "And your last name?"

Nellie's mouth locked tight into silence. No way was she giving
her last name with Interior Police listening. As soon as he had it,
her surname would be on its way to the Interior and a sleek gray van

would come heading in her direction, just as it had for her mother. Crossing her arms, Nellie stood mute, staring at the floor.

"Deller?" snapped the man.

"I don't know her last name," Deller said helplessly. "And I don't know why she's acting this way. She said she'd tell you about Fen —"

"Who's Fen?" asked Nellie, turning toward him.

Deller gaped, his eyes bugging. "Fen, my brother."

"Never heard of him," Nellie said flatly. Sticking a finger into her nose, she pulled out a gooey wad and sucked at it. "Yum, yum," she sang softly, crossing her eyes. "The blind man's hung by the river and the fish are all waiting, the fish are all wait—"

"Slap her," said the bearded man, and Nellie's head was whacked soundly from behind. Stumbling, she fell against the table. Immediately two hands gripped her face, pulling her forward. "Don't play games with me, girlie," hissed the bearded man. "You remember the welcoming committee? You want to see them again?"

He gave her a shove and she staggered backward, wobbling to a halt beside Deller. So crazy wasn't going to work, she thought grimly. Well, she'd just have to keep her mouth shut then. There was no way she could freeze a molecular field with this many people, and the only gate in this underground room was in that doubled bitch. Quickly Nellie slanted a glance at Deller. If only she had some way of explaining this to him. Fists clenched, he looked so desperate and pissed-off she knew he would never think of speaking to her again.

"Okay, so I lied," she said sullenly to the bearded man. "But it's not Deller's fault. He didn't know. I just wanted to make him feel better about his brother, so I told him a story about finding Fen. I never actually saw Fen—"

"You took me through the gate in Fen's old room," Deller bellowed, hurt pouring out of him. "And you opened the gate at the church and we set a fire, and—"

"You imagined it," Nellie said curtly. "He's got a good imagination," she added significantly to the bearded man. "People make up stories when someone they love dies. Believe me, I kno—" Just in time she cut herself off. Jamming her hands into her pockets, she tried to stop their shaking. "I told him stories to make him feel better about his dead brother," she lied steadily to her feet, "and he believed them all."

Face incredulous, the bearded man rose to his feet. "Do you know who we are?" he demanded.

"The Jinnet," Nellie said immediately. "You're the resistance that fights the Interior."

The man leaned toward her. "And have you heard of the 'Cup of Tea List'?" he hissed. "You're getting mighty close to drinking your last cup. Do you want to drink your last cup?"

Coldness oozed up Nellie's throat and she shook her head.

"Let me probe her, Gareth." A new voice spoke up, so mellow it was almost a caress. Without thinking, Nellie glanced toward the woman seated behind the table and then she was trapped, locked into a deepening stare. At that moment, she knew they knew. The Jinnet knew this woman was doubled, and they were gambling that the power that held her was on their side. But a power like this didn't take sides, it used whatever came to it for its own purposes. As Nellie's gaze locked with the woman's, she felt something unseen slip out of the woman's body and into her own brain. Deeper and deeper it probed, jabbing fiercely. Agony rocked Nellie's head, she heard her own groans as if they were a stranger's. Fight, she had to fight to stay ahead of the pain. If she didn't, she would be cracked like a nut and all the secrets she was carrying, even the ones she herself didn't yet know, would be stolen.

Suddenly an intense blur appeared to Nellie's right, moving directly toward the table. Still locked into the probe, she caught only a glimpse of a hazy gold-brocaded dress and the flash of a transparent knife as it rose and descended into the face of the woman behind the table. Abruptly the pain in her own head vanished, and she was able to break the probe. Turning, she scanned frantically for her out-of-sync double. There to her right, she was sure she saw the vague shimmer of a gold-brocaded dress disappearing into the crowd. At the front of the room, the woman who'd been probing her now sat holding her orange-permed head in her hands. The crowd waited, holding its breath as she slowly raised her head.

Nellie could see fear in her eyes.

"She's crazy," the woman snapped. "Out of her head. The reason she didn't tell you her last name is because she doesn't know it. Give her the Double Goodbye, then set her loose in the streets. You'll get no trouble from her."

She's lying, Nellie thought incredulously. *Why is she lying?*

"What about the boy?" asked Gareth.

"The boy is loyal," said the woman. "He'll obey orders never to speak to the girl again."

"You got that boy?" asked Gareth.

Sucking in his breath, Deller stiffened, then nodded.

"Millen," said Gareth. "You've got your orders. Give the girl the Double Goodbye, then dump her on the other side of the river."

"And nothing more," the woman added sharply.

Stepping up beside Nellie, Millen nodded. With a queasy lurch the room upended, and then Nellie was watching Millen's meaty butt as he carried her unceremoniously from the room.

Chapter 15

WHEN NELLIE CAME TO, she was lying with one arm twisted under her body and the heat of the morning sun heavy on her face. She shifted and felt the scrape of rocks beneath her, smelled the scent of wet earth. A sudden wave of pain rolled through her head, splitting her brain like an overripe fruit. Wave after wave followed, so thick they felt solid, and she curled into a ball, riding them out. She couldn't think, couldn't think; there was only the sky-wide pain in her head, the darkness behind her shut-tight eyes, and a single sharp-edged pebble grinding the underside of her arm.

Gradually the headache began to lift. Pushing herself to a sitting position, she huddled with her face pressed to her knees, waiting for the dizzy swing in her head to sort itself out. When it didn't, she crawled to the river and submerged her face. Coolness flooded her skin and the dizziness slowed. Settling onto her haunches, she shaded her eyes against the sun and looked around.

The area looked familiar. Across the river she could see the downtown district and the spire of the Temple of the Blessed Heart with its upraised pleading hands. Relief flooded Nellie and her breathing eased. So, she was still in Dorniver. But how had she gotten to this riverbank? And what had caused the horrible pendulum-swinging pain in her head?

The inside of her mouth was thick with a phlegmy white paste. Spitting some of it into her palm, she sniffed it and immediately recognized the sickly sweet scent of erva. A wave of confusion hit her and she slumped onto the riverbank, resting her cheek in the mud. What in the Goddess's name was so much erva doing in her mouth? She hadn't taken any for at least a year. And none of her previous experiences with the drug had left her feeling as if she'd been kicked in the head with steel-toed boots.

Vague images flickered through her head. She remembered... something about being grabbed and swung upside-down. There had been a room of staring people—an underground room—and Deller had been standing beside her. What had they been doing there? Why had he let them do this to her? And where was he now?

Trailing her hand in the water, Nellie waited, and more images came to her: a table with several seated figures, a woman with a bright orange perm, and the man from the Interior Police. Then one last memory of struggling in darkness while her nose was plugged and a handful of erva forced into her mouth. She'd spluttered and gagged, and then something hard had been pressed to the side of her head and a bright pain had rocketed through her brain, sending her into a long spiral of darkness.

Sitting up slowly, Nellie trickled handfuls of water over her head and face. Her kerchief was gone, but with the exception of the headache, everything else seemed to be all right. She still hadn't figured out how she'd gotten here, but if she filched something to eat the headache would probably let up. Then she would track down Deller and find out what that room of staring people had been, and what exactly had happened to her.

Unless Deller was in on it too.

No, thought Nellie, ditching the thought. Deller wouldn't do that kind of thing to her, not after the trip they'd taken through

the levels to see where Fen had disappeared. First things first—she
would find something to eat, and sleep off this steel-toed headache.
Then she would go looking for Deller. Carefully she ran her fingers
over the stubble on her scalp. It was losing its harshness, starting to
curl at the tips. Hopefully it had grown long enough to cover the
worms unless someone looked real close.

   Clambering up the riverbank, she turned down the first alley
she came to.

SHE SLEPT THROUGH the early afternoon and woke late to the
remains of a half-eaten meat pie and the dregs of a bottle of nevva
juice. Propping herself against a wall she finished the food, then
looked around heavily. The headache had receded to a dull sludge
and the dizziness vanished, leaving the confused irritation that usually followed erva. Her joints ached, and her mouth felt dry and
thick. Why had she been force-fed such a huge dose? And what
was the small object that had sent such a wave of pain surging
through her head?

   With a grunt Nellie levered herself to her knees and peered over
the windowsill. Below her the street stretched empty and listless,
the buildings sharp-edged with sunlight. On the wall opposite a
dribbly spray-painted skull leered silently, its jaws rippling in the
late-afternoon heat. For the past several hours she'd alternated
between dozing and watching through the window. Pullo and
Snakebite had come and gone in the early afternoon. Since then
she'd slipped across the street twice to look in on the place, but the
Skulls' headquarters had been empty, just a few magazines splayed
on the table. She'd considered waiting inside the warehouse, but
a glance at the open magazines had been more then enough to
change her mind. Besides, she wanted to observe Deller first from
a distance, and watch for clues that would tell her if she was still
welcome in his life or if he'd been part of the events that had shoved
the erva into her mouth and the pain into her head.

   When she looked out again he was standing in front of the black skull, shading his eyes with one hand as he stared down the street. Nellie's breath caught in her throat, and a quick bright-winged sensation blew through her and was gone. She couldn't think, couldn't think, her mind like a butterfly trapped in a glass paperweight. Slowly Deller lowered his hand and stood, his face raw amber in the late afternoon light. Then he turned and went into the warehouse and Nellie sank to the floor, her heart thundering, her hands clenching and unclenching.

She couldn't go over there. It had taken no more than a moment to read the set of Deller's jaw, and she knew with certainty that she was no longer welcome, no longer someone he wanted in his life. Eyes closed, Nellie slumped against the wall, riding the quick shallow rhythm of her breathing. When her mother had first disappeared, the pain had been like this—deep ripping claws that came at her every time she succeeded in forgetting, then remembered again. People came and went, they planted themselves like beautiful flowers in your life and then the wind tore them away. That was the meaning of flowers and wind and spray-painted skulls, and nothing would ever change it.

But *why*? Twisting back onto her knees, Nellie stared hungrily out the window. The reason her mother had vanished was obvious, but what had stolen the friendliness from Deller's face? It had to have something to do with last night, and it wasn't fair to punish her for something she couldn't remember. Surely Deller was reasonable enough to understand something like that. Scrambling to her feet, Nellie headed out the door. Warnings buzzed her brain and her stomach felt ready to upend itself, but she ignored it, darting across the overheated street and into the coolness of the Skulls' entranceway.

"Deller," she called softly, hesitating. "It's me, Nellie."

He jumped her as she came through the doorway, leaping without sound. Shoved against a wall, she felt her head slam backward. Dizziness lifted and circled like a flock of birds, separating into endless cries.

"Why'd you do it, bitch?" Deller breathed into her face. "Why?"

She struggled with the darkness that keened through her brain. "Do what?"

"You know what!" He shoved her again, and she cried out at the pain in her head. Slumping to the floor, she covered her face with both hands.

"I don't," she sobbed. "I don't remember anything. I can't remember hardly a single thing from my whole life."

Hunched above her, Deller's ragged breathing slowed. "It's the Goodbye," he said hoarsely. "They got you with the Double Goodbye."

"The what?" asked Nellie, still trapped inside the pain in her head.

"Erva and electric shock," Deller said. "They dose you with erva, then use a shock box to blast your brain so you can't remember anything. It's supposed to knock out about half a day."

Nellie rested her face in her hands, letting bits of quiet come back into her head. "I remember pieces of things," she said slowly. "A room full of people. There was a lady with orange hair. She did something to my head. And a man from the Interior Police was sitting next to her."

"What?" hissed Deller, stunned.

"I saw him a couple of weeks ago." The images in Nellie's head were becoming clearer, coming together like pieces in a puzzle. "He can step out of flux," she mumbled, thinking her way into the memories. "He knows how to travel the levels. That's why I couldn't tell them about Fen or my name, or anything. He would've taken it all straight back to the Interior. Fen would've been gone for good then." She let her hands fall from her face and glanced up at Deller. Thunderstruck, he was standing motionless, his eyes closed.

"You believe me, don't you?" she demanded, panicking.

His face contorted and he nodded. "Yeah," he said heavily, opening his eyes. "Yeah, I've got it." Turning, he slumped into one of the chairs. "Did Mellin do anything?" he asked, his eyes hooding. "Did he hurt you?"

"Besides choking me with erva and blasting my brains?" Nellie asked acidly. "No, nothing else."

"Because Ayne told him not to," Deller said quickly. "They're not bad people, Nellie. They're the resistance. They have to protect themselves."

"Doesn't look as if they're doing a good job," said Nellie. "Interior Police and a doubled bitch sitting right at their big-shot table."

"Ayne's all right," Deller said. "She's psychic. She always probes for the Jinnet."

"She's got no soul," Nellie hissed and watched his eyes widen. "And she's got a gate right in her body. Something comes through that gate and it's *bad*, Deller."

"A gate to another level?" Deller demanded, disbelieving. "How can someone have a gate in their body?"

"I dunno," said Nellie. "I've never seen it before."

"You think she's working with the guy from the Interior Police?" he asked after a pause.

"What else would they be doing?" Nellie demanded.

Deller's eyes grew vague. "The Jinnet's cooked, then. Not just here, either. They're probably infiltrated all over the Outbacks."

"That's what Interior Police are for," Nellie said darkly.

Deller nodded, staring at his feet. "Sorry ... for not catching on last night. And for jumping you just now."

Nellie felt suddenly heavy, thick with knowing. This was it, then. Nodding her head once, she clambered to her feet.

"What are you doing?" Deller asked quickly.

"Going," said Nellie, turning to the door.

"Going where?" Deller stood and his chair tilted over with a crash.

"I dunno," shrugged Nellie. "Somewhere where you're not, so we won't get into trouble with the Jinnet."

"Who cares about the Jinnet?" Deller stepped between Nellie and the door. "I told you before—you're ten times better than all of them put together."

Astounded, Nellie gaped at him. "But what about the welcoming committee? They'll be watching you."

Deller's face twisted. "Yeah, they'd hurt Mom if they saw you at our house."

The heaviness was back, pouring through Nellie's chest and legs. "I'd better go, then."

"Wait a minute." A weasely look crept across Deller's face. "Why not stay in our headquarters? The Jinnet doesn't know about this place, and no one comes here but the Skulls. We can bring you food and blankets and the clothes Mom bought you. You'd be all right here, and we could keep looking for Fen."

Nellie leaned against the wall, waiting for her heart to stop thundering. "I thought you'd hate me after last night," she whispered. "Thought you'd just want to get rid of me."

"I did for a bit," Deller whispered back. "But I didn't understand why. You had your reasons. I should've guessed. You should hate me."

"No." Nellie shook her head fiercely. "You're good to the doubles, and you care about Fen. You're lots better than me."

Deller stared, then gave a short laugh. "Well, that's settled then. From now on we don't hate each other." He ran a finger through the film of erva that still dusted the tabletop. "We'll have to clean this place up. Oh." He glanced at her quickly. "They cut the water off a long time ago. The toilet doesn't work."

She shrugged. "I'm used to it."

Deller's face glimmered with a quick grin. "You're some girl. You can run, scratch and fart with the best of them."

Nellie giggled and glanced vaguely at the wall. "I like farting," she said. "Actually."

"Actually?" Deller grinned back. "And would the Goddess approve?"

Immediately Nellie's face darkened, and Deller ditched his grin.

"Okay," he said. "I've got to talk to the Skulls and get you some stuff. You going to be all right here while I'm gone?"

"Yeah." She shrugged. "Maybe I'll look for some food."

"I'll get you some," Deller said quickly. "Mom'll cook it. It'll get that depressed look off her face. She was really upset when she found out you took off." He paused in the doorway. "Where were you hiding before I came looking for you?"

Nellie blinked, then faltered, "Across the street."

"Maybe you'd better wait there," Deller said carefully. "I'll give you a wickawoo call when I've cleared everything with the Skulls. Just make sure you blow out the candle when you leave."

Leaning toward the candle, Nellie gave it a quick hard gust. When she turned back to the doorway it was empty, the soft thud of Deller's footsteps fading into the late afternoon heat.

THE HALF-CIRCLE OF BOYS sat in the flickering candlelight, their shadows leaping behind them as they watched Nellie engulf the stew Deller's mother had sent. After the stew, there was a bottle of dengleberry juice. Nellie closed her eyes as she drank, trying to ignore the glinting weasely eyes fixed in her direction. Over by the door, Deller was sweeping the last of the erva into a dustpan. A pile of blankets and a pillow sat in another corner, next to a shopping bag of clothes. Setting down the empty bottle, Nellie let out a satisfied burp. It was mid-evening, the heat was letting up and her belly was full. As long as the rats didn't get too bad tonight, things should be okay.

Stepping outside, Deller dumped the dustpan, then set it in a corner. "We've been talking," he said, approaching the table and settling into his usual three-legged chair. "We took a vote and decided to make you a member of the Skulls."

Beside him, Pullo shifted uncomfortably. Earlier that evening the Skulls had held a raucous meeting. Glued to her window across the street, Nellie had twice seen Pullo come stomping out of the alcove, then stand about muttering before heading back in. Now as Deller spoke, he stared morosely at the crack in the window cardboard and scratched the inside of his leg.

"Why?" she asked uneasily, her gaze flicking around the group. "Why do I have to become a Skull?"

"Because you're good enough," Deller shrugged. "And because then you've got to keep our secrets, just like we've got to keep yours."

Nellie scanned the group a second time. "What kind of secrets do you have?" she asked, not bothering to hide the scorn in her voice.

"Nothing like the levels," Snakebite said quickly, his yellow eyes skittering across her face. "But we've got some pretty good stuff. We'll tell you about it if you take us into another level like Deller said you would."

Nellie's mouth dropped and she gaped wordlessly. Ducking her gaze Deller said hastily, "We can talk about that later. For now, we'll get the initiation done and then I have to get home before Mom gets off work."

As if on cue the boys stood and formed a gangly circle, then looked at Nellie expectantly. Eyes slitted, arms crossed, she stared back at them. If they thought for one minute that she was going to do any kind of oogly hocus-pocus that would go against the Goddess, they were out of their Ivana-forsaken minds. Emphatically Deller beckoned to her, and she hesitated, hissing under her breath. Finally she rose to her feet, locked her arms firmly across the jiggle on her chest and shuffled into the circle between Snakebite and a boy with a nervous twitch in his cheek named Gurry.

"Okay," said Deller, looking relieved. "We can get started." Stooping, he opened a box at his feet and lifted out a long shadowy object. Darkness spilled out of the eye sockets and the long bony jaws caught the candlelight in a dull gleam. *Of course*, thought Nellie. *A skull. What is it—a dog?*

"Slow your thoughts and quiet your minds," said Deller, holding out the skull like an offering. "We are now in the presence of the

Lord of Death. All turn and face the Lord of Death. The Lord of Death is our king and prince. All our thoughts and secret deeds are known by Him. Beware, for if you breach the vow of secrecy, vengeance will be swift."

A muffled snicker ran around the group and Nellie felt a flicker of relief. So they weren't serious. This was just a game for a bunch of numbskulls. Beside her Snakebite giggled, and she sucked in her lower lip, fighting to keep a smirk off her mouth.

"Kiss the Lord of Death," said Deller, grinning slightly as he held the skull toward her. Nellie's smirk broadened, taking over her whole face. Pursing her lips dramatically, she leaned toward the shadowy shape. Suddenly her mind tilted savagely and she felt something shift inside the skull, then leap straight toward her face. With a cry she drew back, and the apparition vanished.

"What's the matter?" asked Deller, stepping toward her.

"Dunno," Nellie muttered, warding him off with her hands. "Something came at me out of that thing, like a breath of fire straight into my brain. Looked like the skull, kind of, but made of fuzzy white light."

A well of intense breathing rose around her, the boys' eyes fixed on the skull.

"That never happened before," Deller said dubiously.

"I never seen nothing," Snakebite shrilled.

"Didn't happen when I kissed it," Pullo mumbled.

"Well, it happened now," Nellie hissed, "and I'm not kissing it. That skull isn't dead enough yet. Whatever's still in it is looking for somewhere else to live. If I kissed it, I could get doubled."

"I kissed it and I ain't doubled," Snakebite screeched, dancing from foot to foot. "I ain't, I ain't."

"That's because you're not smart enough," Nellie snapped. "It's looking for someone who can carry its vibes. They're way too fast for you." The boys' eyes fixed on her, a circle of fear. "Don't worry," she added acidly. "It didn't double any of you, or it wouldn't still be in the skull. But you should get rid of it. Throw it in the river. It's evil."

"That's where I found it," said Gurry, his cheek twitching frantically. "In the riverbank by the Temple of the Blessed Heart."

Nellie's eyes widened. "Near the Goddess?"

"The Goddess, the Goddess," Snakebite sang mockingly, breaking into a frantic dance.

"Cut it out," Deller said sharply. "She's a Skull now, like the rest of us. She gets all the privileges."

"We didn't finish the ceremony," Pullo said sourly.

"We did enough," said Deller, setting the skull back in its box. "It's just a ceremony. Anyway, I have to get home, like I said."

"Yeah, me too," said Gurry. "I have to help dad fix the back porch." Shooting sideways glances at Nellie, the boys drifted one by one toward the entrance.

"You sure you'll be all right?" The last to go, Deller stood hesitantly in the alcove. "There's more food by the blankets for later, if you get hungry. You can close this door and push a chair against it. I'll put the padlock on from the outside. It doesn't actually lock, but it keeps the tramps from coming in."

"What if I have to go to the can?" asked Nellie.

"Oh yeah," said Deller, looking uncomfortable. "But if I leave the lock off—"

"I'll just hold it," Nellie said quickly.

Deller frowned, and then his face cleared. "Use that," he said, pointing to a small plastic bucket in the corner. "You can dump it in the morning. I'll come by early and take the padlock off. Then I have to go to work, but I can come back in the afternoon." He paused, outlined in the alcove's dusky gray-brown light. "I had to tell them, y'know," he said slowly. "It was the only way they'd let you into the Skulls. They won't tell anyone else though. They kissed the skull." His voice quickened. "We could take them with us into the levels to look for Fen. It'd go quicker if there were five of us."

"That's a lot of doubles," Nellie said dubiously. "They're already stupid enough in this level."

"They're not bad," Deller said, but she could hear the grin in his voice. "Not once you get to know them. Well, see you tomorrow."

"See you tomorrow," Nellie echoed as the door closed behind him and the room filled with the rasp of the padlock slipping into place.

Chapter 16

IMMEDIATELY NELLIE HEADED for the bag of clothing that sat next to the blankets. Tearing it open she pulled out a soft yellow T-shirt, a pair of blue shorts, some underwear, and a bra. Slowly she turned the bra package in her hands, examining it by candlelight. There on the front was the usual embarrassing picture, but this time the girl looked her own age. Eagerly Nellie opened the box and held up the bra. Swaying in the candlelight, the familiar outline dangled in slim white lines. No mountaintops here. This one was definitely the fried-egg size.

Sliding the straps onto her shoulders, she twisted her arms behind her back and tried to jam the hooks closed. But no matter how she bent and twisted the hooks wouldn't slide into place. Grunting and puffing, Nellie corkscrewed her body this way and that, warping herself into unimaginable positions. *Who was the moron that invented this thing?* she thought, angrily removing the bra and studying every inch of it. A person needed four hands *and* eyes in the back of her head just to get it on.

With a hiss she slid the straps back onto her shoulders and went at it again, huffing and jitterbugging about the room. When the hooks finally slid into place she was sweaty, red-faced and close to hyperventilating. Holding her arms straight out from her body, she took a cautious step forward. No jiggle. She took another careful step. Again, no jiggle. A giggle escaped her lips and she stomped toward the door, staring down at her chest. Even in the room's dim light, she was sure the blobs were squished flat and all the movement had gone out of them. With a triumphant hoot, she began to jump and flail her arms. No more jiggling! She could run, twist and sky-high fly, and with this haircut no one would guess she was a girl unless they got real close. Boys would respect her, and—

Taking another leap, Nellie twisted midair, spinning herself around so she landed facing the table, and saw her double. Seated in one of the three-legged chairs, the girl was wearing the gold-brocaded dress and snapping her pocketknife open and closed. With a yelp Nellie leapt backward, her knees bent and her claws out.

"Keep yelling like that," her double said casually, "and you'll bring the whole neighborhood in."

"There isn't any neighborhood," Nellie said scornfully, trying to ignore the kick-ass thud of her heart. Reaching for the yellow T-shirt she pulled it over her head, hiding as long as she could within its freshly laundered scent.

"There's more going on around here than you think," her double said drily. "This isn't the only warehouse that's been taken over, y'know."

"I've never seen anyone," Nellie flared. "And I've been around here at night."

"Most of the tramps meet one block over," said her double, pointing her knife at the south wall. "At a warehouse right on the river. *Most* of them."

"How d'you know that?" Pulling on the blue shorts, Nellie backed against the wall and slitted her eyes at her double.

"Been busy," her double said tersely. "Doing what you should be doing, but you're too busy hanging around with *him.*"

Unaccountably, Nellie flushed. "What's wrong with Deller?" she asked gruffly, kicking at the blankets heaped on the floor.

"Nothing's *wrong* with him," said her double. "You've got more important things to do."

"Like what?"

"Like finding out things."

"Finding out what things?" Nellie stared, dumbfounded.

Her double sighed. "Finding out what I'm finding out."

Nellie's eyes narrowed. "Oh yeah?" she said coolly. "Well, you can keep your secrets. Take them back to your own level. I've got enough of my own."

Her double snapped the pocketknife closed and leaned forward. "Don't you want to know how I got through the burnt skin where Fen got stolen?" she challenged.

Nellie's eyes narrowed until she could barely see. This double was just about the weaseliest person she'd met in *any* level. "Did you see Fen in one of those machines?" she asked, trying to keep the interest out of her voice. "When I went into that level, there was a hall with a whole bunch of doors, and then a room with machines that had kids in them. Fen was in one of them."

"I'm not telling you what I saw," her double smirked, leaning back again. "At least not yet. There are other things you need to learn first."

"Like what?" hissed Nellie, stung.

"Like the fact city administration has been put on high alert because the skins have been breached so many times lately," said her double.

"Skins again." Nellie rolled her eyes.

"Yeah, skins," snapped her double. "Lucky for you they don't know who's jumping the skins or how, but they're out looking, and if you keep blundering around the way you do, you're going to get caught."

"No one notices me," Nellie huffed. "I sneak in and out of other levels like I'm invisible."

"Oh really?" hissed her double, leaning forward. "Burning down a church is being invisible? Letting a doubled priest do a probe on you isn't being noticed?"

"That was in this level," shrugged Nellie. "And anyway, hardly anyone travels the levels. Sometimes I think I'm the only one."

"What about the men who took Fen?" asked her double. "Or the guy from the Interior Police that stepped out of the store wall? All City Hall has to do is ask the Interior to set some trackers on you."

Nellie blanched visibly. "You travel the levels too," she sniffed nervously. "What makes you think it's me they're after?"

"Because I know what I'm doing," her double said, flipping the pocketknife into the air and catching it. "I don't leave the skins quivering and disrupted like you do. The trail you leave vibrates like a rat scream."

"Oh come off it," said Nellie. "I can ride flux and shapeshift too, y'know. What makes you so much better than me?"

"You don't ride flux," snorted her double. "You find a tiny itty-bitty place flux *spit* on, and play games with it. My whole skin is always in flux. There's always something changing, something new coming through. But then I come from one of the quicker skins. Your skin's the slowest, so things are pretty fixed here."

"Slowest?" bellowed Nellie. Who exactly did this double think she was? "And what d'you mean, *fixed*?"

"Fixed in time and space," said her double coolly. "The next nine skins are fixed and then they break free, at least here in the Out-backs. In the Interior, they're fixed a lot further up. That's what they do there—lock you into a fixed pattern, so all your skins are the same. They're trying to do that in the Outbacks too, but it's still pretty free here."

Nellie's thoughts scrambled, trying to keep up. "Fixed for the next nine levels?" she said. "That makes ten. It was the tenth level where they took Fen. Were they trying to stop him from seeing the levels that aren't fixed?"

"Maybe," said her double.

"Well…" Nellie paused. If she sounded too interested, her double wouldn't answer this next question for sure. "What are the unfixed levels like?" she asked in her best bored tone.

"You'll find out," said her double in an equally bored tone, "when you're ready to vibrate that fast."

Nellie sucked in her breath and tried not to scream. "All this about vibrating faster," she said accusingly. "I can scan vibrations, y'know. So I can tell you're not vibrating any faster than me right now. And when I stepped into your level in the store, the vibrations there weren't that much quicker than they are here."

"I adjust," said her double dismissively. "I'm one of the floaters. There's a few of us. When I feel like it, I can move my whole skin around and adjust the vibes so they're in sync with wherever I end up."

About to make another scornful reply, Nellie faltered. "You helped me," she said slowly, remembering. "At the Jinnet. You broke Ayne's probe when I couldn't."

Her double nodded tersely.

"All my other doubles are always doing the same as me," Nellie continued thoughtfully. "They dress like me and live in the same place. I guess that means they're fixed, right?"

Her double nodded again.

"But you carry a knife," Nellie went on. "You travel the levels and you think different. And there was flux in the store where I first saw you."

"That's my home skin," said her double. "When I float it into a new area, I adjust it to the closest skin so I don't stick out. I've been coming down into the slower skins, investigating."

"Investigating what?" asked Nellie.

Her double shrugged. "Things that interest me. Like I said, there's a lot of flux around here. It's much tighter in the Interior. Those skins are a real bitch to get through."

"I didn't travel the levels when I lived in the Interior," Nellie said hesitantly. "I only started about a year ago. But I know it's easier to get from one level to the next if there's flux."

Again her double nodded. "At least you know that much, but there are a lot of things in the skins that are way past anything you could imagine. They're dangerous. It's not all fun and games. You've got a lot to learn if we're going to pull through this."

"Pull through what?" Nellie couldn't help the scornful note in her voice. Maybe her double knew *some* things she didn't, but that didn't make her the Goddess's announcing angel.

Her double leaned forward, her face tense with exasperation. "They're *after* you, idiot. *Here*, in *this* skin, and the other skins are starting to get interested too. You let that doubled priest probe you, and Ayne. They read your vibes. What d'you think they picked up?" She let out a long suffering hiss. "If they get you, they get the rest of your possibilities too. Not all of us are as stupid as you, but we all get stuck paying for your choices."

"I thought I copy what you do," Nellie snapped.

"It's all relative," her double snapped back. "The possibilities don't all have to do exactly what you do, but they're stuck dealing with the consequences. Except for the ones in flux, of course. Possibilities like me can come and go as we wish, and believe me I'm not here because I'm desperate for your company. I'm just tired of seeing the possibilities suffer because of what you're doing to the skins, and I'm not going to be caught and hauled back to the Interior over your mistakes. I'm here to smarten you up so we can all live easier."

"Oh." Stunned, Nellie wanted to open the closest gate and step through to a level where she didn't have to face the sense she was hearing. So this was why her doubles always froze when they saw her—they were afraid of whatever dumb stupid thing she was about to do next. "Wait a minute," she said, a new thought entering her mind. "If the fixed doubles have to do what I do, how come I can travel the levels and they can't? They don't even know there are levels."

"Dunno," said her double, watching her closely. "That's the big mystery. Something's happening in this skin that's different than the next nine. You're vibrating out of sync with the pattern. For some reason you're not as fixed as the others."

Nellie stared at her blankly. "Well, that's good, isn't it?"

"Yeah, it's good," hissed her double, pointing the knife at her, "*if you smarten up and quit ripping through the skins like a truck. And* if you'll start listening, and let me teach you a few things about living properly in flux."

"Deller knows," Nellie said suddenly, feeling the need to confess. "And the Skulls. I haven't taken them to another level yet, but Deller told them so they'd let me join and stay in their headquarters."

Her double let loose a hiss of swear words, then sat sucking her lower lip until it disappeared into her mouth. "Do they know about me?" she asked finally.

Nellie shook her head. "Last thing I wanted was for him to find out about you. He wants me to take the Skulls into the levels so we can all start looking for Fen."

Her double's face twisted into an expression of delicate pain. "That would be just about the absolutest stupidest idea in all the skins put together," she said darkly. "The only way I'm teaching you anything is if you promise never to show any of it to the Skulls."

"What about Deller?" Nellie asked quickly.

A thinking expression crossed her double's face. "Maybe Deller," she said cautiously. "He's smarter than the others. Smarter than you, at any rate. C'mere."

Fighting the urge to bristle, Nellie joined her double so they stood side by side in the deepening dusk, facing the cardboard-covered window. "First things first," said her double grimly. A faint line of light cast by the split in the cardboard ran down the center of her face. "You've got to learn to listen to the skins."

"Tune in," Nellie said immediately. She already knew this part, it was easy. She just had to let her mind tilt to the right and the molecular field would come into focus like it was doing now, leaping in its dance of energy and color. Even her double was transformed, radiating luminescent wings of orange and sky blue.

"No," her double said tersely. "*Listen*, not see. If you can't listen to *me*, how are you going to hear the skins?"

Chastened, Nellie stood staring at the molecular field. *Listen*? What was there to listen to? Sure there were lots of humming and crackling noises, but that was just the boring old background noise molecules always made. It was the same in every level. Why not find a gate and open ...

"Are you listening?" demanded her double.

Heaving an almighty sigh, Nellie focused on the tiny humming sounds. It was a little like listening to a field of evening crickets, the sound pulsing against her ears in liquid waves, except that sometimes the sound came high and sometimes it came low, and every now and then it seemed to step sideways into a different range altogether.

"What d'you hear?" asked her double.

"Noise," Nellie said shortly.

Her double sighed. "And?"

Nellie shrugged. "Different molecules make different sounds. It depends on their color. And the gates don't make any sound at all."

"Gates?" asked her double.

"Where you go through," said Nellie, pointing to one that hovered midair, a few steps away. "They're like dead space—no vibrations, no color, no noise."

"That's because they are dead space," snapped her double. "They used to be alive, but then some idiot pushed her way through and killed that part of the skin's soul."

Stunned, Nellie protested, "Lots of travelers use gates. How else are you supposed to get to other levels?"

"Ssssst," hissed her double. "You might get into another skin, but you're not *part* of that skin once you enter its turf. Any skin will be dead set against you if you come into it through a wound."

"A wound?" Suddenly Nellie's mind was reeling as she relived the pain she'd felt coming through the gate in the church wall. So it *was* the molecular field that had let out that scream of agony. But why? It wasn't human, it couldn't have thoughts and feelings like people did.

"Yeah, a wound," said her double. "All those *gates* as you call
them didn't used to exist. They were torn open by someone forcing
her way from one skin to the next. The wound suffered for a while,
then closed over and that part of the skin died. Unfortunately the
scar still showed, and you know bullies and idiots—they always
look for the easiest way through anything."

"I'm not a bully," Nellie said defensively. "I didn't know, that's
all."

"Bullies and *idiots*," said her double distinctly. "Idiots think
tuning into the skins is like watching TV. The skins are *alive*, just
like you and me. Now start listening to your body the way you were
listening to the skin."

Nellie scowled. This was getting stupider and stupider. Her
double had seen her travel and knew she could shapeshift, so why
did she insist on treating her like a know-nothing? Sullenly she
turned her attention to the molecular field and focused on her own
body. It was easy enough, she used to do this regularly when she
first discovered the molecular field—tune in and watch the various
energies at play inside her body—but she'd never paid attention
to the sounds they emitted. Now as she listened, she heard the
same chorus of humming crackling noises that the surrounding
molecular field was making.

"It's the same," she said diffidently.

"Not quite," said her double, but she sounded pleased. "Listen
deeper."

Deeper? thought Nellie. How did you listen deeper? Focusing
again on her body's molecular field, she let her mind walk downward into sound as if descending a ladder. As she did sound slowed,
and there was a brief sensation of pressure. Then this cleared and
the sound changed, opening into something entirely different—a
deep kind of calling, many voices swirling through each other in a
vast vibrating ocean of sound.

"Like the stars," Nellie gasped. "It's like the dream of singing
stars I get when flux is coming."

"It is coming," said her double. "Put out your hand."

Nellie stretched out her hand and saw that it was no longer there. Glancing at her body, she saw that it had also vanished. Somehow, without any conscious decision on her part, her entire molecular structure had dissolved and she'd entered a state of pure sound—the voices of her flesh.

"Can you hear yourself?" asked her double.

"Yes," Nellie whispered.

"Now," said her double, "listen beyond yourself. Listen to the skin."

Lifting out of the sound of herself, Nellie opened to the song of the molecular field. On all sides she saw energy leaping and dancing as usual, and yet she seemed to have stepped into a new level of reality where molecules had dissolved their basic structures and colors interwove in a kinetic tapestry. From everywhere came a huge crying out of voices, their eerie beauty swirling around Nellie like a kaleidoscope that had broken its pattern, the vibrations of the surrounding molecular field calling toward the vibrations of Nellie's body until she lost all sense of herself and became part of a vast shimmering river of sound.

Gradually the sensation faded and she became aware of herself again, standing beside her double in the dimly-lit room that was the Skulls' headquarters. Ahead of her sagged the split cardboard that had been taped over the window, to her left leaned a three-legged chair, and behind her she could see the edge of the table. Taking a slow breath, she followed the rush of air through the tunnels of her nose, deep into the cave of her lungs. Everything was as it had been, and yet it was utterly changed. For she now recognized the life that sang in that three-legged chair, and she'd been one with the vibrations that pulsed through the table. For one brief soul-shimmering moment, everything in the room had been part of her, and she a part of it.

Nellie's double sighed, then said quietly, "That was the beginning of listening. Remember—listening will always take you further than

seeing. The eyes tell lies, but the ears are harder to fool. Practice listening to this skin, hearing what it's got to tell you. And no matter
what happens, don't go barreling in and out of the other skins until
I come back and teach you how to sing your way into them."

"Come back?" Alarmed, Nellie turned toward her double. "But
you can't go, you've got to help us find Fen. And what about Ayne
and those people from City Hall you said were after me? If I can't
travel—"

"I've got things to do," her double said gruffly. "You're not the
only possibility, y'know. Just do what I told you—practice listening
to the skin and hearing what it's got to tell you."

Then, as Nellie stared, her double began to disappear. "Wait a
minute," Nellie yelped, lunging toward the ghostly shimmer. "You
can't just—"

But her groping hands slid vainly through her double's fading
outline, and when she tuned into the molecular field she found no
gate where her double had vanished. With a disconsolate grunt,
Nellie settled into her nest of blankets. How could her double be
so heartless, so extremely weaExpiresy, and at the same time know how
to tune into such exquisite, soul-singing beauty? Just the memory
of that eerie ocean of voices made Nellie's breath pause in wonder.
Could she do it again? Well, why not try? Her double had said she
was supposed to practice.

Tuning into the molecular field, she descended into its crackling
hum and felt herself open into a liquid wave of sound. Yes, the
beauty was still here, she could do this on her own. All she had to
do was concentrate and she could sense the vibrations coming from
the closest three-legged chair. That sound over there had to be the
table, and the vibrating cradle of song that surrounded her could
only belong to the blankets in which she was wrapped. Running
along her back was the thick murmur of the warehouse wall, and
beyond it the deepening melody of night settling into the street.
Everywhere Nellie sent her mind, she could hear the faint white
cry of summer heat sinking into the soothing tones of darkness.

Breathing softly, she lay listening to the molecular field croon itself to sleep, touching this sound, then that one with her mind, and running her thoughts along the torn dead length of each gate she encountered.

"I'm sorry," she whispered. "I didn't know how you were made. I thought you were just a thing, like a nail or a stone, but even they can sing and you can't. I know I used a lot of gates, but I swear I only *made* the one at the Sanctuary of the Blessed Goddess. Funny, it only hurt the second time I used it, when I was coming back through. Maybe it went into shock when I tore it open the first time, like when you cut your finger and it doesn't hurt right away. What's it like to be dead? Can you see—no hear—the world of the dead? Can you hear my mother? Is she just dead space now, without feelings, or can she still love the most important person in her life? Does she remember me ... ?"

But the gates gave her no answer and at length, worn out by questions, Nellie fell asleep, the song of the evening air crooning gently against her skin.

Chapter 17

S HE WOKE TO THE SCRAPE of the padlock being slipped from the door. Shock ricocheted through her and she bolted upright, clutching the blankets and staring around herself at the shadowy room. *Where am I? What is this place? What am I doing?*

"Nellie?" hissed a voice from the doorway. "You awake?"

Deller. Pulling the blankets over her head, Nellie sank to the floor in an acid wave of relief. "Yeah, I'm here," she mumbled, jamming her hands into her underarms to contain their shaking.

"Where?" demanded Deller. Cautious footsteps shuffled into the room and she lowered the blankets to see him standing in the doorway, peering about himself. As he caught sight of her he went stock still, then wrapped his arms tightly around himself. "They got Mom," he mumbled, sinking to the floor opposite and hugging his knees with his arms. "They got Mom, and they bombed the Jinnet."

Rigid in her nest of blankets, Nellie stared at his hunched figure. "Your mom?" she stammered. "The Jinnet? What—?"

"I went out last night," Deller said helplessly, still hugging himself. Even in the thick pre-dawn gray, she could see he was shivering.

"To watch the church, see if they had another meeting. There was a Jinnet meeting at the same time. I was supposed to be there." Dazed, he covered his face with his hands. A whimper came out of him, then another. "The resistance is over," he said. "They killed Dad five years ago—left him in a field with the Mark of Silence on him. Now Fen's probably dead, and Mom's gone too."

Nellie's skin leapt with panic. Jumping to her feet she grabbed one of the blankets, darted across the room, and wrapped it awkwardly around Deller. In the soft bewildered heartbeats that followed she found herself on her knees beside him, her hands fluttering about his head, gently brushing his hair from his face.

"Your mom?" she whispered. "They got your mom?"

Shoulders caved, Deller stared at the floor. "I watched the church for a while, but nobody came. So I went to the restaurant." He faltered, and she heard his swallow lock halfway down his throat. "It's gone, just a pile of rocks. There was a crowd, people wailing, cops and fire engines. Someone set off a bomb in the meeting room. Everyone's dead." A deep shudder ran through him. "So I went home, but when I got there, they were taking her away in a car."

"Who was taking her?" Nellie asked hoarsely.

Deller's eyes flicked toward her, slurred with fear. "Ayne. And the extra man who came to the church the night we set it on fire."

"The ninth man?" Nellie asked. "The Interior agent?"

Deller nodded and another shudder ran through him. "There was blood on her face," he said. "I didn't know what to do. I took off after them on my bike, but I lost them after a couple of blocks. I don't know where they took her. And it's all my fault. It's because I took you to the Jinnet. They probably think she knows where I hid you."

Heart thudding, Nellie rocked back on her heels. "No, it's my fault," she whispered. "They took her because they were looking for me. And I swear on the Goddess's name, Deller—I'm not doing anything else until we save your mom and Fen."

Deller's gaze locked with hers, so tight she felt the whole weight of him hanging on with his eyes. In that long stretched moment, Nellie realized he didn't have in him what she had in herself. He'd lost too many people, and one more would bring the twisting weasely passageways of his mind caving inward, leaving him with nothing but wrecked rubble.

"Don't worry," she muttered, giving his shoulder a careful pat. "I'll figure something out. Just don't go working yourself into conniptions."

A tremor crossed his face and he nodded. Standing, she crossed the room and perched on the edge of the table. "If we went back to your place and you showed me where the car was parked, maybe I could read the vibrations," she said thoughtfully. "Pick up something. I don't know what, but—"

"They'll have a watch posted," Deller said dully.

Nellie scowled and scratched her neck intensely. "Wait a minute," she said. "You were there. I bet I could read it through you." Slipping off the table, she crossed the room and stood before him. Suddenly the blood was thudding through her body, and pinpricks of sweat scattering across her skin. What had she just gone and promised? She didn't know if this would work and hope was creeping across Deller's face like the first bit of sun coming into a day. Well, nothing to do about it now but try.

"What are you doing?" he murmured as she fluttered a hand to each side of his head.

"Just think about what you saw with your mom," she said gruffly. "All of it, every second."

"Well," he said. "When I got there they were shoving her into a car, and—"

"Shh," said Nellie. "Words'll mix me up. Just think about it, and I'll see it in my mind."

It was a fierce wild guess, something like the desperation that came to her on a crowded street when someone was on her tail, telling her the turn to the left was a better chance at escape than the one to the right. Still, it seemed to be working. Images were beginning to form in her mind, hazy figures, but she recognized them immediately—Deller's mother, blindfolded, with her hands tied behind her back, being shoved into the back seat of a car. Then Ayne getting in beside her as the ninth man from the church slipped into the front seat. Fighting the giant ache of her heart, Nellie forced her gaze from the blood on Deller's mother's face to the man behind the wheel, concentrating until she could see the shape of his right ear, the curve of his nose and his upper lip.

C'mon, scaredy cat, she thought grimly. *It's just vibrations. You're a bunch of vibes, he's a bunch of vibes.*

Abruptly all sense of her surroundings, even her own body, left her, and she was slipping through the brief thickness of the man's skull into the warm ooze of his brain. Vibrations pulsed everywhere, she was caught in a sudden maze of light. Holding herself steady, not wanting to get lost in the mad wild pulse, she scanned the closest vibrations and tried to form a cohesive picture from the images she was picking up. Then without warning her body was back, the heat of Deller's scalp again pulsing between her fingers.

"The Temple of the Blessed Heart," she gasped, letting her hands fall from his head. "The big church downtown. I saw a picture of it in the agent's mind. That's where they took her."

"The Blessed Heart?" asked Deller, staring at her. "That's next to City Hall. And police headquarters."

"So?" asked Nellie.

"So they're both major connections to the Interior," he said, white-faced. "City police are your last cup of tea. That's what they say at the Jinnet."

"D'you think the Temple is connected to City Hall and the police?" demanded Nellie.

"It's got to be," Deller said grimly. "They're taking Mom there, and the cops are next door. I'm sure the Goddess doesn't know about it, though," he added quickly, slanting her a glance. "Just the priests."

Nellie nodded, her stomach an ooze of fear. Why would the God-dess permit such evil in Her Temple? Why didn't She strike all the priests dead? "Well," she said, getting to her feet. "The cops don't know what I look like, and neither do the priests. If I borrowed your clothes, I'd look like a boy and—"

"Borrowed my clothes?" demanded Deller, thunderstruck.

"You can't go," said Nellie, looking down at him. "You're tired, you've been up all night. And it's your mom. You'll be too crazy worrying about her to keep your head straight."

Deller stared at her, his eyes red-rimmed and grim. "I'm coming," he said.

Nellie's shoulders sagged with relief. "Okay," she mumbled. "Actually my head's a little crazy right now. Maybe you can help me keep it straight."

In the dim morning light, she saw the briefest of smiles touch Deller's mouth. "C'mon then," he said softly, and got to his feet. Slowly he held out his hand and stood waiting as if expecting something. Uncomprehending, Nellie stared at it until he reached further and slid his hand around hers. Warmth shot up Nellie's arm like shock.

"Oh," she whispered, and almost sat down on the floor.

They headed out the door.

ABOVE THE HORIZON the twin moons were two smudged thumb-prints, fading into the dawn. Deller biked steadily through the early morning streets, passing delivery trucks and vendors setting up their carts. Here and there the odd man could be seen sleeping off a holiday dose of erva, and halfway down an alley Nellie caught sight of a newspaper boy standing blissfully in one of the naturally occurring mindjoys that were scattered everywhere at this time of year. Then, coming around a corner, a glimmering undulation between two garbage pails caught her eye. Flux! A fierce longing flared through her, but she gripped the bike seat firmly and fastened her gaze to the pair of brass hands that rose in the distance above the Temple of the Blessed Heart. Just seeing those dawn-lit hands quickened her breath. There was the Goddess, holding the entire city in Her hands, praying for them all. Surely this kerfuffle with Deller's mother was some kind of bizarre mistake that could be sorted out with a little faith.

As they neared the downtown district, they began to encounter city maintenance crews setting up decorations for the festivities that were to take place that evening. With a pang Nellie realized it was the seventh of Lulunar and she'd missed the pageantry and games mounted the previous evening to celebrate the descent of the Goddess's twin sons into the underworld. Downtown streets would have been packed with audiences watching theater troupes act out the story of the twins' separate searches through the netherworld, while clowns with sad faces mimicked the brothers' desolate return to the land of the living without the longed-for reunion. Tonight there would be a festival to celebrate their individual homecomings with fireworks, free mindjoy booths and mirror masks for one and all.

Several blocks from the church, Deller dismounted from the bike and walked it into an alley, looking for a place to hide it. As she waited for him, Nellie leaned casually against a store wall and watched a nearby vendor set up a cart of baked goods. Various sweet and spicy scents invaded her nose and her stomach gave a long grumbling burp. She'd had nothing to eat since the previous night, and her head was giving off the silvery ache that came with missing breakfast. Already wearing his mirror mask, the whistling vendor bent down to unpack a box of supplies. Immediately Nellie's hand shot out, snatching two fruit pies from his cart. Then she slipped into the alley and handed one to Deller, who'd just stashed the bike behind a large garbage bin.

"I remembered something," he mumbled, demolishing it in several bites. "That shock box Millen used on you? It was Hadden who brought them into the Jinnet—the guy you say is Interior Police. He must have gotten them from the Interior."

"Did he get them to use erva too?" asked Nellie.

"Erva's always been around," shrugged Deller. "But the Double Goodbye—that was his idea."

They turned down another street and the Temple of the Blessed Heart came into view, facing them from several blocks away. A myriad of gables and spires, its gray stone outline dominated the skyline, dwarfing City Hall and police headquarters, which stood to either side. Nellie's eyes darted between the three buildings, so closely juxtaposed. She'd never before considered a connection between them. Surely Deller was dreaming. The Goddess wouldn't allow it, She *wouldn't*.

Several police cars drove past, and Deller turned his head, obscuring his face. "Uh, why don't we use the alley?" he said, turning down a lane that led into the parking lot behind City Hall. Their feet scuffed loudly in the early morning quiet. "Ever been in this church?" he asked as they passed City Hall and began to cross the parking lot. Nellie shook her head. "Me neither," he said. "Gurry's brother was one of its altar boys for a couple of years. He told Gurry he'd found a secret door, but he wouldn't say where. And over there," he added, pointing to the river that flowed behind the church. "That's where Gurry found the skull one day while he was waiting for his brother after a service."

Nellie shrugged, disinterested in skulls and altar boys. "Where can we get in this early?" she asked, staring up at the church.

"Gurry used to talk about a door at the back that didn't close properly," said Deller. "His brother and some friends used it to get in one night. They wanted to check out the secret door, but a priest caught them and they had to take off."

"Which door was it?" Quickly Nellie scanned the back wall of the church. She could see at least five entrances.

"Dunno." In the growing light Deller looked pale, but the grim set of his mouth remained unchanged. They approached the church, quieting the scuff of their feet until they were almost on tiptoe. From behind came the sound of a car pulling into the parking lot. Abruptly Nellie turned and glanced around. No more than ten vehicles were scattered about the vast parking area shared by City Hall and the church.

"Seen any of these cars before?" she asked. Deller turned to look and his eyes widened.

"That one," he said softly, pointing to a blue car that matched the one she'd seen in his memory.

"So, they *are* here," Nellie whispered, her fear deepening within her. It looked as if she was going to need a lot more than faith to carry this off. If only, she thought, her eyes flicking toward the twin moons, her double in the gold-brocaded dress would step out of thin air right about now and give her some advice on what to do. But doubles never seemed to be around when you actually needed them. *Listen*, the thought came to Nellie, and she shrugged. Well, it was something. Turning to the church, she let her mind tilt to the right and tuned into the molecular field. Instantly she was hit with such a roar of energy that she staggered backward, an arm raised to her face.

"What's the matter?" Deller demanded.

"It's the church." Nellie lowered her arm to find herself tuned back into solid reality, Deller standing beside her, staring at her in confusion. "It sounds like all the demons in hell screaming at me," she stammered. "I was trying to listen to it, and that's the sound it makes. Like it's made up of demon screams."

They glanced simultaneously at the church. "Why would it sound like that?" Deller asked uneasily.

"Dunno," said Nellie, her face twisting. "But I can't… hear the Goddess anywhere. I don't think She's in there, Deller. Why wouldn't She be in Her own holy house?"

Deller's shoulders sagged. "So," he said carefully, not meeting her eyes. "Does that mean you want to go back?"

Nellie's eyes skittered across his face. "No," she said quickly. "I'll just concentrate on hearing the Goddess. She's got to be in there somewhere."

Tentatively, she tuned back into the molecular field and was again hit by a barrage of screams, hisses and long drawn-out sobs. Within seconds her mind began to buckle and an ugly wave of panic reared through her. Where was the Goddess, Her pure and holy spirit? Why wasn't She here to welcome Her chosen ones, two children who'd come to rescue a *mother*? Blinking furiously, Nellie fought to get a grip. Scaredycatness and loneliness weren't going to help her here. The Goddess was in there somewhere and so was Deller's mother, and—

Her mouth dropped in slow astonishment. Of course! The Goddess was with Deller's mother, protecting her from harm. That was why She hadn't had time to banish the evil from the Temple walls—She was busy with more important things. With renewed determination, Nellie sent herself into the soundscape before her. The Goddess had one job, and she had another. If she could just figure out some way to listen to *bits* of the wall instead of the whole building, she might be able to pick up something helpful. Flicking her mind lightly along the wall, she flinched from one vibration to the next, processing the images that came to her. The actual layout of the place seemed pretty ordinary. She'd located several rooms, a maintenance closet and a hallway. And there, two doors down along the outer wall, she could see it quite clearly in the molecular field—an open space in the doorjamb where the lock hadn't quite caught.

"Over there," she said, pointing to it. "It's that door right there."

Quietly Deller ran toward it, tried the knob, and gave her a nod. By the time she reached the door he was inside, holding it ajar. She slipped in after him, and he edged the door shut. Together they turned to face the gloom behind them.

No one else seemed to be around. The hall that stretched ahead of them was obviously empty and lit only by an EXIT sign at the far end. Silence pressed down, so intense it was like someone breathing. Without speaking, Deller pointed down the hall and raised an eyebrow. Nellie shook her head. They were standing just shy of a three-way fork, the hall splitting to the left and right as well as running straight into the heart of the building. If Ayne had Deller's mother imprisoned and was subjecting her to the same kind of probe Nellie had experienced, there was no time to waste guessing and backtracking.

With a deep thinking breath, she knelt and pressed her hands to the floor, then opened her mind to the molecular field. The barrage of screams and groans was immediate, and everywhere she looked energy leapt in a manic dance as if the building was on fire. *Pain*, Nellie thought suddenly. The Temple of the Blessed Heart was in utter agony.

"Can you feel it?" she hissed at Deller.

"Feel what?" he hissed back.

Lucky you, she thought, and focused on the vibrations entering her palms. Faint images surfaced into her mind, obscured by the uproar in the molecular field—nothing she could see clearly, but the fear coming from them felt recent. With a sinking feeling Nellie realized that if Deller's mother had been brought here, she wasn't the only one. The Temple of the Blessed Heart was probably used regularly for interrogations. In that case this trail may or may not have been left by Deller's mother, but the likelihood was that anyone brought in here who was feeling this much fear would be taken to the same destination.

"C'mon," she hissed at Deller and veered down the left corridor, stooping every now and then to press her hands to the floor. The trail seemed to grow clearer as she followed it, heading down a flight of stairs into an even more shadowy hall, then turning to the right. Nothing else changed. The walls kept up their screaming, the floor continued its throb of malevolence. Abruptly the trail she was following faded as she picked up a stronger one, its images vivid and undeniable—a blindfolded woman with her hands tied behind her back, being shoved through a nearby doorway by a woman with bright orange hair.

"There," Nellie said, pointing to it. "She's in there."

Deller lunged toward the door, and she had to jump him and drag him back. "Don't be an idiot," she hissed into his ear. "Let me scan it first."

For a moment he stared at her, his eyes blank with terror. Then the Deller she knew returned to his face and he nodded, slumping against the wall. Swallowing hard, Nellie turned and peered through a small window set high in the door. A gasp escaped her, and immediately Deller pressed in behind her, leaning over her shoulder.

"Can you see her?" he hissed.

Nellie shook her head. The room before her was well lit and empty of human presence. Cupboards and medical equipment lined the walls and there, positioned along the far wall, were the three birdlike machines she'd seen near the quarry.

"No one's in there," she mouthed at Deller. "But I can feel her."

Turning the doorknob, she edged the door open. Nothing stirred. Then in the silence, she heard a muffled groan. Glancing at Deller, Nellie saw his face pale. "Wait here," she whispered, but he shook his head. Together they slipped into the room and eased the door closed behind them.

Another moan sounded. Quickly Nellie turned toward it and saw a second door in the wall to her left, partially obscured by a cabinet. Crossing the room she gripped the knob, about to turn it, when another sound sent her whirling back around. Across the room someone was coming out of what appeared to be a supplies closet—a man with blond hair, narrow blue eyes and a wide thin mouth. *Hadden.* At the sight of him Nellie's brain tilted savagely, filling with the eerie singing of stars, and then she saw a second head composed of brilliant light that overlapped Hadden's—slightly bigger, with a long jutting jaw. *Another doubling*, she realized with a surge of panic. Was everyone who hung out in the Goddess's house in cahoots with the devil?

Hadden's eyes widened as he saw them, and then a grin crossed his face. "Gotcha," he said, turned to a button on the wall and pressed it. Instantly an alarm signal went off, the high-pitched beeping tearing into Nellie's brain.

Without hesitating, she yanked open the door before her. As she tore into the next room, two figures came into view—a woman with bright orange hair who was leaning over a second woman with a bloody face, strapped to a chair. Neither looked up. Ayne was hissing, her concentration broken by the alarm, but her focus remained on Deller's mother who sat slumped with her eyes closed. Frantically Nellie glanced about the room. Small and almost empty, there was only a bare bulb overhead, the chair at the center of the room and some ominous-looking equipment on a nearby table. Obviously an interrogation room, Nellie realized, and its only exit was the one through which they'd just come. A hot spurt of urine ran down her legs as she saw that door open and Hadden rush in. Gibbering softly, she backed away from his grin. There was nothing she could do here. He could travel the levels too, and the last thing she needed was to face him *and* his double. They both knew this place better than she did.

Unless ... Turning to Deller, Nellie saw him struggling with Ayne. Quickly she raced over to him and grabbed his arm. Then she placed her other hand on his mother's shoulder. Mustering every raw nerve in her body, she focused and took them out of sync with the surrounding vibratory rate. Immediately the room disappeared, and they found themselves standing in a murky blur that reverberated with shrieks, howls and groans.

"What is this?" yelped Deller, backing into her.

"I told you," Nellie yelled into his ear. "It's what the church sounds like—all the demons in hell screaming."

"You've got that right." Beads of sweat dotted Deller's forehead. "It's making me dizzy. I—" Glancing down, he saw his mother huddled on the floor. "Mom," he whispered. Reaching for her arm, he helped her to her feet.

"Deller?" she murmured, swaying slightly.

"I'm here, Mom," he said, then shot Nellie a glance. "What happened to the chair?" he hissed. "Where are we?"

"Out of sync," she hissed back. "Between levels. The chair's back in our home level."

Understanding crossed his face and he nodded. Turning from him, Nellie scanned the surrounding blur, watching for any sign of Hadden. He'd probably jumped to the next level looking for them, and with any luck would continue onward for several levels, keeping up the search. She would give it a few minutes, then—

But no. Halfway across the room she could see a vague outline solidifying into narrow blue eyes and a thin-lipped sneer. "Gotcha," Hadden said again, starting toward them.

Putting out her hand, Nellie brought Deller and his mother back into sync with the molecular field. There was no helping it now, she had only one option left, regardless of what her double in the gold-brocaded dress had said. As the room came back into focus, she saw it was empty except for Ayne who was standing beside the interrogation chair, staring grimly at the spot Hadden had disappeared. Glancing toward Deller, Nellie saw his eyes fix on Ayne, then flick toward her. Horror flashed across his face as he realized what she was about to do, and then he nodded once. It was all Nellie needed and she darted toward Ayne, skidding to a halt in front of her.

For one endless, screaming-crazy moment she stood inches from the woman's thunderous face and bright orange perm. Then Nellie tuned into the molecular field and threw the full force of her terror at the gate hovering midair before her. To her profound relief it opened without the slightest sensation of pain. Tuning back into solid reality, she saw Ayne's body divided down the middle, the two parts standing several feet apart.

There was no blood or sign of tearing, no internal organs hanging loose. The division had taken place as cleanly as if the woman had been made of plastic. *Ever seen what happens to a body when its soul dies?* Nellie remembered. Her eyes skittered across the look of fear frozen into both halves of Ayne's face. Then she turned and grabbed Deller and his mother by the arm.

"C'mon," she hissed, and they stumbled together through the gate framed by Ayne's body into the unknown.

Chapter 18

FOR A MOMENT NELLIE felt everything about her—the room, Ayne's divided body, even her own body—dissolve into a panorama of quick, high-singing vibrations. Then the solid world returned, but in a completely altered form. Instead of standing between the divided halves of Ayne's body, Nellie found herself stepping out of a set of metal brackets that rose approximately a foot above her head. In front of her lay a small room that was obviously an office. Filing cabinets and bookcases lined the walls, and a desk, with a computer stood to her left. Seated at the desk, with his back to her and completely engrossed in the screen before him, was a man wearing headphones. Turning to warn Deller and his mother, Nellie saw Deller's eyes already riveted to the man's back. Beside him stood his mother, eyes closed and swaying slightly. Nellie's gaze lingered briefly on a cut beneath the woman's left eye. It was still bleeding and looked deep, but for now it was going to have to wait. Reluctantly she turned her attention back to the room.

The brackets through which they'd emerged were positioned several feet from the nearest wall. A red light was blinking on the right bracket, probably signaling their arrival. Clearly the brackets acted as a kind of a receiving gate, but why, thought Nellie, would they connect to a gate in a human being? She'd expected to have to deal with whatever it was that had stolen Ayne's soul, not a mechanical device. And where was her double, and Deller's and his mother's? The vibrations through which they'd traveled en route to this level hadn't been much quicker than their home level's. This meant they couldn't have gone more than one or two levels, and everything should be more or less exactly the same as the place they'd just left—unless they'd hit a major pocket of flux, or somehow jumped to one of the unfixed levels her double in the gold-brocaded dress had mentioned. But those started at the eleventh level, which would mean a much quicker vibratory rate.

Without warning, Deller's mother gave a quiet moan and slumped against her son. As Deller steadied her, Nellie's eyes darted toward the man at the computer, but the music blaring from his headphones had blocked the small sound. Still, they had to get moving. Catching Deller's eyes, Nellie pointed to an open doorway across the room, then tiptoed toward it. A quick glance through it revealed a reception area with a large desk, the usual office equipment and a few chairs. Beyond the lobby she could see the beginning of a hallway, and to her right another door. The entire scene ached with emptiness. The man at the computer seemed to be the only person around.

Of course, thought Nellie. It was the seventh of Lulunar, the day the Festival of the Return was celebrated. Businesses and offices would be closed, and everyone would be outdoors at the various carnivals. The guy at the computer was either a workaholic or an utter pagan. Gesturing to Deller, Nellie slipped into the reception area, then leaned against a wall and opened her mind to the molecular field. Hadden would be searching for them, might even at this moment be coming through the set of brackets in the office behind her, but she had to get a feel for this place, figure out its vibratory rate and how many levels they'd gone. But as solid reality dissolved into glowing silhouettes of energy, she felt only more confusion. No onslaught of wails and screams hit her, and as far as she could tell the surrounding vibratory rate matched her home level's exactly.

That meant this *was* her home level, but from the lack of wails and screams in the molecular field it was obvious they were no longer in the Temple of the Blessed Heart. How was that possible? Almost against her will, Nellie glanced toward a long window that ran the length of the opposite wall, and her jaw dropped. She was obviously on the upper floor of a very tall building, for the view before her was tremendous. More importantly, it wasn't a tremendous view of Dorniver's downtown area, or any of its meandering suburbs. Instead she saw, stretching toward the horizon, a city whose streets and buildings were far too sophisticated, utilitarian and *orderly* to belong to any Outbacks city. And yet, Nellie thought, scanning the main river, parks and downtown area, the landscape looked familiar. To her right she could see the planetarium and Museum of Natural History her mother used to take her to, as well as a rec center at which she'd taken swimming lessons. With deft familiarity, her eyes followed the gridwork streets past the Goddess's Redemption Cathedral toward a suburb where she'd lived until she was eight. This was Marnan, one of the Interior's largest cities and the last place she remembered being happy, before she and her mother had started moving so much, *running* from city to city.

They were in the Interior. Numb with shock, Nellie turned to face Deller as he led his mother into the lobby. How in the Goddess's name was she supposed to explain this? Here she'd been trying to help them, and had made the situation ten times worse.

"Where are we, sweetie?" Deller's mother whispered. Eyes half-open, she leaned heavily on her son's shoulder. Under the harsh overhead lighting, the cuts and bruises on her face were clearly visible, and her skin had a grayish pallor.

"I don't know," Nellie said helplessly. The soaked patch between her legs had turned cold and was beginning to rub. Desperately she squeezed her legs together and hoped no one would notice the smell.

"Just one of your levels?" With a grimace, the woman touched the bloody cut under her eye.

"Sort of," said Nellie, watching Deller who'd turned and was peering through the office doorway. Suddenly he tensed and backed toward them. "Hadden," he mouthed as voices broke out behind him.

"Anyone come through here lately, Lars?" demanded a familiar clipped voice.

"Uh uh," said another voice carelessly. "Not for hours."

"You sure?" asked Hadden, his voice loud and irritated. "I was following three, in a group—a middle-aged bitch, a boy and a girl. Couldn't really get a fix on the girl. A lot of her waves were pretty high up. She breached a contact point and left it dysfunctional. Took me a while to get it working again."

Contact point, thought Nellie weakly. So that was how they thought of Ayne—merely an entry and exit point.

"You think she's the one they're looking for?" the other man asked quickly.

"I don't know," replied Hadden. "You're sure they didn't come through here?"

"Been here for hours," the other man assured him. "No one's showed."

"I'll have to call headquarters then," Hadden said. "Could be the contact point screwed up and downloaded them somewhere else in the system. The receiving stations will have to be notified."

"There's a direct line at the front desk," said the other man. "It's a Goddess freak day and everyone's on holiday, praying to their star charts."

Nellie's eyes slitted. A pagan, just as she'd thought. She turned toward the hallway, intending to run toward it, then felt a hand grab her arm and whirled to find Deller pulling her through a second doorway close to the reception desk. Quickly his mother eased the door shut behind them. Huddled in the dark, they listened as Hadden stalked into the lobby and picked up the phone.

It sounded as if it was going to be a long, very muffled conversation. Restless, Nellie let her mind tilt to the right and began to scan the molecular field. They appeared to be standing in a small storage room. Outlines of several filing cabinets glowed quietly in the dark, and she could make out rows of shelving along the far wall. Further probing revealed what was probably a small lamp sitting on top of a filing cabinet. Tuning back into solid reality, Nellie crossed the room and touched the object. Yes, it was a lamp, and it appeared to be plugged in. Cupping her hands around the knob to muffle any click it might make, she turned it on.

The room lit up with a gentle glow. Immediately Nellie's eyes flew toward the others, who were still standing by the door. As the light hit him Deller whirled, then relaxed and nodded. His mother simply opened her eyes and closed them again. It must have been twelve hours, Nellie realized, since the woman had had anything to eat. Glancing around, she spotted a box of sugar cubes next to some coffee supplies on a shelf. Carefully she opened the box, wincing as the cardboard rasped slightly, then tiptoed to the door and placed a cube against Deller's mother's mouth. The woman's eyes flew open, and she took the cube from Nellie and fit it carefully between her swollen lips. Handing the box to Deller, Nellie watched him lift another cube to his mother's mouth.

She turned from them and began to prowl the room. Part of a secretary's work area, it was consumed by shelves of office supplies, a photocopier and a row of filing cabinets. Stopping in front of the latter, Nellie scanned the labels that appeared on the drawers. *MB129QS. Detta 093. Quadrant 74QA.* What kind of codes were these? Curious, she pressed a release button and slid open a drawer packed with file folders. But the files were labeled with incomprehensible technical jargon, and none of the diagrams in the folders made any sense. Bored, she moved on to the next filing cabinet and opened the top drawer. Pulling out the first file, she almost grinned as she read the label. *Breeding Program?* Was the government of the Interior getting into the dog-breeding industry?

Slipping the file back into the drawer, Nellie flipped to the next one and read the name Gemma Abreen on the label. She opened the file and saw the photograph of a seven-year-old girl in the top right-hand corner and her case history typed into the appropriate boxes below. Unease rippled through Nellie and she scowled. What would a seven-year-old girl have to do with a breeding program? Opening the next file, she saw another photograph and name—Phillip Acker, fifteen years old. His mother was an engineer, his father ... *See File PRADS01* was typed into the appropriate box. The next several files revealed a similar scenario—a child's photograph with an address, birthdate, and mother's occupation, and a similar reference to the father's identity: *See File JQFR1011* or *Refer to File MTZFN1201.*

Nellie's heart began to thud painfully. Mysterious unnamed fathers—it had been a sore point between her and her mother. While Interior children didn't live with their fathers, they were usually given the basic facts about their lineage, including their father's name, caste and medical history. But all Nellie's mother would say about her father was, "He's with the stars now, honey. It doesn't matter what his name is—he belongs to the Goddess."

Nellie shivered once, uncontrollably, then got a grip and began leafing through the files until she reached the back of the drawer. The last file contained the case history of a boy named Sean Edden and she shifted to the next drawer, continuing her search. She was looking for the letter K—K for *Kammer, Kendricks, Kidder* ... And then, there it was—*Kinnan, Nellie Joan.* Soundless bells tolled in her palms, blackness oozed through her brain and cleared. Slowly she pulled out the file and opened it.

There was her photograph, taken when she was eight, approximately two years before she and her mother fled the Interior. The home address listed was for an apartment she remembered as having bright yellow walls and a landlady two floors down who owned a pet canary named Holy Moley. Her school had been just around the corner, a two-minute dash. Nellie's eyes roamed the page, scanning her uneven academic record and the lists of her recreational activities and closest friends. Why would anyone want to keep track of her friends? And why had a dark stroke been drawn through the box that listed siblings? She had no siblings. It had been another sore point to pester her mother about.

Without warning, Nellie's eyes locked onto her mother's name: *Lydia Stella Kinnan. Occupation: elementary schoolteacher. Terminated in Dorniver, traitor's death.* The death date given was sixteen months previous. As Nellie read it, the floor wobbled under her feet and she slumped heavily against the filing cabinet. *Deaddeaddead, my mother is dead.* Finally it was official, more than a deep dark question hovering at the back of her brain. For a long moment she stood caught in a nothing place, sucking her pain into a small black box and burying it deep within herself. Then she forced her eyes to return to the page and scan for details about her father.

There was the appropriate box, but a heavy stroke had also been drawn through it. Nellie whimpered in dismay, then glanced up, terrified at the sound she'd released. Her eyes locked with Deller's, and they waited, strung like live wires across the muffled staccato of Hadden's voice. Finally Nellie shrugged and Deller shrugged back. Handing the box of sugar cubes to his mother, he crossed the room and stopped beside her. Instinctively Nellie's arm shifted to cover the page, resisting when he tried to move it. Then her eyes fell on the gap in his hand that had once held his missing finger. Everyone had something missing in their life—with Deller it was his father and brother, with her it was her mother and her past. Slowly she let her arm slide off the file.

Deller glanced at the page and his eyebrows rose disbelievingly at the sight of her name. "What is this?" he whispered.

She shrugged, not able to speak the words *Breeding Program*, and flipped to the file's second page. Filled with diagrams of the human brain, it was marked with small Xs and arrows. Tiny print gave complex medical explanations. Nellie scowled as she stumbled over the unfamiliar terminology. *Biotelemetric, electromagnetic, biochip, nerve chip, radio-transmitter*—what was this but fancy talk for some kind of machinery that had been stuck inside her head? Shrill stars sang in her ears; for a moment she felt everything she knew and understood slip completely away from her.

"Nellie?" Deller whispered, gripping her arm. The warmth of his hand brought her back to herself, but she shrugged him off and glanced again at the page before her. According to this file she'd been part of a secret government breeding program that wouldn't even list her father's coded file number. Her mother had been murdered for trying to rescue her, and her brain was filled with technology she couldn't begin to understand. Shakily Nellie flipped to the file's final page and read the last typed entry: *Contact lost near Dorniver.* The date listed was the same as the one given for her mother's death. A single hand-scrawled phrase dominated the bottom half of the page: *Operation 9Q4L incomplete.* Quickly she flipped back to the previous page. There it was—the code 9Q4L, written next to a profile of her brain showing two implants inserted into the right temporal lobe. Was this the reason her mother had taken her and fled to the Outbacks, then died a traitor's death—for trying to save her from the completion of Operation 9Q4L?

Clutching the file, Nellie stared at the cabinet drawer. There were so many folders, surely one file marked incomplete wouldn't be missed. But what if she was caught with this information on her? Any Interior agent would immediately know who she was. Longingly Nellie traced the phrases typed onto the first page. There was her mother's name, her own name, the name of her school and her former best friend. She was real, she did exist, and this file was her only evidence that she'd once belonged with people who'd known and loved her. It felt like missing breath.

Without glancing at Deller, she returned the file to the drawer and tucked it into place. She took one last look, straightening the file's edges, matching it to the previous one. As she did, the following file sagged and she reached for it, intending to straighten it too, but then her heart stopped beating and she was falling through a long silence. When the falling stopped, she found herself once again standing before the filing cabinet, her eyes focused on the new file, repeatedly scanning the label. *Nellie Joanne Kinnan*—the name came at her like a whisper that had been buried deep underground. Sliding the file out of the drawer, she opened it.

The photograph was obviously recent. The girl facing the camera had long blond hair. Her eyes were gray and curiously slanted, her nose thin and snubbed at the tip, her lips smiling but unsure of their meaning. Something about the corner tuck of her mouth told Nellie this girl could get pretty weasely. Maybe that was why they looked so much alike. But then maybe it was because the girl's birthdate was the same as Nellie's, and her mother was also listed as Lydia Stella Kinnan, an elementary schoolteacher who'd died a traitor's death. Her father's name had been blacked out, as had the box listing siblings.

Nellie Joanne's current address was unfamiliar, but Nellie read it several times, imprinting it to memory, as well as the incomprehensible phrase, "Black Core Program: Advanced Stage." Then she flipped to the second page and saw the same diagrams of the brain, only this time operation 94QL was marked complete. Further operations had followed. A third page revealed a full-scale drawing of the human body with Xs marked all over it. Nellie's face blanched as she saw some of the sites. The girl was a walking implant factory.

Nellie stood in a terror vast and silent as a slowly spinning universe, and listened to her heart beat. She had a twin. Somewhere in a past she could barely remember they'd probably lived together, shared a bedroom, played with the same toys, and breathed one another's air. While the details had been forgotten, she finally recognized the sensation of absence that had always been with her, sliding across the edge of her thoughts like a reflection in a mirrored mask. In some deep buried part of herself she'd always known about Nellie Joanne, had always missed her.

Slowly she slid the file into the drawer and closed it. Turning, she saw Deller standing inches from her and staring openmouthed, and his mother beyond him, still leaning against the door listening to the uneven rumble of Hadden's voice. Frozen, Nellie stared back at Deller, her mouth also open, filled with the same silence. It felt as if it had been years since she'd opened the first filing cabinet drawer, as if she'd traveled several universes since reading the label *Breeding Program*. Through the door came the muffled click of a phone being returned to its cradle. Footsteps stalked out of the lobby, down the long tiled hallway of her mind, and faded.

"He's gone," Deller's mother mouthed.

Nellie nodded blearily. Crossing the room, she grabbed several sugar cubes and shoved them into her mouth. Grimly she fought off the urge to gag, sucking and swallowing until her head cleared and her blood quickened. "I guess we should try going back now," she whispered. "Are you okay enough to do that?"

With a grimace, Deller's mother closed her eyes and murmured, "Dizzy, but I'll try."

"C'mon, Mom," Deller said, slipping an arm under her shoulder.

Quietly Nellie eased open the door and tiptoed across the lobby. Peering into the office, she saw the man still working at his computer and the set of metal brackets just beyond him, close to the far wall. An attack of shivering hit her and she hugged herself fiercely. What would happen this time when they stepped between the brackets? Would they be sent back through Ayne, or downloaded somewhere else in 'the system'? And if they returned through Ayne, where would that be—to a laboratory full of waiting lab-coated men and priests?

It was only when she was a third of the way into the room that she realized the man at the computer was no longer wearing headphones. Fortunately the floor was carpeted and he was clicking furiously at his keyboard, but as she reached the room's halfway point a phone sitting next to him began to ring. The man reached to pick it up and his eyes fell on her, frozen mid-step. Briefly he sat, mouth open and staring at her, and then she felt him tense, about to spring.

Sending her mind into the molecular field, Nellie brought it abruptly to a standstill. Shock reverberated through the molecules in her immediate vicinity and she wondered helplessly what this was doing to Deller and his mother. For a long stretched moment she stood fixed in position, watching the man who sat facing her, frozen in his chair. Then she braced herself and revved the vibratory rate back up to its normal speed.

The man at the desk continued to sit with his hand stretched toward the phone, a woozy expression on his face. Whirling, Nellie grabbed Deller and his mother and began dragging them toward the metal brackets. "Wake up," she hissed, panicking at the stunned looks on their faces. "Wake *up*." When Deller continued to stare blankly at her, she slapped him. Abruptly his eyes cleared, and he glanced swiftly around himself.

"I'll go first," Nellie hissed at him. "You bring your mom." Then she turned and stepped between the brackets. Immediately she sensed what seemed to be a large pattern of vibrations with many smaller patterns pulsing within it, as if she was being offered a selection of destinations. Scanning them, she found one that felt familiar and focused on it. As she did, a long vertical seam appeared before her. Quickly she sent her mind into it and began to push. Easily, without pain, the gate opened, and she stepped through it.

She was back in the Temple of the Blessed Heart all right, but in the interim Ayne had been moved from the interrogation room to the laboratory. The first thing Nellie saw as she stepped free of the gate were the three birdlike machines, which had been moved from their original position in a corner to the middle of the room. Beyond them stood a priest in his emerald green robe of daily office, leaning against the door that led to the hall. Several lab-coated men were also standing about, facing him. A discussion was in progress and no one had noticed her arrival.

"We've got the kids doped and ready in the van," said one of the lab-coated men. "There's a strong alignment between the Susurra and the Moons tonight, and we're going to check out any new levels that might bring into range. But Hadden said one of the machines wasn't functioning properly, so I want to give them a quick test before we head out."

Leaning forward, he flicked a switch on the stem of one of the machines, and all three began to emit a loud hum. At the same moment, Deller and his mother stepped through the divided halves of Ayne's body. When she saw the scene before her, Deller's mother let out a cry, and the men whirled toward them.

"Get them!" shouted the priest.

Gibbering softly, Nellie rode out a wave of panic. There was no possible way she could freeze a molecular field with this many people. Behind her stood an open gate, but there was no point in heading back into the Interior. As the men lunged forward, her eyes fell on the birdlike machines. Swiftly, without thinking, she grabbed Deller and his mother and stepped into the space between the machines. A howl of dismay went up from the men and she heard one of them call out, "They're not stabilized. We won't know how to bring you ba—"

Nellie's brain tilted to the right and her head filled with the shrill voices of whirling stars. Heat permeated her body and her vibratory rate shot up. Dimly she felt Deller's mother's hand tighten around her own, and then the birdlike machines, the shouting men and the laboratory disappeared.

Chapter 19

FOR WHAT SEEMED LIKE uncontained infinity, stars whirled and called out inside Nellie's head, heat built inside her body and her vibratory rate continued to increase. Then the stars vanished and she saw what appeared to be level after level rapidly materializing and dematerializing around her. The first few resembled the laboratory scene she'd just left, with lab-coated men shouting at her from beyond birdlike machines. But before she could tell what was happening to her doubles, she'd passed through the nine fixed levels and entered what appeared to be a world of ancient broken-down buildings occupied by gargoyles. Next, a realm of darkness and fire materialized, inhabited by the looming figures of demons. This passed, and she was surrounded by humanoid reptilians that watched her through cold predatory eyes. Then they were gone, and she'd entered a landscape filled with vivid, strange-singing birds.

On and on Nellie traveled, her vibratory rate continuing to increase as she passed through levels as exotic as they were different. One moment she faced figures of blue spiraling smoke, the next she was surrounded by entities that leapt and danced with the jagged radiance of lightning. Finally she jerked to a halt, teetering in the rush and whirl of her own mind, and tumbled forward. Sobbing, she pressed against the ground beneath her, holding onto it with her body, begging it to remain in place. When nothing changed and her vibratory rate remained constant for several minutes, she opened her eyes and sat up.

She was immediately conscious of heat and a mild thrumming sensation. Squinting against a brightness that seemed to come from everywhere, Nellie gaped at the surrounding landscape. In the distance a row of high white cliffs hemmed a gleaming lake, and an abundance of glittering transparent vegetation grew everywhere, giving off flashes of prismatic light. Trees stretched into impossibly delicate shapes and flowers were patterned like snowflakes. Under her feet was something that looked and felt like sand, but glowed like tiny crystals.

Reaching down to scoop some of it into her palm, Nellie gasped and lifted both hands to her face. Glittery and transparent, they glowed like the surrounding landscape, as did the rest of her body. Sticking out her foot, she watched it give off a flash of brilliant multi-colored light. Upon entering this level, her entire body appeared to have been transformed into a crystalline substance that matched the landscape. *Just like*, Nellie thought, excitement catching in her throat, *when I'm shapeshifting and I turn into a crystal girl.*

As she turned her hands, watching them sparkle, she became aware of a mild thrumming sensation that seemed to be coming from her body. Kneeling, she pressed her hands to the sand and felt it emitting the same quick pulse. This was obviously a level vibrating at a very high rate—even the air seemed to shimmer and hum. Touching her throat, Nellie felt her pulse racing at three times the normal rate and yet she didn't feel tired or overwhelmed.

Turning, she saw Deller and his mother lying nearby, their eyes closed. Though their bodies had also been transformed into a crystalline state, their limbs were dull, without the gleaming luminescence of her own. Gently Nellie patted their faces. When neither stirred, she pressed the inside of their wrists and felt their pulses also racing at three times the normal rate, but harsh-edged and erratic.

"Deller," she shouted. Taking him by the shoulders, she gave him a good shake, but his eyes remained closed, his mouth slack and open.

"They'll be dead in a couple of hours," said a voice behind her, and Nellie whirled to see her crystalline double standing several feet away. As with everything in this place, the girl's transparent body glimmered and thrummed. Dressed in a short white tunic and sandals, she cocked her head to one side and observed Nellie curiously.

"No, they won't," Nellie snapped back, surging to her feet. "I won't let them."

Her double shrugged and tossed her long glowing hair, then turned and pointed a short ways off to several humps in the ground. "That's where we buried the others," she said nonchalantly. "They show up every now and then; we don't know from where. Never even wake up, just lie there and die."

Nellie's eyes flicked desperately over the row of humps, counting. Nine. Had they all been children sent here by the bird-like machines? "Deller can't die," she stammered. "Or his mom. They're my friends."

"We're all friends here," her double shrugged. "You'll see."

"What if I give them some water?" Frantically Nellie pointed to the far-off gleam at the base of the cliffs.

"They can't drink it," her double said carelessly. "We've tried, but it won't go into them. They're not made for it. I think you're okay though," she added. "If you weren't, you'd be out of it like them. Besides, you look like me, so you're probably someone who was supposed to be with us but got lost. I bet it won't take long for you to learn oneness."

"Oneness?" Nellie asked warily, but instead of answering, her double reached out and touched her arm.

"Come," she said, and instantly Deller, his mother and the glittering landscape vanished. Before Nellie could even blink, she found herself standing inside a large room. Clear crystalline walls arced upward into a single point and thrummed quietly. Through them she could see the white cliffs, shrunk to pinpoint size and decidedly further off. With a flash of panic she pivoted, seeking her double, and found herself facing a crowd of crystalline children and adults, all dressed in white tunics. And, Nellie realized, all giving off the same quick thrum she felt coming from everything else.

"Yes," said her double, stepping out of the luminescent crowd and nodding to her. "What you're feeling is the oneness of this place. We're all one here—the air, the sea, the land, the animals and the people. When one of us has a thought, we all have it. When I wish for something, we all receive it. There's no discord here, we understand each other completely and we share everything."

Startled, Nellie stepped back. "You read my mind," she whispered.

"When you have a thought, we all have it," her double repeated. "You'll learn to receive our thoughts too, you'll see."

Behind her the glimmering crowd shifted and thrummed excitedly. A scowl crossed Nellie's face and she slitted her eyes at them, wondering if they were in the process of sharing one of their thoughts. If so, it was probably about her. Uneasily she took another step back. "That's very interesting," she said, scavenging her mind for something polite to say. "But I have to get back to my friends and help them. If you don't mind—"

"They'll die," her double said dismissively, "and we'll bury them. Forget them. We're your friends now. You're one with—"

"Yes," Nellie snapped, her panic getting the better of her. "Fine, you're my friends, that's just fine. Now will you please tell me how we got here, so I can get back—"

"I thought us here," said her double with a look of surprise. "How else do you travel?"

"You thought…" Nellie stared around herself in bewilderment. "You mean you had a thought and it happened, just like that?"

"Of course." Her double stared back with equal bewilderment as a confused-sounding thrum rose from the glimmering crowd behind her.

"So if I thought—," began Nellie eagerly, but her double cut her off with a wave of the hand.

"You can't think someone alive when he's dead," she said. "It has to be something that can happen. Your friends can't carry the vibrations of this place. It's too fast for them."

"But they can't die," Nellie shouted, her fear splitting wide open. "They took care of me, they loved me, they're the only ones who even looked at me after my mom died. What about the rest of you?" she demanded, turning to the crowd that pressed close, listening anxiously. "Why don't you say something? Will you help?"

"They don't talk," her double said quickly. "We don't need to. We communicate through thoughts, like I told you. I'm only talking to you now because you haven't learned oneness with us yet. When you do—"

"I don't want to learn oneness!" Eyes slitted, Nellie backed away from her double. "I'm not one with you, I'm one with myself."

Hey, don't get uptight. The voice spoke inside Nellie's head, shimmering like light. Startled, she glanced around, seeking its source, and saw the crowd part to let a second girl through. Coming to a halt beside Nellie's double, the new girl watched in amusement as Nellie's eyes darted between the two figures standing before her. With their long blond hair and sarpa eyes they were almost identical, but a closer inspection showed the second girl's face to be narrower, her lips fuller and as well a tiny mole that sat on the right side of her neck—all in all, she was a mirror image of the photograph of Nellie Joanne that had been in the Breeding Program file folder.

"Are you another double?" Nellie asked hoarsely.

I'm Nellie Joanne, said the voice inside her head. *What's a double?*

"But aren't you in the Black—?" Nellie faltered, then stopped. No, that question didn't make sense. This wasn't a fixed level, so there wasn't any Black Core Program here, and neither of these girls had scars on their scalps. Hungrily she watched them. They stood so naturally together, as if nothing would ever change it. Almost angry, she blurted, "Where's your mother?"

"Dead," said her double easily. "But we have many mothers here. What does one matter?"

A giant ache blew through Nellie and she swallowed hard. "How did she die?" she asked finally.

"She was standing beside me about a year and a half ago, and she just fell down," said her double casually. "Then her body disintegrated into the sand crystals from which we all come."

Nellie closed her eyes and stood for a moment, just letting her pain be. So, it looked as if Lydia Stella Kinnan had died simultaneously in every level. Dead was dead was dead, there was no getting around it. *Deller,* she thought in renewed panic, coming back to herself. *I've got to get back to him.*

"Will you help me?" she asked, ignoring her double and appealing to Nellie Joanne's. "Deller's heartbeat is way too fast, and his mother was hurt before we got here. I'm scared they're going to die. If you could just think me back—"

They're not one of us, her twin's double shrugged. *Let them die and become one with—"*

Shock swept through Nellie and she staggered backward. "How can you say that?" she screamed. "They love me, they're the best people in my whole level—"

"Level?" interrupted her double with a frown. "What's a level?"

"It's another place," faltered Nellie. "Different from this one. It's where I come from. You all live there too, except your lives are very different there. In that level..." She looked directly at her double. "...you're like me. I'm you."

Her double scowled in open confusion, and then her face cleared and she shrugged. "Of course," she said. "We're one."

"No," said Nellie. "Not like that. We're the same person, but—"

She stopped and stared at the two girls. They looked happy and had no scars. Their world seemed peaceful and safe and was filled with such beauty. Turning, Nellie gazed through the crystalline walls toward the white cliffs that shimmered in the distance. She could feel the thrum deepening in her body, pulsing through her blood. What her double said was true—she was adapting, she could stay here if she wanted. Deller and his mother would die, but it would be like going to sleep. They probably wouldn't even wake up and she would finally be safe, free of the Interior, with somewhere to sleep and food to eat. Sure, it was kind of a dumb place. The whole level was like a mindjoy, with that trancelike thrum going on all the time. But maybe she could handle it. She might even learn to like being a bunch of thrumming crystals and becoming one, whatever that meant.

But hadn't her mother died fighting the oneness of the Interior? Hadn't she been killed for thinking differently than the people around her?

Nellie turned back to the glimmering crowd and stared at them. They returned her stare, their eyes fixed on her like a single pair of eyes, the same expression of detached curiosity sharing every face. But it wasn't their obvious sameness that had the warnings running lightfooted up the back of Nellie's neck. It was something entirely different—an invisible presence that hovered over the group and seemed to be reaching toward her, though not a single person could be seen raising their arms.

Tuning into the molecular field, she saw it—a mass of bright prismatic light that glowed in the floor and the walls and reached up into the crowd, completely engulfing it. Though she squinted fiercely, not a single individual figure could be seen within it. As her double had said, the crowd standing before her was one—not only with each other, but with the walls, the floor and the entire landscape that surrounded them. And even, Nellie realized in horror, glancing at her own body, with herself. No matter how she squinted and peered, all she could see where her arms and legs should have been was more of the all-pervasive brilliant light. With a shudder, she tuned back into solid reality and watched the crowd take on the illusion of separate bodies.

"You're … not me," she stammered, turning to her double. "And you're not my twin," she said to Nellie Joanne's double. "And somehow you're putting me into a trance, stopping me from thinking normal, so I'll forget about Deller and let him and his mom die. That's not oneness. Real oneness is listening to everything around you and loving it—the people, the air, even the dirt in the ground. You don't forget about people and let them die, and you let them think different from you if they want to. You don't have oneness, you have sameness. And sameness is evil. This whole place is evil."

As Nellie spoke she stepped back, and the crowd surged after her as if drawn by an invisible string. The thrumming sensation deepened within her body, and she thought she heard a delicate chorus of voices speaking deep within her mind. *Be one with us,* they singsonged. *Come and be happy with us. We feel nothing but joy and peace. We'll lift you up—*

Focusing on her fear, Nellie picked it up and threw it directly at the gleaming crowd. A startled hum rose from them and they drew back, scattering. Instantly Nellie felt herself released from an invisible hold. *Think,* she told herself fiercely. *Think of Deller and his mom.* Closing her eyes, she pictured their sprawled forms and took a running step forward. A rushing sensation filled her head, and then it faded and she was standing in the crystalline sand, staring at the far-off cliffs. At her feet lay Deller and his mother, stretched out and motionless.

With a sob she fell to her knees and felt their wrists. A faint, barely discernible rhythm pulsed against her fingertips, and she almost swooned with relief. Gripping their hands, she whispered,

"It's all vibrations. This place is just a different pack of vibes from home. And what we passed through to get here—that's all vibrations too. I just have to find the trail."

Desperately Nellie scanned the surrounding molecular field, squinting at its brilliance. There had to be a seam in it somewhere, some kind of gate to mark their entry point. Sending her mind back and forth, she probed the radiant play of energy. Abruptly her mind snagged on something and she sent her thoughts back over the area, scanning it. Yes, she could feel some kind of seam, and when she probed the vibes along it she picked up traces of Deller, his mother and even a slight whiff of the Temple of the Blessed Heart.

Swiftly Nellie sent her mind into the seam and drew it open, then grunted and ducked as a scream of pain hit her. Her mind reeled, swimming in the aftershock, and she realized she'd just opened a freshly created gate. At their entry into this level, they must have unwittingly torn open part of this skin's soul.

Well, there was nothing she could do about it now. Wrapping her arms tightly around Deller and his mother, Nellie closed her eyes and pictured the three of them passing through the gate. Again a rushing sensation filled her head and then she was passing directly into the gate's pain. Briefly her mind buckled and every molecule in her body seemed to cry out in fear, and then the gate and its torment were behind her and the levels were once again flashing past. Ignoring panoramas of angels and lightning like beings, Nellie tightened her arms around Deller and his mother and hung on. "Please, blessed Goddess, Mother of us all," she whispered as strange exotic animals took shape about her, then humanoid reptilians and demons. *Hear my prayer, Ivana, hear my prayer.*

Finally the fixed levels appeared, laboratory after laboratory zooming by, and then a completely familiar range of frequencies surrounded her. Jerking to a halt, she felt the floor solidify beneath her knees and looked up to see several men staring at her from the other side of a birdlike machine. Along the far wall, four small children could be seen standing listlessly, watching their own feet.

The kids in the van, Nellie thought quickly. The men must have brought them inside to wait while they stood guard, hoping for her return.

Abruptly, one of the gaping men was shoved aside and a green-robed figure reached around the stem of the nearest birdlike machine and flicked the on-off switch. The machines' dense hum shut off and a brief silence descended on the laboratory.

"Gotcha," said the high priest of the Temple of the Blessed Heart, a grin twisting his face.

Chapter 20

HEART THUNDERING, Nellie lowered Deller's head, then his mother's, to the floor. Quickly she pressed her hands to their throats and immediately felt a pulse in each one, strong and beating at its normal pace. Relief flooded her, so intense she almost swooned. Leaning into Deller's face, she hissed, "C'mon bozo, wake up. We're back in the temple and they're all around us."

Deller's eyes flickered dozily across her face, then shot wide open. Letting out a startled yelp, he reached up and gave her a hard shove. "What's with you?" he croaked, scrambling to his feet and backing away. "You're like … glass. Shiny."

Looking down, Nellie saw that she was still in a crystalline state. Though their journey back through the levels had returned Deller and his mother to flesh and blood, her glittering body was still giving off a rapid high-pitched thrum. To make things worse, she had no way of explaining her current condition to Deller since he'd probably lost consciousness before they reached the crystal level and had no awareness of it.

"It's just me, Deller," she stammered awkwardly. "I'm not doubled, or nothing." But the look on his face didn't change, and a long deep heaviness poured through her as she turned from him to face the gaping men.

As she focused on them, Nellie realized her thoughts were racing at ten times their normal speed and were clearer than she'd ever felt them. Without touching her throat, she knew her pulse was three times its regular rate. An old kind of knowing filled her, a wisdom that lived not in flesh and blood or the synapses of the brain, but in a particular range of frequencies. And when she turned her gaze this time upon the green-robed priest, she didn't need to tune into the molecular field to see he was doubled.

Immediately she sensed that the entity living within him existed in an energy state that vibrated at an extremely rapid rate. Ordinarily she wouldn't have been able to look directly at such brilliant frequencies, but in her crystalline state she could clearly see the tightly slanted eyes that peered through the priest's, and the long jutting jaw that extended from his lower face. *Sarpa*, thought Nellie in a flash of blinding instinct, her hands lifting to touch her own eyes. Then, *The skull Gurry found—its head is exactly the same shape.*

"That's right, little star," the entity hissed through the priest's mouth. "You'll find our bones buried beneath many of the sacred places in this land. For this was our kingdom once, and so it shall be again now that we've found you. We've been searching years for you, little star, and now we've got you."

Fear swept Nellie as she realized the entity had read her thoughts. "Me?" she faltered, staring at it. "Why were you looking for me?"

"One of the deeper mysteries," said the entity as the priest took a step forward. "Soon all will be revealed to you, and you'll discover the great purpose for which you were bred. But for now, don't fight me, little star. You haven't got my strength. Just let these men take charge of you and we'll fulfill your destiny."

Abruptly the scene before Nellie blurred slightly, and she felt a surge of quick high vibrations enter her brain. Then her vision cleared and she heard a girl's voice exclaim, *That was a real rush, coming through all those different places. What were they—levels? Where are you now? And who's that guy standing there scowling at you?*

Startled, Nellie glanced around the laboratory in search of the speaker, but saw only Deller, his mother and the men. Suspecting a trick, she glanced toward the doubled priest and saw his face contort with rage.

"Don't think you can fight me by calling on others," the entity hissed through the priest. "I come from a place more powerful than anything you can summon to do your bidding. Your powers are limited, little star. Your father is one of our greatest lords, it is true, but your mother pulls you down to the lowest order. You're only half sarpa, not of my rank. You can't defeat me."

"I'm not cal—," Nellie started to protest, just as another surge of vibrations shot through her brain and the girl's voice spoke a second time. *Hey Nellie*, it persisted. *Can't you hear me? It's me, we're linked by the oneness, and I can feel something really weird where you are. Who's that guy you're talking to?*

With a start, Nellie realized that her crystalline double had somehow found a way into her head and was communicating through thought. *I'm in trouble*, she thought rapidly, her eyes on the doubled priest, wondering how much he was picking up. *There's a man near me with a thing from a really high level living inside him, and it's after me.*

Probe him, her double said immediately.

Are you nuts? hissed Nellie. *That thing is big time, its vibes are even faster than yours.*

Nellie, you're not just one with me, her double shot back. *You're one with all of us here—the people, the animals, the air, the land and the sea. We're all one and we're all linked to you. Go on, probe him so we can find out who he is.*

Well, what did she have to lose? Taking a deep breath, Nellie focused and sent her mind tentatively toward the doubled priest. But despite her caution, the entity sensed her approach and sent a counter-probe. The malevolent tendril of energy hurtled toward her, knocking her to her knees. Crouched against the floor, she grunted and writhed as the hostile probe jabbed at her mind.

"Don't fight me," roared the doubled priest, leaning between the birdlike machines. "I'll crush you and leave you so stupefied, you won't even know what's happening when we call out your soul and transform you into our greatest star."

At that moment a clear bright hum entered Nellie's head. Surge after surge of energy followed like waves on a shore, and she could feel the presence of hundreds of minds swirling about her brain, trying to get oriented. Coming together, they fused into a single line of radiant energy that soared directly at the hostile probe. Immediately she felt the pain in her head falter, but the probe renewed itself, jabbing with twice the strength. Screaming, she clutched at her head with both hands. She couldn't take this. No one could absorb this much evil and survive. If it didn't stop soon—

But new vibrations were entering her mind and sending themselves at the hostile probe—energy that lapped like water, blew like a fierce wind and pressed with the great weight of the ground beneath her feet. Shrill cries resounded through Nellie's head and she felt the minds of birds and animals dart and leap at the malevolent force that continued to pierce her brain. And woven through these new vibrations was the ongoing presence of the people of the crystalline level, sending themselves in an unbreakable thrum deep into the entity's probe.

Gradually the pain lessened, and finally Nellie felt the entity release her mind and retreat. For a long moment she continued to be filled with a dense crystalline light that swirled into every corner of her mind, permeating the frightened agitated vibrations of her brain, soothing and healing them. Then it also withdrew from her head, leaving her breathless and crouched on the laboratory floor. Slowly she looked up.

Twisted across the priest's face was a look of such malevolence that she scuttled backward, passing the nearest birdlike machine in a blur of fear. With a roar the priest sprang after her, landing between the machines. Instinctively Nellie's eyes darted to the on-off switch on the stem of the nearest one, and then suddenly she was standing next to it and flicking the switch. A click sounded, the three machines began to hum, and the rage on the priest's face changed to terror.

Then he was gone. Quickly Nellie flicked off the switch. Silence descended on the laboratory, edgy and thick, and then one of the lab-coated men whimpered and dashed toward the exit. The others followed. The door swung closed behind them and their feet pounded rapidly down the hall, leaving the laboratory full of a sudden emptiness. Slowly Nellie turned to face Deller and his mother.

They were standing well back from the birdlike machines, staring openmouthed. *Rerraren*. Nellie saw the thought cross their faces, and a deep loneliness shuddered through her. "It's just me," she whispered, lifting her crystalline hands toward them. "Shapeshifting is just something…sarpas do, I guess. But I'm not like that thing inside the priest, even if it said I was. I'm like my mother, I believe in the Goddess, and I won't hurt you, or nothing like that."

"Of course you won't, Nellie sweetie," whispered Deller's mother, her face blanching as she clutched at Deller's arm. Blood still trickled from the cut under her left eye. "Of course not," she added reassuringly, but she didn't come any closer, nor did Deller. Helplessly Nellie stared at her glittering hands and wondered how to transform them into flesh and blood.

Just think them back, said her double inside her head, *the way you moved yourself over to that machine by thinking it. We'll probably lose the oneness when you do it, though. I've never been one with someone in another level before. I never even knew there were levels.*

There are zillions of them, Nellie thought at her quickly. *When you learn how to travel, you can visit me here.*

Maybe, said her double dubiously. *The people in your level seem odd to me. Besides I'd have to bring along everyone from this level—the oneness, you know.*

Oh. Nellie faltered, trying to envision it. *That could get a bit complicated. Well, here goes. I'm going to try and think myself back into a human being. Goodbye.*

Goodbye? What does goodbye mean? asked her double, but before Nellie could reply, the crystalline radiance had left her body and it had returned to its flesh and blood state.

"That's more like it," Deller whispered, and she was startled to see tears glimmering in his eyes. He flashed her a weak grin. "For a second I thought you were going to tell me you'd gone and turned into the Goddess."

Nellie's jaw dropped, and then she gave him a scowl of absolute disapproval. His grin broadened.

"C'mon," she snapped, slitting her eyes at him. "We've got to get out of here."

"What about the kids?" asked Deller.

Nellie's eyes shot toward the four children, who were still standing in a submissive line along the far wall. Thoroughly drugged, they'd been so quiet she'd forgotten their presence. Even the priest's sudden disappearance hadn't roused them. Fleetingly— very fleetingly—she considered taking off and leaving them, then remembered the oneness of the crystal level and the way it had come to her rescue.

"Okay," she said gruffly. "But we have to get them moving *fast.*"

Crossing the room, she opened the door and peered into the hall. Gloom and silence stretched in both directions, with only an EXIT sign glowing at one end. "C'mon," she said, beckoning to the children. When they didn't budge, she grabbed the nearest one by the hand and began to lug him toward the door. Immediately the others followed, shuffling along sleepily. Behind them came Deller, supporting his mother, whose harsh breathing underlined every step she took. Easing open the door a second time, Nellie stepped into the hall and started leading the children toward the EXIT sign. As the door clicked shut behind them, her heart jumped so hard she thought it would upend her stomach. A glance over her shoulder showed six shadowy figures following her quietly through the darkness. If the lab-coated men had left the building, she thought rapidly, they should be all right. It was the middle of the night, and even with the kids they would be able to travel Dorniver's back alleys without being seen.

But as they drew close to the EXIT sign, lights went on up and down the hall and a male voice called, "Stand where you are." Squinting through the brilliance, Nellie peered at several men who were standing under the EXIT sign—one lab-coated man and two police officers.

"There's a bunch at the other end too," Deller hissed.

Turning, Nellie saw a second group of men at the opposite end of the hall. "Sweet blessed Goddess," she whispered, her eyes locking with Deller's. What was she supposed to do now? The abilities that came with her crystalline state were gone, and there was no way she could find and open a gate, then get everyone through it fast enough. Desperately she shoved the children toward Deller and his mother and snapped, "Everyone put a hand on me." Then she took them all out of sync with the surrounding vibratory rate. Immediately the hallway disappeared and they were surrounded by a murky blur that stretched endlessly in every direction. A second later they were hit by an agonizing barrage of shrieks and moans.

"Not this again," grimaced Deller as the children whimpered and crowded against their legs. Abruptly Deller's mother grabbed her stomach and bent forward.

"It's like a sickness," she moaned. "Gets into you and makes you feel desperate."

Stumbling, she fell heavily against Nellie just as Deller and the children sank to their knees. Frantically Nellie tried to pull Deller upright, but he sank again, white-faced and trembling. "Get up," she yelled, but he remained crouched at her feet, his arms over his head. For one brief, terror-edged moment, Nellie almost kicked him. Then she straightened grimly and stared at the surrounding blur.

It's all vibrations, she thought fiercely. *Those wails and screams are vibes, and so am I.*

Drawing her thoughts together, she sent her mind deep into the surrounding soundscape. The church was thick with the sound of pain—moans and screams that pressed close, trying to merge with her vibrations. As the groaning sobs passed into her, Nellie's nausea grew, but instead of fighting she focused on the cries, listening as each told her its story. Suddenly she realized what the sounds were—the pain and terror of the victims who'd been interrogated, tortured, and used for experiments in the Temple of the Blessed Heart.

A sob broke from her own lips. Opening completely to the wails that surrounded her, she thought, *I understand, I know who you are, and I swear someday I'll tell everyone your story so they know what happened to you.* Immediately the cries stopped shoving themselves at her and begun nuzzling like small children seeking comfort. *Help us find our way out*, Nellie whispered to them wonderingly. *Please, I need your help.*

Instantly, a corridor opened ahead of her through the blur, a passageway of clear bell-like sound. Bewildered, Nellie stood staring at it. She was sure the church hallway didn't run in this direction, and that the new corridor was traveling directly into the nearest wall, but the whimpering voices continued to bump against her, urging her forward. *Help Deller's mom*, she thought at them. *And Deller and the kids.* Immediately the voices surged downward and surrounded the six crouched figures. Then as Nellie watched, Deller, his mother and the children got to their feet and stood staring about themselves. One of the children raised a hand and began patting at the voices in the air.

Joining hands, Nellie and the others stepped into the radiant corridor of sound. As they did the voices moved in behind them, absorbing their vibratory trail until every trace of their presence had been erased. On all sides the bell-like sound continued to resonate, and they found themselves propelled forward at breakneck speed until they were suddenly stepping free of the temple's outer wall, into murky darkness and a light-falling rain.

In quiet astonishment Nellie leaned against the solid wall, watching the children mill about her as the corridor of sound faded into nothingness. It was gone, the great gift of love and pain that had lifted and carried them out of the very bowels of danger, and all she wanted to do was turn and crawl back into it, live inside its bell-like sound forever.

"C'mon," Deller hissed, pulling at her arm. "I'll handle Mom, you take the kids, and let's get our asses out of here."

Quietly, their heads swimming with exhaustion, the small group made its stumbling meandering way across the parking lot into the pre-dawn rain.

Chapter 21

NELLIE SAT ALONE on a riverbank, staring out over the quiet rippling water as a nearby wickawoo called out low in its throat, the last song of the day. It was dusk, the twin moons starting to show above the sepia-blue horizon, their pearly whiteness approaching half size. From a ways into the trees came the crackle of a campfire and muted voices as Deller and his mother cleaned up after the evening meal. Having been the one responsible for cooking the rather dismal lump of fried eggs, rice and cheese everyone had eaten, Nellie had been dismissed from the washing up chore and had wandered off to the riverbank to do some private personal thinking.

They were camped in the bush with a guide, approximately one day's journey from Dorniver. After their escape from the Temple, Nellie and Deller had located his bike and helped his mother onto it. Followed by the four children, they'd wheeled her carefully across town to the house of a healer in the Snake-Eye district. By the time they'd arrived, she'd been sliding off the seat, barely conscious. The healer had immediately sent for several other women and they'd placed Deller's mother in a deep sleep, then encircled her, laying on hands, singing and burning sweet-smelling herbs.

Refused entry into the room, Nellie and Deller had taken up position in the hallway. Having gone two nights without sleep, Deller had soon drifted off, his head sliding down Nellie's shoulder until it rested in her lap. His closeness had been warmer than anything she'd imagined. To get a grip, she'd concentrated on tuning into the molecular field and probing the room behind her.

The molecular field had revealed the glowing figures of five chanting women seated around a sixth who gave off such a pale light Nellie had initially thought she was dead. *Listen*, she'd told herself fiercely and tuned deeper into the scene, following sound downward into a quieter darker realm. There she'd seen two figures in the distance—a woman leaning against a man with sarpa eyes who held her gently in his arms.

No! Nellie had thought, and in a flash of fear had sent her mind toward them, intending to break them apart. But at that moment the door to the bedroom had opened and one of the healers had come out into the hall.

"You leave her be, child," she'd told Nellie sternly. "This is her time to choose if she wants to continue living in her body, or pass on to the next world. It's not your place to interfere. She's been invaded in harsh ugly ways and we can't change that, we can only work as much healing into her mind and body as we're able. Then she has to decide if she wants to live on with the memory of what happened to her, or leave it behind."

The healer had gone back into the room and closed the door, and Deller's mother had continued to lie silent and motionless for two full days. Finally she'd woken, and after a meal and further rest, Deller had been called into the room. Impatient, Nellie had sat another full hour in the hall before she'd been allowed through the door. The woman she'd seen lying on the bed then had looked pale and thin, but the smile she'd given Nellie had carried the deep peace of two days of rest. Beckoning Nellie closer, she'd taken her hand.

"Nellie," she'd said in her husky voice. "Deller's been telling me what you went through, trying to rescue me, and I know about how the two of you've been sitting outside my door. Now I want to put what I'm saying next very clearly, so you won't go changing it in your head. I don't know if you're a child of the gods and what that could mean if you are, but it doesn't matter. From now on I want to wake up and find you in my home every morning, y'hear? No more taking off. You put your whole heart on the line saving me in that church and now I'm ready to put my whole heart into loving you, but you've got to realize it's a different kind of loving, day by day. More like an open door than a windstorm. Takes a different kind of strength, keeping that door open, always coming back to the same people instead of blowing wherever the wind takes you."

A smile flickered across Nellie's mouth as she remembered the way Deller had stood beaming at her from the other side of the bed. There hadn't been much time to stand around relishing the moment. Men had arrived to discuss moving them to a safe house in Shor, a small city several days' journey to the south. By that point, the children they'd discovered in the Temple had been returned to their families in West Daven, and volunteers had been found to watch over Deller's house. It hadn't been difficult—with the bombing of the Jinnet's headquarters and the news of infiltration by Interior agents, new resistance cells had been springing up everywhere.

A deep shudder ran through Nellie as she thought of everything that had happened, and she wrapped her arms around her knees and rocked fiercely. Abruptly she stopped and glanced up at the moons, halfway visible above the kwikwilla trees. A wistful look crossed her face, and she thought, *Fit them together and you'd get one person. A whole life, happy in itself.*

In spite of the events of the past few weeks, there were still so many things missing, so many unanswered questions. She'd seen official documentation stating that her mother was dead, but not how she'd died. She knew she had a twin, but the knowledge was like a gaping hole inside her gut that demanded a solution. And the things the doubled priest had said about her father—well, Nellie didn't want to think about that, pure and simple. A breeding between her mother and some creepy sarpa from a level higher than she'd ever traveled? A destiny that was so important, the sarpas had been pursuing her for years to fulfill it? What had the sarpa inside the doubled priest meant when it said it wanted to turn her into their greatest star? You had to be dead to be a star—stars were the souls of those who'd devoted their entire lives to the Goddess. Only Ivana could decide who became a star in the afterlife, not the sarpas.

Nellie shuddered again. One thing was clear—the sarpas were after her and she had to keep clear of all doubled people, especially priests and Interior agents. That shouldn't be too difficult. She could usually spot Interior agents a long ways off, and the sarpas seemed to be restricted to inhabiting doubled people. Maybe they'd once lived in this level as solid bodies, but she was willing to bet they couldn't any longer. She'd seen the hunger in the eyes of the doubled priest at the Temple. That sarpa had really wanted to get its hands on her directly, and if it could have shapeshifted into solid form, it would have done so.

Nellie shook her head, rumbling deep in her throat. The whole thing was beyond confusing, into another category of thinking and being she couldn't comprehend. The sarpa in the Temple had been evil, no doubt about it, but Outbackers seemed to revere people with sarpa eyes, calling them the Goddess's children. Was it possible the Goddess had once mated with a sarpa? Could there be good and bad sarpas? Or were they all bad, but some of their descendants good? Wonderingly Nellie traced the outline of her eyes. Was she actually one of the Goddess's descendants? Could her destiny in some way be connected to Ivana?

This whole thing connected to the Goddess somehow, Nellie was sure of it. Ivana held everything—all of life, truth and knowing—in Her divine hands. But then why did She allow such evil to go on in Her holy house? Small ripples of thought flicked across Nellie's face as she remembered the pleading hands that sat atop Dorniver's church spires. Maybe one of the clues to this puzzle was in those hands. Maybe they weren't blessing the churches as she'd originally thought, but trying to escape them. Maybe those hands were a message from the Goddess telling everyone that She wasn't a building, She was a presence that stretched everywhere you looked. *For Ivana,* Nellie thought excitedly, her pulse quickening, *was the molecular field, great hands of energy that held everyone and everything, even the people who didn't believe in Her. That was what the hands on top of the spires were saying,* she thought, a glad smile crossing her face: *Reach beyond what you can see. Reach into the molecular field, with all its love and hope glowing in every molecule. Reach into what you feel, into your soul, into other levels, even into the afterlife like the twin sons if you have to, but reach and you will find what has gone missing in your life.*

Slowly Nellie unwrapped her arms from her knees and knelt facing the twin moons. It had been three weeks since her last remembering session, and in spite of the friendship she'd received from Deller and his mother, there was still an ache in her to be touched by her own mother's hand. Hugging herself tightly, she began to rock. "Blessed Ivana," she murmured. The words spoke themselves deep into her mind and she closed her eyes, imagining the Goddess' hands atop a church spire, high above Dorniver's roofs. "Blessed Ivana," she sighed. "Mother of all mothers, mother of all sad and lonely children, come to me, come."

Hunched and swaying, Nellie forced herself deeper and deeper into herself, digging into her mind for that moment when worlds connected and she could find her way through. *Old women,* she thought furiously. *Think of their stinky garlicky mouths and the inside of a church, smelly with incense and old carpets.* An ache started in her knees and they creaked protestingly but still she rocked, pushing against some invisible inner barrier. "Blessed Ivana, blessed Ivana," she whispered, but all that came to her was the loneliness creeping up her arms and the hot burn of her knees against the ground. What was wrong? Why wasn't her mother coming to her? Was Ivana angry with Her humble devotee?

Placing the heels of her hands against her closed eyelids, Nellie pressed hard. Suffer, she had to suffer the way the Goddess suffered for Her people. Surely then Ivana would grant a lowly request to call one dead mother from the grave. *Nellie, sweet darling*, her mother would whisper—

"Nellie," murmured a voice, and soft fingertips grazed her forehead. Yearning pierced Nellie, she cupped her hands and lifted them pleadingly the way the Goddess did. Her mother was coming back to her, was even now descending onto this riverbank—

"Look at me, bozo," commanded the voice, and Nellie's eyes flew open to see her double in the gold-brocaded dress standing before her with a weasely smirk on her face. Instantly she was on her feet, her claws out and ready to lunge, but the other girl simply waved and faded into thin air. Breathing heavily, Nellie sat down with a thump, and sure enough her double reappeared, wearing the exact same smirk.

"What did you do that for?" Nellie hissed. "I was *remembering*."

Her double shrugged. "Thought it would be interesting."

"It's not interesting," Nellie snapped. "Interrupting people's *hearts* like that."

"Keep that in mind next time you see the possibilities," replied her double coolly. "Besides, you don't need to do it anymore. You've got someone else now."

"Doesn't mean I've got to forget my real mother," Nellie spat.

"I didn't tell you to forget her," said her double. "I said you don't *need* her anymore. Let her rest, like the dead should."

"What about you?" asked Nellie, pointing. "You wear the remembering dress *all the time*."

For a moment Nellie's double regarded her impassively. Then, in a single movement, she shucked the dress and stood naked, holding it out to her. "Here," she said quietly. "Take it back. But I can already tell you it won't work. I've tried and tried, but she doesn't come. We don't need her anymore. That's why she isn't coming to you. Now that you've found love in this world, she can rest in hers."

Sinking her face into the dress, Nellie stroked it like a live thing. It was true, what her double was saying—she could feel it, some kind of longing slid out of her and gone. "But isn't it evil?" she whispered, breathing in the dress's musky scent. "To let her go like that? To *forget* her? Think of her all alone in the dark, suffering without any love. Think of how she died."

"She's not dying anymore," her double said softly. "That's finished. She stopped suffering a long time ago. Now she needs to rest, and for us to let her go."

With a heaving sigh, Nellie lay down on the riverbank and curled up with the dress. An enormous exhaustion settled around her, curling up like a second presence, and for a moment she seemed to feel a hand pressed to her forehead and the quietest of voices whispering, *Nellie Joan. Goodbye, my sweet Nellie Joan.* Then it was gone—the presence, the great gray exhaustion and that moment when invisible doors opened and worlds connected. Hugging the dress tighter, Nellie licked tears from her mouth. "I've still got my twin," she said thickly. "Nellie Joanne."

"Me too," said her double, sitting beside her.

"You knew," Nellie accused, lifting her head to glare at the hunched figure. "Why didn't you tell me about her?"

Her double shrugged. "Something you had to figure out in your own skin."

"Thanks a lot, Miss Snotty Ass." With a sniff, Nellie started to get to her feet.

"Okay," her double sighed heavily. "I'll tell you this much. Nellie Joanne used to live with me until I started school. That's when they took her away, but I still saw her at training sessions."

Nellie sat down eagerly. "Black Core training sessions?"

Her double shot her a quick glance but remained silent. Nellie's eyes slitted, and then she blinked them into a wide-eyed innocence. "Why can't I remember her?" she wheedled, trying a different tack.

"I can't remember even one little thing. When I saw her name on the file, my head felt like it was blowing up, but I wasn't surprised, neither. Somehow I knew, but I just couldn't remember."

Her double nodded.

"D'you think she can remember me?" Nellie asked pleadingly.

"No," her double said firmly. "She's fixed, even worse than you. Remember, there's no flux in the Interior."

In bewildered silence, Nellie stared at her double. "But not all the levels are fixed," she said finally. "I saw Nellie Joanne in the crystal level, and she wasn't fixed there. If we went into the Interior and found her, maybe we could unfix her and bring her to live in the Outbacks."

"You'd need a lot of flux for that," her double said darkly. "The skins are like stone there. And anyway, you've lost your identity tattoo."

Nellie shrugged carelessly. "I'll get a pen and draw one on."

"There was an implant under it," said her double. "Remember the bump under the cat's head? It had all your vital statistics and case history. Without it, they'd catch you at the first checkpoint."

"Well, we have to do something," Nellie snapped. "What if I just thought myself there, like they do in the crystal level?"

"Can't," said her double immediately. "The vibes are slow here, so it takes a lot longer between thinking about doing something, and then doing it. In the crystal level it's so quick, you just think something and it happens."

A weasely expression crossed Nellie's face. "What if I shapeshifted into a crystal girl and thought myself there?" she asked cagily.

"Uh-uh," said her double. "When you've got flux you can shapeshift into any form, but you can't hold it. The reason you stayed in crystal form in the Temple was because of your mind link to your crystal double. That's broken now."

"Oh." Moodily Nellie stared at the twin moons. "That mind link is why the crystal people all think at each other instead of talking, isn't it?" she asked finally. "The vibrations are so quick that by the time someone thinks a thought, it's already spoken into everyone else's mind."

Her double nodded and Nellie shuddered. "No wonder they're all the same," she grumbled. "No one can have private thoughts."

"It's different," shrugged her double.

"Yeah, but they don't think outside themselves," Nellie protested. "Deller and his mom were dying and they didn't even care. I know they helped us in the Temple, but it was evil of them not to care when people were dying right in front of them in their own level."

"Maybe," said her double. "But maybe they aren't afraid of death the way you are. And maybe they just don't know any different. None of them travel to other levels, remember?"

Sitting up, Nellie stared at the twin moons. "What are the levels?" she asked huskily. "D'you think that all of them put together are one big... *thing*? A kind of oneness like in the crystal level, but a oneness that lets each level be different? And inside each level, it lets each one of us be different too? At least in the slower levels."

"Unless your level gets fixed," said her double.

"But who's fixing the levels?" Nellie asked. "The Goddess?"

"No way," her double said emphatically. "You'll find out someday, when you're ready."

Quiet relief flooded Nellie. She'd learned enough lately to last her for a good long while. "I bet that's why those men jumped Fen in the tenth level," she said eagerly. "Like you said, everything after the tenth isn't fixed, and they probably didn't want him to find that out. But they didn't come from the eleventh level, their vibrations were way too fast. Were they from a floater level, like you?"

Her double shook her head. "It's something else, something I can't tell you about. You don't know enough yet, and it would bust your brain."

"Oh." Nellie let out a small hissing laugh. "You've busted it a couple times already, in case you haven't noticed."

Her double snorted, her eyes dancing across Nellie's, and got to her feet. "I've got to go," she said. "The others, y'know." Her eyes strayed longingly over the gold-brocaded dress and then she said quietly, "You did good in the Temple. You listened."

Brief brilliance sang in Nellie's throat. "Here," she said gruffly, holding out the gold-brocaded dress. "Take it. I've got other clothes."

Her double accepted the dress, running a hand over the gold embroidery. "I had my own, but I threw it away when the remembering stopped working," she said slowly. "I kept this one mostly to bug you, but somehow I got used to wearing it."

"It's like a song," Nellie said wistfully. "It sings. About her."

"Yeah," sighed her double. Sliding on the dress, she stood glimmering in the moonlight. "You've decided, haven't you?" she said. "You're going back to the Interior to find Nellie Joanne."

At her double's words a vivid flash of fear hit Nellie, and then she nodded. Her double sighed knowingly.

"Take Deller with you," she said. "He's got sense, more than you do, and he'll have connections there through the Jinnet. And whatever you do, make sure you listen." She stared at Nellie, her face earnest with moonlight. "Listen to the skins," she said. "Listen to your *own* skin. Can you hear it?"

Reaching out she took Nellie's hand, and Nellie felt herself washed with a liquid wave of sound. Voices swirled through her, a huge crying out, and for a moment every molecule in the air seemed to open and she was looking into every level at once. Countless girls with sarpa eyes stared back at her, the closest dressed in yellow T-shirts and blue shorts, those further out furred like animals or with wings on their backs. One spiraled gently like smoke and another seemed to be made of fire, flickering in all the colors of thought.

Without warning, the girl in the gold-brocaded dress sang a shrill clear note and stepped directly into Nellie. Then, in a rapid flickering sequence, the rest of her doubles also broke into song and stepped into and through her. Suddenly Nellie found herself shapeshifting through mad gorgeous shapes—gargoyles and angels, a girl who flowed like water and another who seemed to be composed of the scent of a susurra flower, a great flying serpent, and then for a moment, a glittering figure made of a myriad brilliant crystals. With a triumphant hoot, Nellie finally realized what shapeshifting was.

"It's love," she bellowed gleefully. "It's all the levels reaching out and touching each other with love."

Gradually the endless sequence of doubles stopped passing through her and retreated into their own levels. The singing voices faded and the air closed into itself again. Bit by bit Nellie felt the molecules of her body reassert themselves, first her bones, then her heart and lungs, her nervous system and finally her skin. Opening her eyes, she saw the girl in the gold-brocaded dress standing beside her, still holding her hand.

"Now *that*," said her double with a grin, "is what I call flux."

About to respond, Nellie was interrupted by the cracking of twigs and whirled to see Deller coming toward them through the bush. A grin crossed his face as he saw her, and then he fixed on the girl in the gold-brocaded dress and went bug-eyed.

"Hey!" he yelped, coming to an abrupt halt. "Are you a double?"

Absolute silence descended onto the girl standing beside Nellie, and she gave him an icy glare.

"Uh, Deller," Nellie said hastily. "It's kind of, well… relative, y'know?"

"Relative?" he asked, confused. "You mean she's your cousin?"

"No." Nellie slitted her eyes, scowled and fidgeted. "I mean, like… Well okay, I'm *her* double."

The air relaxed as the girl in the gold-brocaded dress gave an approving nod.

"Oh." Deller's eyes darted between them. "Yeah sure, I get it. So, does that mean we're in another level?" He glanced around eagerly. "Where's my double?"

"We're not in another level," Nellie said impatiently. "And if you shut up and don't ask too many questions, she might help us find Fen."

A very weasely expression crossed Deller's face and he glanced quickly at Nellie's double. "D'you know any easy ways into the Interior?" he asked.

Relief hit Nellie, so enormous she almost sank to her knees. As usual, Deller was way ahead of her. She wasn't even going to have to ask him if he would come along on her search for Nellie Joanne.

"You can't go through the skins," her double said quickly. "A watch has been placed on them and even if there wasn't, the skins are too tough to get through in the Interior. You'll have to get there the normal way." She turned toward Nellie, her gray sarpa eyes intent. "You don't know," she said quietly, "how important this is. How important *you* are—more even than the rest of your doubles. You have to *listen*, to the skins, to your own skin."

Utterly bewildered, Nellie stared at her double. Their eyes locked and then she heard a voice shimmer deep within her mind. *You're not half bad, y'know,* it said lightly, *for a double. My slowest double, that is.* A dense brief humming started up around the girl in the gold-brocaded dress, she grinned a fierce weasely grin, and was gone.

"Hey!" Deller yelped, stepping forward and running his hands through the air. "Is there a gate here?"

"She doesn't need gates," said Nellie, staring at the place her double had been standing. What in the Goddess's name had the girl meant when she'd said Nellie was the most important double? What had happened to everything being relative? "She won't show me how she does it without them though," she added glumly. "She's kind of a crabby person, actually."

"Well." Deller grinned at her. "She *is* your double."

Nellie slitted her eyes at him, but he ignored her, settling down on the riverbank and pointing west. "See that?" he asked.

Sitting beside him Nellie glanced in the direction he was pointing. "See what?" she asked grumpily.

"That constellation," he said. "It's the Five Children, the ones who didn't get turned into moons and ended up living normal lives. It's sitting right over the Interior. All we have to do is follow it, and it'll take us where we need to go. It'll be like a promise. We're going to find them alive—Fen and Nellie Joanne."

Nellie sat watching the scattering of tiny stars, her heart thundering like an ache, like anger, a knife-edged knowing she couldn't put into words. What they were about to do was absolute foolishness. It was sliding off the cliff edge of hope. It could steal breath and end heartbeats. And it would take her straight into her most frightening memories.

"What about your mom?" she whispered, hugging her knees. "She told me no more running off. And she'll be too scared to let you go."

"We'll have to sneak off," Deller said glumly. "I don't like it, but I don't know any other way. We'll hang around a couple of days when we get to Shor to help her get settled, then take off. Lucky for us Shor's closer to the Interior than Dorniver." He sighed, rubbing his face with both hands. "I know she told you to stick around, but you're not taking off really, if you're with me. She'll be mad. She'll be out of her head with worry. But she'll understand why we went. And think how happy she'll be when she sees us coming back with Fen." He stared up at the Constellation of the Five Children, transfixed. "It'll be worth every minute of her worrying, she'll see."

"Yeah." Doubt still hung over Nellie like a thick veil. "But what if ... " She paused, swallowing.

"What if what?" asked Deller, turning to look at her.

"Well ... " Again Nellie paused. "What if what the doubled priest said in the Temple is true?" she burst out unhappily. "What if I am half sarpa?"

"That's good, isn't it?" shrugged Deller. "My dad had sarpa in him too, remember? Lucky for Fen it all went to him."

An astonished look crossed Nellie's face, and he leaned toward her, bumping her shoulder with his own. "The way I see it," he continued, "if you're half sarpa, you'll be able to figure out what they're likely to do next. We're bound to run into a few of them again somewhere, especially since they're looking for you. And I bet they've got something to do with whatever's happening to Fen and your sister. Plus, being half sarpa, you can do things the rest of us can't. I mean, Nellie—, " Deller gave a short laugh. "When those guys took off through that laboratory door, it wasn't the human part of you they were running away from. Anyway," he said gruffly. "Your heart's all human, I know that for sure."

Suddenly Nellie found herself engulfed in a tight hug, Deller's heart thundering against her own. Just as quickly he withdrew, and they sat breathing rapidly, staring out over the quiet rippling water.

"Well," said Nellie, her hands fluttering nervously, patting her short bristly hair, her face, her throat. "*Well.*"

"We're going to find them, Nellie." Deller turned toward her, his face shadowy in the sepia-gray dusk. "We're going to find them and bring them back, you and me."

"And the Goddess," Nellie said firmly. Getting a grip, she raised a finger and waved it in his face.

"Sure." With a grin, Deller hooked her finger with his own. "We'll let Her come along too."

Watch for the exciting sequel to *Flux*

In *Fixed*, Nellie and Deller leave the Outbacks and head into the Interior, intent on rescuing Deller's younger brother Fen. Caught by the security police, they are taken into one of Detta's underground military bases. There Nellie becomes a subject in one of the dreaded experiments performed in K Block and learns the truth behind the "great mysteries" of the Goddess Ivana and its relationship to her own past.

Using her ability to enter other levels of reality, Nelly confronts the mysterious elite who control human minds through doubling and discovers the real reason the levels are fixed.

Award-winning books
by Beth Goobie

The Lottery

ALA Best Book nominee
CLA YA Book Award nominee
International Youth Library White Raven List

*"…an ambitious, thought-provoking homage to
both Shirley Jackson and Robert Cormier."*
—Booklist

Before Wings

Canadian Library Association
Young Adult Book Award
Mr. Christie's Silver Seal Award winner
Governor General's Award finalist
for Children's Literature

*"Beth Goobie just might be the best YA writer in the country.
She is, certainly, the most intense, most poetic."*
—Tim Wynne-Jones